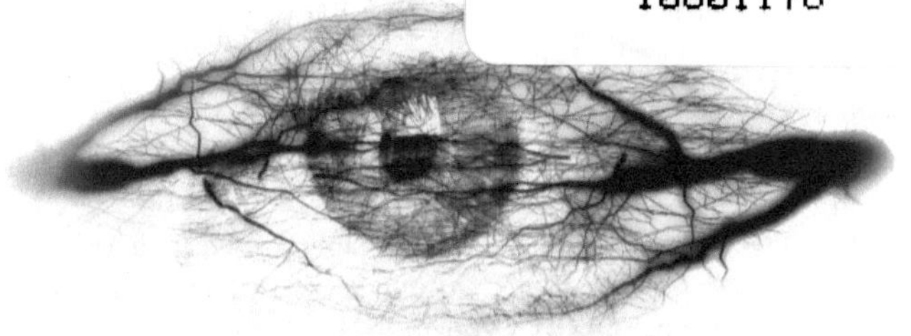

THE CRUX

Anthology

COMPILED BY
RACHAEL RITCHEY

RR PUBLISHING

ACKNOWLEDGMENTS & INDIVIDUAL COPYRIGHTS

The stories within this anthology were submitted as new and original works by the authors. Each author has given permission to print their original work in this anthology and reserves all rights to their individual story.

"Chosen for the Fox-dance" Copyright © 2018 by R. J. Rodda. Printed with permission from R. J. Rodda.

"Ealiverel Awakened" Copyright © 2018 by Joy E. Rancatore. Printed with permission from Joy E. Rancatore.

"Blue Rose" Copyright © 2018 by Audrey Driscoll. Printed with permission from Audrey Driscoll.

"Elixir" Copyright © 2018 by V. P. Grey. Printed with permission from V. P. Grey.

"Vanished" Copyright © 2018 by E. E. Rawls. Printed with permission from E. E. Rawls.

"The BUSS Stop" Copyright © 2018 by K. R. Ludlow. Printed with permission from K. R. Ludlow.

"The Cave of Legix" Copyright © 2018 by David Jesson. Printed with permission from David Jesson.

"A Mystery Wrapped in a Riddle" Copyright © 2018 by Deb Whittam. Printed with permission from Deb Whittam.

"A Journey with Death" Copyright © 2018 by Briar Shea. Printed with permission from Briar Shea.

"The Paths We Choose" Copyright © 2018 by R. J. Llewellyn. Printed with permission from R. J. Llewellyn.

"Daddy Forgot Water" Copyright © 2018 by Barb Taub. Printed with permission from Barb Taub.

"Restore" Copyright © 2018 by Angie Thompson. Printed with permission from Angie Thompson.

"The Knight Errant" Copyright © 2018 by Sha'Tara. Printed with permission from Sha'Tara.

"The God Strain" Copyright © 2018 by Gary Jefferies. Printed with permission from Gary Jefferies.

"Lost & Found" Copyright © 2018 by Victoria Lynn. Printed with permission from Victoria Lynn.

"The Forever Door" Copyright © 2018 by Rachael Ritchey. Printed with permission from Rachael Ritchey.

Compiled, Designed & Edited by Rachael Ritchey
Proofreading assistance by S. Huggins & Joy E. Rancatore

Thank you to everyone who participated in the Adventure Sci-fi & Fantasy Short Story Contest! Congratulations to these authors who have been included in *The Crux Anthology!*

Thank you to our guest judges, authors Morgan Wylie & C. M. Banschbach! Couldn't have done it without you!

CONTENTS

AN INTRODUCTION

Hello, kind reader! You've found yourself on the edge of an adventure. Or many adventures more accurately. Within the pages of this anthology, you will be welcomed into the stand-alone short stories of sixteen different authors. Some contributors are seasoned authors, but for others, this is their first published work, and I'm pleased to introduce them all to you through this Adventure Science Fiction and Fantasy Anthology.

Most of the stories have a link to the author available under the title so that you can find and connect with them outside the pages of this book or find their other works. The first three entries are the Adventure Science Fiction & Fantasy Short Story Contest 1st, 2nd, and 3rd place winners, and the rest of our stories are placed randomly!

The anthology is the product of a short story contest I hosted at the beginning of 2018, and herein you'll discover the culmination of our joint effort to provide you with a variety of adventures in both science fiction and fantasy. The contributors are from around the world, which is pretty epic! And each one has been amazing to work with through revisions and edits. We truly hope you'll find something to enjoy in each one.

So, what might you find in the pages of this book? You'll battle with faeries against evil, wake on an unfamiliar planet, fight for survival after an apocalypse, have the strangest conversation with aliens half your size, uncover mysteries, and so much more!

****

The ASF Short Story Contest and anthology project was organized with the goal of donating any profit from the sale of this book to Compassion International, a non-profit organization helping underprivileged and poverty-stricken children around the world. Any profits from the sale of *The Crux* will be donated toward Compassion International's "Where Most Needed" fund.

https://www.compassion.com/

- Rachael Ritchey
Author of the Chronicles of the Twelve Realms Series

How To Read This Book

The best way is front to back, but if you're a fan of just science fiction OR fantasy, each story has been marked by its basic genre category. Skip around to what you're in the mood for. Enjoy! The flavor of each of these stories reflects the voice of the author, and you're sure to find gems in these pages!

Thanks for reading with us and supporting a good cause!

FANTASY

CHOSEN FOR THE FOX-DANCE

By R. J. Rodda

https://www.wattpad.com/user/rjrodda

On the misty morning of the much-dreaded Fox-dance, Tarryn hurried through the crowded workyard, searching until she found Pom. She snared his dirty little hand just as the grim-faced Hattavah strode out of their master's enormous house. Soldiers moved to flank him as he unfurled the list.

"Benson."

A wail rent the air. Tarryn turned to see Cate running into Benson's thin long arms. He staggered back, stroking her dyed brown hair as her foot stamped against the flagstones. One soldier marched over and commanded Cate to be quiet. She pinched her mouth shut and stilled her body.

"Pom."

Tarryn froze. Pom put a black long-horned beetle on her shoulder, and it crawled onto her bare neck. She tried to catch it and failed. Pom giggled as he retrieved it, his light-grey eyes dancing at her until she forced a smile back. She'd fail to save him, but she had to try.

The Hattavah watched her approach, his hand resting on the whip tucked into his belt. She swallowed. He'd used that whip on her before, the time she'd been caught stealing. How strong and capable he looked in his sleeveless, silver-trimmed black tunic. Close up, he was not that much older than her, the hair on his chin more scruff than beard. He cleared his throat and read out five more names. Newcomers. Strangers. Then the Hattavah looked at her. "Tarryn."

All her breath deserted her. She'd been utterly betrayed. Why? She wasn't lazy, like Benson.

The Hattavah rolled up the list. "If you are chosen, you have until the afternoon to say your goodbyes and dispose of your belongings. The rest of you, back to work."

Tarryn stepped forward. "There must be a mistake. Pom is only seven years old."

The Hattavah pointed to the tattoo on his neck, the fire-snake crest of their master. "I don't make the list."

"I know that, but you're not like the rest of us. You could save Pom if you tried."

"You too, of course. Why not Benson as well? And everyone else? I'll just tell Lord Rustavan to cancel the Fox-dance and hold a picnic instead." His deep-set, dark eyes glared at her.

Tarryn drew back. He wouldn't help. Hadn't he kicked Pom to the ground before, on Lord Rustavan's orders? Even if Pom seemed to have forgotten, she had not.

The other slaves milled around the workyard, crying, exclaiming, commiserating.

Cate's piercing voice rose above the confusion. "It should be the Hattavah's daughter. Why does she get to live and not you?"

In between them all ran Pom, his small pale face alive with excitement as he chased a bright yellow butterfly. He veered so close to the solid stone outer walls that the snapleaf vine guarding them flapped its leaves at him, just missing. Pom skidded to a stop before backing away.

Tarryn had to try again. "I know you don't care about the rest of us, but you talk to Pom sometimes."

"He talks to me. He shows me his bugs." The Hattavah scratched his clipped brown hair, and she glimpsed his wrist, covered in scars. "I suspect the Tasker picked him. Perhaps Pom's been annoying him. If so, twenty silver coins should be enough. You're allowed to send messages outside the gate now you're chosen. Gather the money and he'll be free."

Twenty silver coins. No one she knew had that much, and Pom was an orphan. She had to try something else. "Is it true that there's a pavilion behind the woods?"

The Hattavah raised his eyebrows. "Yes, but it's inside the walls. There's nothing for you there."

So he thought. After the Hattavah had gone, Tarryn took Pom by the hand and slipped away. "Let's see if we can make it to the other side of the woods."

Pom grinned, shrinking the dark smudges beneath his eyes. "Easy, if we go to the stables first. I'll get the scraps bucket for the cows."

"No, I'll get it."

They carried the bucket to the stables, past a group of soldiers lighting fire snakes. With all the hollering, only one looped his beard in her direction. Tarryn rushed on.

"We must run," she told Pom, as they dropped the bucket. "As quickly and quietly as possible. Imagine you are a bug trying to escape a boy." "I'll be a cricket."

"No hopping," she warned.

He ran fast for his age. They made it to the edge of the woods, and she'd almost relaxed when she spotted a soldier with his back toward them. Two red finches lay dead at his feet.

Tarryn put a finger to her lips, but Pom pranced ahead, reaching the shelter of a large spreading bush when a leaf crackled beneath his foot.

The soldier let out a shout. "What are you doing here, sleck?"

Tarryn caught up to Pom, and together they raced through the darkness of the trees until they reached the clearing. She let out a shaky laugh. The white marble pavilion stood before them, ancient and glorious in the sun. They'd made it, almost. Except for the enormous moss-covered boulders that elevated the pavilion and barred the way. Pom could never climb those in time.

Seeing a large crevasse, she made haste to hide him in it. "Don't come out until it's quiet, then go to the pavilion. You'll be safe there." If Lady Kiki's words could be trusted.

Tarryn scrambled upwards, for once grateful for her lanky legs. Her flimsy shoes scrabbled to grip the slimy boulder. She lunged forward in desperation, somehow finding a handhold to lever herself up with, but the largest boulder was still ahead.

"This is fun, sleck. A real hunt."

She gulped and kept climbing. An arrow whizzed towards her, nicking her shoulder. A cry leapt to her lips. She strangled it just in time. Whatever he did to her, she must keep silent, else Pom would come out. For a second, only a second, she paused.

"I've got you now."

A rough hand grasped her leg. She kicked with all her might, so hard that he cursed and let go. Her forehead smacked the pavilion with a dizzying crunch. Her head spun, her shoulder ached, but her heart sang. "I'm safe."

Behind her the soldier snorted, a derisive, ugly sound. "No, you're not."

He snatched at her arm. She moved just in time. Of all the soldiers, it would be Garve. Except for coin day, when a certain freckle-faced girl visited him, Garve seemed to delight in following her about, looping his scraggly orange beard at her while saying words that made her blush. Now, for the first time, he'd got her on her own.

Tarryn dashed for the far corner of the pavilion, less impressive now that the sun had vanished. "Lady Kiki told me in the day of trouble I'd be safe in the pavilion of her God. She must have meant here."

Garve hauled himself onto the cracked marble floor. "This is a She-Fox pavilion for the Wayvolk, not slecks like you."

Tarryn saw the etchings of the Fox carved into the white pillars, even as Garve got her. All these years she'd been wrong. She would dance after all. Pom too, unless he stayed hidden, which he wouldn't. Tarryn's heart plunged even as her thoughts raced. What if she was in the right place after all? Did she need to do something, say something, to unlock the power of the pavilion? She had to try. She pretended to trip and dropped to the floor in a half-roll, holding her bleeding shoulder, moaning as if she could not bear the pain.

"Get on my back," Garve snapped.

Before he could yank her away from the pavilion, Tarryn cried out, "Please protect us!"

"Quit your whining." Garve jerked her toward him as the sun re-emerged from the clouds. Out of the corner of her eye, she saw Pom next to a pillar of the pavilion. She bit her tongue. It couldn't be. She frantically motioned him away. He moved forward, kicking a pebble with his foot that shifted enough to bump a larger rock that fell with a crash.

Garve's jaw dropped. "What's that?"

A brilliant light shone from the heavens, so full of radiance that the features of Pom's face melted. Garve's grip on her tightened. "Is that you, Mollen? Come back to howl against me? It was an accident, I swear." Pom kept coming.

Garve let go of Tarryn and backed off the pavilion onto the rock. He'd forgotten the slipperiness of the moss. With a misjudged foot he skated on the edge of the largest boulder before skidding down it at tremendous speed. He landed with a thud at the bottom, his head at a strange angle.

A shudder trembled through her, even as Pom cried out. "Why'd he do that?"

"I don't know." The shadows returned, edging Pom's scrawny body. How ordinary he looked now, his tawny hair slick with sweat. "How'd you get up here so fast?"

"I found the stairs," Pom answered with a grin, and she shivered. He hadn't realized then what had just happened.

"Stay here. Don't look down." Tarryn made herself search Garve's body to find his money pouch. Then she returned to the pavilion, hiding behind a pillar while she untied her breast bindings. With the cloth she wrapped up her wound, sucking in her breath as she did so.

Pom bounded over to her. "What's wrong?"

"I thought I saw a sun-spider," she improvised.

"Where? I won't frighten you with it this time, promise."

"No, they're too dangerous."

Pom went looking for the sun-spider, but she dragged him away. "One last run."

They snuck along the edge of the woods, found a patch of flower-mushrooms, and picked some. If anyone stopped them now, they could say Cate sent them. It was possible, with all the strange dishes she prepared for the Fox-dance.

A peculiar quiet now hung about the workyard. Hidden by the trees, Tarryn watched until the few people still around seemed distracted and then signaled Pom. They ran to the guardhouse. Only Poddit was there. This should be easy.

"Let us out, and you can have two silver coins," Tarryn said, discarding the mushrooms. Pom picked them up and threw them at the nearest snap-leaf. The wide green leaves closed over them. How strange. Usually they only ate flesh and insects.

Poddit's bony fingers reached out toward the coins and then whipped back as if stung.

"Hello, Hattavah," piped up Pom.

"Tarryn and Pom." The Hattavah approached her with such purpose she shrank back onto the guardhouse. "Go back inside now, and I'll pretend I didn't see you trying to escape."

They would die if she obeyed. She had to think of some way out. "Why me? Because I steal? Because I'm a winter kit?"

"Mostly because of your hair."

Her snow-white hair. Tarryn drew in a ragged breath. "I could've understood if it had been because I steal, but not because a Wayvolkan Lord wanted my mother, and I got his hair. That's not fair."

The Hattavah stared at her until her stomach twisted upon itself. He must understand. Didn't Tallie, his own white-haired winter kit, live only because her mother, Lady Belvana insisted on it?

"The Wayvolk want their rightful heirs protected," he said at last, "but I am not Wayvolk."

Tarryn held her breath. Was he saying he would help them?

Pom ran up, a rainbow leaf beetle on his palm. He put it onto the Hattavah's finger. "Look how sparkly it is. Tallie can have it."

The rigid expression on the Hattavah's face faded. "She'll like it, but Mezia won't."

Pom's eyes grew large. "Don't tell her. She squashes all of Tallie's beetles."

The Hattavah blinked. "How do you know that?"

Tarryn crossed her arms around Pom, drawing him close. "Tallie tries to play with him sometimes when he's supposed to be scrubbing the floors of her room. That's why he takes so long and gets into trouble."

"Tallie gets scared by herself," Pom explained.

The Hattavah's nostrils flared. "She's never alone. Either I'm with her or Mezia."

Pom shook his head. "Mezia goes away and Tallie cries."

Tarryn wiped away the sweat beading on her forehead. "Tallie begs us both to stay with her. I have before, for as long as I've dared."

The Hattavah's eyes flashed. "Why didn't you tell me?"

"I spoke to Mezia. She told me I was a three-coin sleck and to go away. She said you wouldn't care about Tallie being left alone, but if I kept bothering her, she'd make sure you'd punish me. I believed her."

The Hattavah frowned. "She said that?"

Pom bounced up and down. "I want to play with Tallie."

The Hattavah shot a glance at Tarryn. "You have about an hour left. I suppose you could."

Tarryn bit her lip. "Let me take Pom outside the gate. I'm sure to find someone who'll want him. If he's in the dance with me, all I'll do is protect him. I don't care about gaining honor in the afterlife. I won't do what Lord Rustavan says."

The Hattavah stiffened. "I can't just let him run away. I'd be sent to bring him back." He scratched at the ground with his leather boot then let out a sigh. "I suppose I could use some of the money I've saved for Tallie to instead pay off the Tasker." He scooped up the two coins abandoned by Poddit, who had edged as far away from them as the guardhouse allowed. "Take Pom down to the fish market street. Leave him at the cottage with the flowers painted on it. The lady there, Val, will welcome him."

Wild hope surged through her. Pom would be safe.

She would be safe. The Hattavah would let them go free.

"Not you, though," he said, pinning her with his eyes. "You are required. Lord Rustavan wants you to act the part of Queen Alleska."

"The Queen who fought against the artic foxes?" Tarryn whispered, picturing herself against the vicious, unnaturally-sized She-Fox with the vivid bi-colored eyes. She wouldn't last long.

"Yes. As you said, you look Wayvolkan enough with your white hair, despite your small nose and green eyes."

Everything turned dark within her except the part of her heart that throbbed for joy that Pom would be saved.

"Come back straight away."

Tarryn nodded even as she decided to run. She had nothing to lose.

"If you don't, I will hunt you down and bring you both back. Pom will lose his chance."

There was no hope for her then. Tarryn followed the foul smell of fish and found the cottage.

A middle-aged olive-skinned lady opened the door, her canceled slave tattoo visible above the collar of her dress. "I'll take him, but not as a runaway. I need his paper. Lord Rustavan is too powerful a man to cross."

"The Hattavah said he'd fix it," Tarryn assured Val even as she worried. He wouldn't forget with all the commotion of the Fox-dance, would he? She would have to remind him, though the mere thought of talking to him again made her stomach coil.

Tarryn gave Pom a fierce hug goodbye. A sign opposite Val's house caught her eye, and she made one final stop before returning. The rest of the chosen had already assembled.

Lord Rustavan appeared. How diminished he seemed next to the Hattavah—shorter, podgier, almost grandfatherly with his trim grey beard, but there was no kind twinkle in his eye when he saw her.

"Where's your long white hair?" Lord Rustavan shook her, so hard the pain in her head flared, before shoving her at the Hattavah.

His firm grip steadied her. "A soldier probably had fun with her. Is that so, Tarryn?" He made a show of inspecting her blood-stained bandage.

"He hunted me."

"Weak and ugly," Lord Rustavan jeered, digging his fingers into her arm. "You're supposed to be the star attraction."

The Hattavah coughed. "Her hair will grow back. Why don't you save her for the next dance? I could get some of those jackals infesting the forest instead."

"The She-Fox against wild animals? That's not her way."

"It'd be unexpected, a thrill for the audience, a shock for her."

Lord Rustavan sniggered. "True, Hattavah, but this sleck deserves death, hair or not."

"Death is what she'll get. I promise that by the time of the next dance, she'll be ready."

Lord Rustavan let her go.

Tarryn staggered over to the walnut shelling table and picked up her hammer.

"A clever trick. Don't try it again."

The Hattavah. She swiveled toward him. "Val needs Pom's paper."

"I said I'd fix it," he snapped. "After the dance."

She bobbed her head as guilt made her add, "Garve's dead."

"Did you kill him?"

"No! He slipped off a boulder chasing me. His body's just lying there in the woods, and with everything going on, they might not even notice he's gone."

"So?"

Tarryn swallowed and let her eyes meet his. "He had a sister who visited him."

His lips twitched. "A sister? A fun-girl more like."

"Probably," she agreed. "Still, she deserves his body more than the jackals do."

His eyebrows danced upwards. "I'll see he's found if you tell me one more thing: did he chase you before or after you stole from him?"

"Before," she exclaimed, heat flooding her cheeks.

The Hattavah smirked at her until she half-smiled back and then he left. Pom was safe. She was safe, for six months. Surely, by the time of the next Fox-dance she'd be long gone.

Avlyn sidled beside her at the walnut shelling table, her short black hair tucked behind her large ears. "I can't believe you got away with that. I can't even persuade the Tasker to give me shoes."

"It wasn't him. It was the Hattavah."

Avlyn snorted. "I'd sooner believe the She-Fox herself intervened."

"Or Lady Kiki's God," Tarryn murmured. "Why don't you go to the pavilion and pray for shoes? It seems to work."

"I'm more practical than that. I've told the Tasker I'll do anything he wants for them, and he said he'd see."

Tarryn moved away from her. "We should get to work." Behind Avlyn, she saw a withered snap-leaf, the very one that had eaten the mushrooms. She stared at it, and then her knees beneath the table began to jig.

That night at second meal, Tarryn sat with Avlyn at her usual table. Holding her nose, she took a mouthful of lek-duck soup as a soldier on the other side of the dining room shouted out her name and Pom's. She put down her spoon and held her stomach. "How can they bet on us dying? The monsters."

"Speaking of monsters," Avlyn said, her high-pitched voice lower than usual, "there's the Hattavah."

He was sitting down at his lonely table in the corner.

"All he does is obey orders."

Avlyn's eyes goggled. "Have you forgotten how you could hardly walk after he beat you?"

"No." Her back still prickled at the memory. "That was the Tasker's fault. Every time the Hattavah tried to stop, he was ordered to keep going."

Avlyn let out a scornful laugh. "So that makes what he does okay, does it? I'm sure he enjoys it just as much as the Tasker."

Tarryn made herself eat another spoonful of soup. "I don't think so."

"Has being chosen for the Fox-dance addled your head? The Hattavah's like a fire snake, pretty in a savage sort of way, but dangerous. Too dangerous for girls like us."

"I know." Tarryn met the Hattavah's cool stare from across the room, and he motioned for her to join him. Avlyn tittered and tugged at an imaginary beard. Heat fired Tarryn's cheeks as she went to stand awkwardly by his table.

"I promised Lord Rustavan you'll be ready for the next choosing." The Hattavah picked up a sharp little knife and attacked the plump whole fish that poked its head out of his soup. No foul-smelling bones for him. "Don't try to run. You won't succeed, and I'll just have to drag you back and punish you. What do you have to live for anyway? Pom's safe. The She-Fox, for all her antics, is quick when she pounces. You'll hardly feel it, and then you'll be free of all this. If I didn't have Tallie, I'd volunteer."

"My mother risked everything in taking me to Lady Kiki to live. I won't just give up and wait to die."

The Hattavah dropped his knife with a clatter. "You give me no choice. You'll be collared and assigned to the dungeons."

"Collared?" Tarryn asked in horror, feeling the soft skin on her neck. "Why?"

"So the soldiers remember who you are. From now on, you are forbidden to go outside at all, let alone near the gate."

Tarryn's mouth sagged. Six months, trapped inside with a collar. How could she escape then?

"I've also warned the soldiers to stay away from you. They so much as loop their beards in your direction and you tell me."

Tarryn stared blankly at the Hattavah then trudged back to her table as if through snow.

The next day, the Tasker himself took her to the trapdoor that led down to the dungeons. "Not sure what's worse down there." A cruel grin exposed the furry blackness on his teeth. "Is it the camo spiders, the scorpions, or the foxes? You'll have to let me know."

His laughter echoed in her ears as she hunched her way down the stone steps to the stench below. Ferrin, a shrunken man with six earrings in each ear, met her at the bottom and patted her shoulders with glee. "Welcome, welcome. Good of the Hattavah to get me an assistant. I can't bend as well as I used to, and the creatures miss it, they do. They need someone quick and agile."

"That's me."

He cackled and put her to work moving the fire snakes to a larger enclosure.

After she'd been in the dungeons for a week, Lord Rustavan came. The Hattavah was right behind him, a cobweb stuck on his hair.

Lord Rustavan removed his shirt and laid down on a low stone table in the centre of the gloomy room. "Get the spiders."

Tarryn snagged a camo spider by its leg then hovered, uncertain of what to do next.

"He likes them crawling on his back."

She stared at the Hattavah for a second, not sure if he was joking, then put the first spider down on her master's mole-dotted skin.

"More."

She got out ten more and put them on, even as she tossed a bemused glance at the Hattavah, who shrugged in reply. Lord Rustavan let out a gagging sound, and anxiety seized her.

"What's wrong?" she whispered to the Hattavah.

"Nothing. He's enjoying it." Something like a smile skimmed across his face.

She gave him an uncertain grin back before racing to shepherd the spiders, who kept wandering away.

Lord Rustavan returned to the dungeons often for more.

One time, the Hattavah lingered behind long enough for her to ask, "How's Pom?"

"I don't know."

"You haven't visited him?"

His forehead scrunched. "Why should I?"

"He's little and alone with strangers. He'd like to see you. He thinks of you and Tallie as his friends."

The Hattavah's lip curled. "I don't have friends. All Pom wants is someone to listen to him rattle on about his bugs. He doesn't need me for that."

"That's friendship for kids," Tarryn ground out. "If you won't go see him, let me."

"Is that what this is about? No."

Tarryn gritted her teeth and went and collected the spiders. If it wasn't for the Hattavah, she'd have found a way to see Pom the day after the Fox-dance. If she'd run off after that, why did he have to care? Thinking of Pom reminded her of the flower-mushrooms. She had to gather them soon.

That night, Tarryn outlined her plan in whispers to Avlyn as they lay side by side on their lumpy pallets. "You'll help me, won't you?"

Avlyn pulled her blanket up to her mouth. "The Hattavah said if I help you escape, I'll be chosen for the next Fox-dance. I won't risk that."

Tarryn's collar seemed to tighten around her neck. "I thought we were friends."

"We've never shared the oath." Avlyn rolled away from her, and Tarryn scowled. She'd do it alone then.

The next day before dawn, Tarryn got the fire snake she'd hidden in her sack and crept over to the soldier snoozing beside the outside door. She lowered the snake onto his shoulder. He woke up with a start and began shrieking and failing about. Tarryn snuck past him and made for the woods. Once there, she lit the lamp she'd borrowed from Ferrin and found her first flowermushroom. Her confidence rose. Just a few more.

A light flared behind her. She spun around. The Hattavah. That didn't surprise her but Avlyn beside him did.

The Tasker appeared, a gloating look on his round, hairy face. "Caught her trying to escape, did you?"

The Hattavah looked as if he'd just eaten lek-duck soup. "Yes."

"Well then, what are you waiting for? Whip her good, so she doesn't try again."

The forest filled with gawking slaves and soldiers. The Hattavah cleared his throat, twice. "That didn't stop her stealing. I've a better idea."

The Tasker only lengthened his smile. "I wasn't asking for your opinion. That was an order."

"Your orders don't count when they go against Lord Rustavan's. He wants her unmarred for the Fox-dance. I'll do what's necessary to stop her running away."

The Tasker hissed and stalked off. The Hattavah glared at the crowd until they dispersed, and she was alone with him. In the creeping dawn, he loomed larger and more frightening than usual, the trees behind him dark and menacing.

Her breath hitched. "What will you do to me?"

The Hattavah leaned against the nearest tree. "Not what you deserve. Tallie had me up all night, and just as I got to sleep, I had to come chasing you."

At the lightness of his tone, Tarryn relaxed, picked up a stick and slashed the air with it. "Because of Avlyn, you mean. What a three-coin friend she turned out to be."

"The Tasker put her up to it, but I supported him. I can't fail Lord Rustavan."

"So what, you'll tie me up until the Fox-dance?"

"Something better. If you promise to stop trying to escape, I'll give Val the money to send Pom to school."

The fight inside her dimmed. Pom would have a brighter future than one she could ever hope for, despite Lady Kiki's words. Could she give up trying to survive, for him? Tarryn snapped her stick in half.

"You seem to think death is the worst thing that can happen to you. It isn't. Not in this house and or even out there."

Tarryn looked over at him. "I'll never be ordered to do the things you do."

The Hattavah made a strangled sound. "You really think so? You're like one of Pom's newly hatched monarch butterflies. Soon you'll open your wings and you'll dazzle the Wayvolk. You'll be a fully-grown forbidden winter kit, already caught in their net. When that happens, you'll regret every day you didn't dance."

A cool wind numbed her cheeks. "You think I'll end up like my mother; the longer I live, the more miserable they'll make me."

He fisted his hands and said in a voice so low she could hardly hear him. "That's my experience, apart from Tallie."

Tarryn threw the sticks up into the air and let them fall to the ground. "You win. I promise I won't run."

The Hattavah allowed her to return to working in the kitchens. At first Tarryn was overjoyed, but between Cate's temper, soured by Benson's death, and Avlyn and her new shoes, Tarryn often wished herself elsewhere.

The months flew by like a stink bug and her hair grew back as white as ever and nearly as long. On the night before the Fox-dance, Tarryn slipped out to the pavilion. "Lady Kiki's God, thank you for giving Pom sanctuary. Can I have it too?"

Something flooded within her, a feeling, an overwhelming impression. Lady Kiki's God did not like her stealing.

"I must steal," Tarryn argued. "They've taken everything from me. This is the only way I can get something back." The feeling possessed her insides. "Is that what you demand? That I stop stealing?" A small price to pay. She swallowed and then surrendered. A trickle of peace crept into her heart and she remembered the one good thing she had done. Pom lived free because she'd persisted until her voice was heard. Now she needed to summon that same courage for herself.

A dark figure leapt onto the pavilion. She jumped back. The Hattavah.

"What are you doing here? Who are you meeting?" He scanned the gloomy trees, his body tensed for action.

"No one."

"I don't believe you."

"It's true."

"Then why are you here?"

Tarryn looked down at her tattered sandals, shadowed in the moonlight. "I came to pray for sanctuary. Last time I prayed, Pom got it but not me."

"You prayed to the She-Fox to rescue you from the dance?" His tone was incredulous.

She winced. "To Lady Kiki's God. She said when I was in trouble, I'd find safety in the pavilion of her God. I thought she meant here."

"If you can pray here, you can pray anywhere."

Tarryn buried her face in her hands. "You're right." She lifted her head to say, "Am I definitely on the list tomorrow?"

"Yes."

"I have no hope then."

"You'll carry a sword."

Tarryn grimaced. "So?"

"If you still want to live, you could try to use it. Aim for her eyes or her mouth or her legs. If you wound the She-Fox badly enough, she'll retreat."

"A warrior could do that but not a kitchen slave like me. I'm skilled with a walnut hammer though, and they really hurt if you slip. I could fight the Fox with one of those, pretend she is a nut I have to crack."

The Hattavah flattened his lips. "I don't think Lord Rustavan would let Queen Alleska wield a walnut hammer. An actual sword would give you some sort of chance."

"I've never even held a sword," she protested. "I will die tomorrow, there's no point denying that. As you said, even if I miraculously survive, there is no sanctuary for me."

"What do you mean by 'sanctuary'?"

She sucked in her lips. "I've always wanted to live, but you've made me see that isn't enough. I want to be able to walk without fear."

"And that's it? That's all you prayed for?"

"That's impossible enough." She fiddled with the collar on her neck. "When I was with Lady Kiki, I had the best kind of sanctuary—a chest full of books in a room of my own. I wore a soft sky-blue tunic and a silver necklace. I had money to spend at the markets, and I wasn't forced to eat lek-duck soup."

"That soup's foul. What does Cate put in it anyway?"

"Not any duck, I know that much. I should take some to the dance with me and feed it to the She-Fox. It might actually kill her."

"She's not as easy to kill as that." The Hattavah hooked his thumb through his belt. "I visited Pom the other day with Tallie. He showed me every bug in his collection. He misses you, but he enjoys school and he's happy."

"I'm glad." Moisture pricked behind her eyes. Pom, happy. She'd hold on to that tomorrow when she faced the She-Fox. She wished the Hattavah would leave so she could look at the stars and grieve her short life.

Instead, he insisted on escorting her back to the kitchen. As Tarryn made her way to her pallet, she saw by the firelight the sleeping mound of Cate, her freshly darkened hair fanned out over her face. Her feet stilled. Dye. Hair dye. Cate probably kept the mixed-up dye in her box of things on the bottom shelf. She could get it out and put it on her hair.

Half-way there Tarryn froze, remembering the promise she'd made to Lady Kiki's God at the pavilion. She moved forward anyway. By the time she reached the box, the thrumming in her chest was so strong she could hardly breathe. She sighed and went and jogged Cate's arm.

"What are you waking me up for?"

"Can I use your hair dye?"

To Tarryn's amazement, once Cate realized why she wanted it she volunteered to put on her hair. "You're lucky I made too much. It's not easy to catch a leech just whenever you want one."

Tarryn held back a groan as her hair was painted with something that reeked of fermented herrings.

When she finished, Cate crowed, "You don't look like Queen Alleska now."

Tarryn's lips curved upwards even as Cate's shoulders drooped. "It won't be enough, though. This time you'll dance. You take the morning off. We'll have to learn to manage without you now anyhow."

A whole morning off. Tarryn made herself a hot bath in the washroom, pouring bowls of water over her ashgrey hair until the putrid stench lessened. When the water cooled, she got out and helped herself to two fresh tunics. One she dressed in, the other she tied over her hair.

When the Hattavah read her name at the choosing, Tarryn pulled the tunic off her hair in one defiant swoop.

The Hattavah gasped then went straight to her. "What will Lord Rustavan say?"

"I don't care."

"I do," he said in a strained voice. "I promised I'd have you ready for the dance. He'll punish me for sure."

"Who disciplines the Hattavah?" she asked with a touch of mockery. "The Tasker?"

"He'd like that. No, Lord Rustavan. He prefers more creative punishments than whipping, and now Tallie is here, I'm afraid …" He trailed off. "We must go to him now. He's built the whole dance around you."

All her cockiness left her. Tallie punished because she'd dyed her hair? She couldn't let that happen. She followed the Hattavah to the front of their master's house, seeing for the first time the huge, sculpted head of the SheFox above the arched doorway. On the wall beside it was a colorful mosaic of a stately Wayvolkan Lady. Tarryn halted and a lump rose in her throat. Lady Kiki.

"Hurry up." The Hattavah took her elbow and marched her over to where Lord Rustavan was inspecting slaves gathering blood wort from the garden.

The Hattavah flung himself to his knees. "Forgive me, master. I've failed you. I heard Tarryn praying to Lady Kiki's God to be spared from the Fox-dance. I never dreamed he had the power to change the color of her hair."

Lord Rustavan snagged a lock of Tarryn's hair and sniffed it. "Haven't you heard of dye, Hattavah? Because she has. No god did this."

The Hattavah sprang to his feet. "You dyed your hair?"

"Yes, because I don't want to dance. I want to think up new treatments for you, Lord Rustavan, like black long-horn beetles."

"Intriguing," Lord Rustavan said in a bored tone. "Do they nip, spider girl?"

"Never. I can apply them after the Fox-dance to help you relax after the thrill of it all."

Lord Rustavan gave a dry laugh. "Nice try. You can gather them before the dance and give them to Ferrin." He stroked his beard. "Why did you pray to Lady Kiki's God?"

Fear threatened to eat her, but she lifted her chin. "I'm the girl you promised your sister you'd adopt."

A sneer twisted Lord Rustavan's face. "Lies to soothe her passing. As if I'd ever acknowledge a fungirl's winter kit. You got to live. That was enough."

She clenched her teeth. "You're killing me now. If you do this to me, I hope Lady Kiki comes back and howls against you."

Lord Rustavan snarled. "She'd never do that. She didn't even believe in any of that. Her worthless God made her question everything, even me and how I live. Yet all I have, all my wealth and power, is because of my true devotion to the She-Fox. I give her all the blood she wants, and she rewards me by letting me do exactly as I please. She created you slecks to exalt me, and exalt me you will."

At the ferocity of his tone, Tarryn took a step back. The Hattavah was beside her in an instant, pressing down on her head until she sunk to the soft green grass. "We both acknowledge your greatness and your right to command us." He bowed, then straightened, resting his hand on her shoulder. "You said once if I wanted a girl among the lesser slecks, I just had to ask. I'm asking now, for her."

A coldness crept up Tarryn's body as she remembered Avlyn's warning. *He's too dangerous for girls like us.*

An ugly smile spoiled the neatness of Lord Rustavan's face. "You want to lengthen your beard with her? What about my dance?"

"There was a pale-haired girl among the slecks the High-Priestess sent over this morning."

"There was." Lord Rustavan's boot hit Tarryn's knee, hard enough that she whimpered. "You've awoken my sister with all your ranting, spider girl. I can feel her hot breath on my neck." He fingered his lip. "You deserve to be punished for that. As the Fox says, the best revenge is not a quick death."

"Wise is the way of the Fox," the Hattavah and Tarryn responded in unison.

Lord Rustavan slapped the Hattavah's back. "Take her and have your fun with her. When you tire of her, give her back. She can live to entertain."

"I'd rather dance," Tarryn spat and tried to stand.

The Hattavah kept her down. "I want to own her." Tarryn's chest iced up and she struggled to breathe. She touched him on the wrist and he flinched. "I don't want to be a fun-girl, yours or anyone else's. I'll do anything else you want. I'll take care of Tallie. I'll bring you bed tea." The Hattavah did not answer, and she scrambled to think of something he'd value enough to change his mind. "I'll swear friendship with you." She held up three shaking fingers. Surely friendship freely given was worth more than forced fun.

Lord Rustavan mocked. "Did you hear that Hattavah? She'll be your friend."

The Hattavah shoved her hand away. "I want you for Tallie, not me. Are you willing?"

Tarryn blinked. "I am."

"For Tallie?" Lord Rustavan jeered. "Why lie about it?"

"I'm not lying."

Tarryn found herself believing him. He never looked at her the way the soldiers did.

"Tarryn is not only clever, she fights for those weaker than her. She'll take good care of Tallie. Please let me buy her."

Lord Rustavan glowered. "I should have known. Always for Tallie, never for yourself."

"Everything I do is for you and her."

The harsh lines on Lord Rustavan's face softened. "That's true. You have proven yourself worthy of my trust, time and again. Your swift obedience is an example to all. Take the girl as your reward."

The Hattavah bowed again as he praised Lord Rustavan's generosity.

Bile rose into Tarryn's mouth. Lord Rustavan grabbed her ear and yanked her to her feet. "Don't you ever mention Lady Kiki to me again. You're some other Lord's brat, not mine. Your life is more than you deserve."

Tarryn nodded even as her eyes widened. Was that why Lady Kiki had taken her in? No. Lady Kiki had saved her because she believed even a winter kit's life was precious.

The Hattavah took her to the Tasker's room to get her collar removed and her tattoo canceled. "You'll be a servant, not a slave."

Tarryn's jaw dropped as excitement jolted through her. "You're buying me to free me?"

"I hate slavery."

For the first time she saw the flecks of hazel in the darkness of his eyes.

"I'll do everything I can to make you happy, to make you want to stay. You'll have your own room. Tallie will be in it most days, but you'll have time off too. You'll get wages, to buy your own tunics and books to read. You can visit Pom. You can even go to the pavilion in the daytime if that's what you want."

Tarryn could not stop smiling. "You must be right. Lady Kiki can't have meant that pavilion. With my first coin, I'll get the book she quoted and figure out what she meant."

"I'm sure you will. You always seem to find a way."

After her tattoo was canceled, the Hattavah took Tarryn to her new room, with her own pallet, her own wooden chest and a window with a forest view. Her heart filled with fireflies of happiness, and she wanted to share them with him. "You freed Pom and me. You listened to me. You got me everything I said I wanted."

The Hattavah rubbed his forehead. "I collared and trapped you."

"You've been a friend to me as much as you could."

"You really want to swear the oath with me? Bound as I am to serve Lord Rustavan in whatever he asks, because of Tallie?" He searched her face, until she was sure enough to nod.

The Hattavah held up his three middle fingers, curved, his thumb holding down his little finger. "I will always be your friend. I'll watch your back. I'll keep your secrets. I won't lie to you or laugh at you. I'll do everything I can to make your life better."

Tarryn returned the oath and their fingers hugged. She felt the gentleness of his touch and also his strength.

When the door shut behind him, Tarryn danced for the joy of it all until she collapsed onto her pallet. Sanctuary. She'd found it at last and in the most unexpected place.

FANTASY

EALIVEREL AWAKENED

By Joy E. Rancatore

http://www.joyerancatore.com/

Elspeth has accepted her calling—Faerie Shepherdess. She journeys to Temple Taepaeum where she must pass several Trials to awaken all her power in order to begin her Training.

Four days Elspeth had traveled without tire through the Kingdom of Riefaerlie. Ctesias, the unicorn king, had carried her on his back as she slept the final night. She slid along his muscular flanks, free from moisture despite his exertions, and breathed deeply of the spicy air dancing through her wavy black hair. She envisioned Temple Taepaeum beyond the walls ahead. Her Training awaited her.

Prophesied at birth to be a mighty Faerie Shepherdess, Elspeth grew up surrounded by humans afraid of what their eyes could not see. Now she entered the Faerie realm to train for her Calling. Her future remained veiled to her, but this Training would reveal much and awaken more.

She recalled the rich conversation she'd shared with Ctesias the night before. They spoke through her dreams as he galloped ahead of the wind under shimmering moonlight—a journey of nearly three-hundred miles.

They had conversed about the Faeries and the many creatures of the forest. Their words turned toward darkness as he advised her about Maelphaeus and his Legions. She sought his counsel concerning some of the visions her dreams brought to her. He set her mind at ease on many topics, but only smiled at her query regarding the destiny she shared with his own Eail, unicorn princess.

Elspeth knew of Eail and the prophecy that bound them, but she'd first glimpsed the filly only the day before. On her journey through the dense forest, she had sensed a mighty presence and sought the sanctuary of a Wary Willow. Its stringy red vines snaked around her body, covering her from sight, even as the spindly branches parted. She gazed down an arrow-straight cliff into a perfectly round meadow. The entire area glowed with an ethereal light, the source of which Elspeth couldn't ascertain. The grass within pulsated with an oddly yellowgreen light that danced and changed with the colors of the multitude of flowers swaying all around in an unfelt breeze. Sapphire, ruby, jade, turquoise and amethyst hues swung a wild fling while brooding trees overhung the glade as much as they dared. In the exact center of all the color and light, a mother unicorn nursed her foal.

Elspeth's blood-red lips parted as a quick inhale of air swept past them. The foal turned and looked her way. Their eyes locked and the flaming glow encircled her green irises. Elspeth raised her eyes to the crimson streak she knew wrapped the length of the tiny horn; the marking matched the one encircling her left forearm— the one she'd been forced to keep hidden.

"Eail," she breathed.

Elspeth and Eail were destined. For what, she couldn't see. The goosebumps along her limbs assured her their meeting need not be feared. She smiled a greeting even as the foal tucked chin to knobby knee in acknowledgement, her mane falling forward in a waterfall of colors.

Elspeth recalled one of her recurring Visions. In it she rode onto a battlefield astride a white unicorn with a rainbow mane and red glowing horn. Together they faced all the Hosts of Evil. Though she never saw the end, Elspeth knew together they prevailed. That unicorn knelt before her now.

Eail gazed to Elspeth's right until the girl left the security of the Willow to follow her directions. She'd been told her path lay toward the rising sun beyond the Meadow of Eternal Luminescence wherein Feleroli, mighty Queen of Light, dwells. As Elspeth looked back, she understood the light originated with the unicorn mother.

"Feleroli," she whispered. Ever watchful of his precious family, Ctesias had met her nearby and offered his speed for her journey. She recalled how he had smiled down on her, his golden horn shining in the sunlight. Or, perhaps, the horn cast its own rays. He was taller and broader than any horse she'd ever seen. He had to stand at least twenty-four hands above the grass.

Now he blessed her where she stood facing impenetrable gates. "You are the prophesied, Shepherdess of the Fae. Long have we looked for your coming. Great trials await you beyond these gates; your strength to face them rests deep within you. It is time for that Force to awaken before your Training can begin."

"King Ctesias, greatest of all Light Beings, your goodness and mercy fills my heart with thanksgiving." Girl and unicorn king faced one another, heads bowed, until Elspeth flung her arms around his mighty breast. He embraced her with his towering neck and gifted her with courage, wisdom and peace.

Ctesias turned and faded back into the forest, the light of his golden horn casting a cape-like glow from his retreating silhouette.

The gates in front of her served as her first test and would open only to the Chosen. She surveyed the black wooden doors. They appeared menacing, unbreachable. No handles; no wise riddles. Elspeth approached to examine intricate runes etched deep within the wood. As she touched them, they moved. Swirling and changing as they eddied about, they sang her a visual ballad of loss and hope, destiny and sacrifice.

Ethereal music hummed and joined the runic dance until each symbol flew freely, filling the air around the Shepherdess. Floating runes lifted her tousled locks and encircled her forest green eyes, now glowing red around the rims. She joined the song in a new tongue—

Riefaerlish. The words rolled over her lips in time with the melody, and she understood the praises they sang to Dhae, Creator of All.

Ollihesttapha naaman sucre diliea unicristos aman gumpturi paer cristum nomen ti, nomen mi, alli hominas eminestifa sumonumen tuah, Dhae.

Trees rustled to a deafening crescendo as nature joined the chorus. Leaves took flight, wrapping her within their cyclone. Her pale skin glowed, and her voice matched the urgency of the newly freed words and animated nature. She embraced her Calling. Her tartan skirt billowed around her as she twirled. Matching plaid half-sleeves covered her lower arms, revealing muscles flexed above as she raised rippling fingers to the heavens. Eyes closed, Elspeth bent and swayed, rose and leapt. Music swelled within her and guided her feet, faster and faster—in, out, all around. She, the words, the tune, the leaves, the trees, the gates—all were one. One in all. The notes climbed ever higher. No end appeared; none was desired.

Melodic praise to Dhae reverberated from this union and soared. The music gamboled over the gateway into its guarded mystery. In response the gates sprang open, and Elspeth glided through with the song's crescendo.

Her voice reverenced to a whisper before trailing away with the fading runes. They and the magical gates returned to their stalwart position as Elspeth surveyed the path ahead. A glen sloped toward the narrow entrance of a cave. Steep mountain walls climbed beyond her sight on either side. Behind her the gate faded away, its music a faint perfume on the wind, the apparition of a dream slipping away upon awakening.

As she drew nearer, the cave's mouth gaped—its blackness reaching out and enveloping her. Instinctively she closed her eyes. A moment later, they opened to a dull red glow. Reaching toward the source, Elspeth gripped the half-sleeve covering her hidden mark—an intricate pattern of curls, runes and vines feared by most people. She inched the cover down from her elbow toward her wrist, revealing a bright red light. The Force Ctseias mentioned was indeed within her and it was waking—like a dragon from its strengthening slumber. She held her arm aloft to discover a close but passable tunnel. This light guided her cautious progress as her steps left footfalls not even the Audaerie could hear.

At each twist in the passage, Elspeth confronted another Vision—her dreams awakened. Daemon Legions flashed in her inner eye. Blood rained upon the moors of her childhood. Lailiana and her precious Faerie sisters littered the Garden of Light with wings, limbs, hair and blood—pools of blood.

The white heat of terror that had blanketed her every night of her existence burned deep within Elspeth's soul. Sweat beaded along her forehead and dripped beneath her long, thick tresses. A nauseating pain deep within doubled her over, making the trek more burdensome. She stumbled into the wall when a hairpin curve in the tunnel caught her off guard. Recovering, she turned nearly back the opposite direction to follow the passage.

At that moment, Elspeth saw Him—Maelphaeus— as clear as if he stood flesh-to-flesh with her. He, the creator of her nightly horrors, looked down on her with eyes black as coal. His evil laugh sent shudders through her being; his breath seared the skin of her slender neck. This apparition towered over her with treacherous reality. Her glowing arm faltered—faded to a mere whisper of light— and she tripped on a stone. Terror and fear seized her breath in a scream at the dim outline of his wrinkled face, now inches from her own—more razor-sharp teeth than anything.

A hole opened beneath her, swallowing Elspeth in an eternal fall where Maelphaeus now adhered himself to her skin in a battle for her mind and soul. The putrid stench of Death from his mouth mixed with the sickening scent of her burning flesh. Casting away the terror viciously clawing at her heart, Elspeth clung instead to the images of her beloved sister-friend, Arabel, and all the peoples who looked to her for protection and guidance. All of Lailiana's wisdom morphed into a tangible reality for Elspeth. Love, loyalty, empathy and compassion washed over her as never before. She took on her rightful title— Elspeth Ealiverel, Shepherdess of the Fae, and protector of those in her care. This shored up her anger and hatred toward Maelphaeus. She halted, hanging suspended beneath him for a split second. In that blink, she saw his fears.

Soaring upward, she thrust him above her as power surged through her. Hard, fast he flew backward. The tunnel came back into sight, the ceiling closing in rapidly. With his fanged mouth hissing Daemons and Death and Destruction to be consumed in her Light, he struck the stone, shattering into nothingness in the brilliant illumination of her red mark—the Ealiverel.

"Out of Nothingness you came; to Nothingness you shall return. I shall protect the Light, Maelphaeus, King of Darkness!"

Her voice soared higher than the winds atop the tallest mountain and dove deeper than the lowest thunder. She drifted back down to the earth inside the passage, a captivating image of might both beauteous and terrifying. The walls reformed to their original state around her as her arm's glow dimmed.

She stood taller under the certainty of her Calling. She must triumph over the Evil One, but she ought first to be trained to understand and control this great Force. It was time to meet her Master, the One the Faeries dared only name in whispers—Minestio. The Mystery.

A thin streak of light gleamed ahead. Elspeth sprinted toward it. As she reached the opening, she gasped in awe. Above her towered a stone staircase, green with moss and narrowing as it rose. Atop it rested a building, pure white as Ctesias' silken mane. Light shone down upon it from somewhere out of sight, but the Temple itself glowed with a golden pulsing light. From countless archways and artistic designs etched into the moldings of the Temple's façade, a song drifted more mysterious and magical than the one at the gate now far removed. It summoned her, played for her, drew her to the massive red door that spanned half its front.

Elspeth Ealiverel, unisomuntia; unisomuntia.

Elspeth climbed the stairs rapidly, though they were high with barely a toehold on each step. The melody aided her, strengthening her footing with each note. She climbed as the song reached its crescendo when she crested the stairs and stood firm in front of the Temple Taepaeum. Her voice matched the climax swirling about her very soul as she sang her solo, *"Unisomunmia! Unisomamia!"*

The great arched door of the Temple opened, welcoming her. She strode in without pause, chin and shoulders high, though unaware what awaited her.

Greeting her was a cobbled entry lined on either side with gurgling fountains, long and low and filling her nostrils with a softness sweeter than any she'd known. She closed her eyes and breathed deeply, filling her being with peace and joy.

When she opened them, her gaze drifted along a grassy expanse softly sloping toward a mirror-like pond. A mighty rushing reached her ears and drew her sight across to a breathtaking waterfall, filling the pond beneath from a source unseen. It seemed to flow from the air itself. Within the cascades of water flitted Aquaerie Sprites, their round bottoms bouncing from stream to stream. She smiled at the sounds of their child-like laughter and singing.

A gentle tugging on her tartaned skirt brought Elspeth's attention back to her nearer surroundings. A wee Seelie in a brightly colored dress gazed shyly up at her Shepherdess' rosy cheeks. In her tiny, melodic voice Analeighlia spoke, "The Master much wishes Elspeth Ealiverel should retire to her chambers to refresh herself and ready for the commencement of her Training."

At that, the red-haired maiden turned to lead Elspeth to her room. She smiled after the bright red curls bouncing ahead of her and recalled her own dear Arabel. Her heart ached as she longed for the late-night talks when they shared their dreams. She gave thanks that Arabel was in kind James' care. They were born for each other. She'd known it from the first time he had happened upon their little hideout beside the stream.

But that was a home far away and long behind. She had much to learn and become to keep that homeland safe and protected. They climbed an ever-circling staircase. As she pondered how much higher they could possibly ascend, Elspeth spied the landing. Open to the entire expanse of the Temple grounds beneath, the chamber's view caught her breath.

Directly across from her flowed the waterfall. The Aquaerie waved, their merriment and joy clear as the water in which they danced. She smiled and waved in return before looking to her left. A bed clothed in silver silken linens extended across the room's width. Faerie fronds and Wary Willow vines draped above it. A soft breeze caused the lovely scent from below to caress Elspeth's skin. She looked up to see more Faerie fronds floating above. They were joined in groups of three and seven, each twirling gently so as to breathe just enough movement into the surrounding air.

Beyond the bed stood a great wardrobe, ancient and ornate and as red as the Temple's entrance. Nearest to her, Elspeth spied a smooth white stone basin large enough for her to stretch out and bathe within. A miniature double of the waterfall across the way sourced the everflowing water of this pool. Analeighlia's laughter rippled like the water as she noticed the delight on Elspeth's face.

"Aye, 'tis for ye. Cast off the grime of yer journey and sink within the cleansing waters therein. Ye'll find new clothing in yon wardrobe, then ye'll dine."

Elspeth followed Analeighlia's gaze to a previously overlooked cushioned chaise and ornate table centered before the view. To the right a deep brown door, strong and sturdy, barred the way to mysteries untold.

"What lies beyond that door?" Elspeth queried as the wee Seelie began to descend the stairs.

"Yer Training," she replied simply. "It will open to ye once ye're rested and readied."

Elspeth eyed the door for a moment more as curiosity held her attention. Soon, though, lavender and vanilla rose from the bath behind her, drawing her toward its intoxicating scent. She stood a moment, touching the smoothness of the bath before plunging her hand beneath the fall. The water's warmth filled her with an inexplicable longing for its cleansing powers to cover her whole being.

As she removed the garments of her travels, she cast off the anxieties, uncertainties and hardships gathered along her way. Any residue remaining drifted away from her body as she sank into the water's depths. She closed her eyes and laid back against the edge, allowing the waterfall to flow over her hair and down her face and neck. She breathed in the purity of the water itself, deep into her lungs. It filled her with a power she'd never known.

She slid down into the water and opened her eyes to Visions of beauty and Faeries of Light, fields of flowers and unicorns. Eail whinnied a greeting from her meadow. Elspeth watched her grow into a mare of exquisite beauty and grace and power with her red-patterned horn shining forth and exuding well-wishes and friendship like a beacon. She remained within the water's embrace for what felt like decades before floating to the surface where the breeze of the fans carried her up and out to the floor.

She stood and dried beneath the wind's caress before crossing the room to the wardrobe, her hand exploring the softness of the bedding as she passed it. As she took hold of the knob shaped like the head of a unicorn, Elspeth heard again the lyrical whinny of Eail. She found within one set of clothes—men's clothes with feminine tailoring.

Her stomach reminded her brain that it desired sustenance. She turned back toward the chaise and table, now topped with a feast—roasted venison with a thick gravy lay in the midst of potatoes and carrots with tiny pearl onions mixed in. She found a silk robe to cover with before crossing to lay back on the soft cushions as she ate, filling herself as if she hadn't eaten in many moons. She tipped up a heavy earthen mug. The whiskey it contained coated her throat with warmth.

Soon Elspeth found herself drowsy with food and drink and glided back toward the luxurious invitation of the massive bed. As she slid into a cocoon of warmth and softness, her final thought was of the door and the Training that lay in store. It was a musing of eager anticipation and not one of worry.

Elspeth drifted off into her first dreamless sleep. When she awoke from what seemed an eternal, peaceful slumber, the season had changed. She cast off the linens and padded in bare feet to her clothes.

She first slid into a corset more comfortable than any she'd ever experienced and socks both thin and warm. Next came leather breeches sewn for a woman's figure. Over her head, she slipped a long red tartan tunic before donning and lacing up a leather vest shaped to rest beneath her tunic-covered bosom.

Elspeth gazed down at the red markings encircling her forearm. They stood out now, bared to the world. A restless readiness stirred within her. It radiated throughout her being, not from the pit of her stomach but from this tattoo that had marked her from birth. She breathed deeply, ready to face her future and accept her Calling.

She took up the final piece—a wide leather belt. This accessory, the vest and the fitted breeches perfectly matched the brown of her wavy locks. Beside the wardrobe she found boots with fur tops and pulled them on to complete her new look.

Elspeth marveled at the comfort and flexibility of the clothes. She could scale mountains, traverse many miles, run through dense forests and fight any foe in them. After a final glimpse across to the waterfall and its merry Sprites, she strode to the door. As she locked her eyes on the wooden façade without a handle or knob, the egress unsealed for her.

She faced then her own reflection and marveled that this door should contain a mirror. What part could this play in her Training? As she admired the clothing she now wore, Elspeth reached out to touch the reflection of her visible mark. Rather than feeling smooth glass, she felt a slight give like semi-solid water. She pressed harder, and her hand sank through. Elspeth spared not a glance for the luxury behind as she followed through to whatever lay beyond.

She stood on a small ridge in a glade with trees looming ahead. Once through, she turned to see only a path into more forest behind her. No door existed in this realm. When she looked forward once more, she found herself face to chest with a man, muscular and intimidating. His skin was darker than any she'd ever encountered. He towered taller than Ctesias with shoulders nearly as broad.

Gaping scars and jagged marks of battles past covered his otherwise smooth head. One scar began at his left temple and continued its deep gorge through his eye, down and across his nose and mouth to his neck just above the right shoulder. It was hard to look anywhere else. Though much of his eye beneath the gouge was missing, she glimpsed a hint of yellow-green. His other eye glinted a goldish-brown that glowed in the sunlight.

"At last, Elspeth Ealiverel." His voice boomed, shaking her and taking her by surprise.

She worried she'd come to the wrong place, for she believed his countenance held much hate and loathing. Surely this wasn't the one to be her Master. There was something in his penetrating gaze, something that left her uncertain. A seed of distrust planted itself within her heart, and she narrowed her eyes.

"How many ages have passed ere I arrived?"

"Time and space are fluid here, as the ebbing and flowing tides course in and out and drift up and down the coastline of Aê." His voice shook her soul as he answered. After a moment's pause during which his unequal eyes pierced through her, he answered one of her unspoken questions. "I am your Master and Trainer, the One whom the Lesser Faeries call Minestio."

Elspeth did not hide the wariness in her eyes. She was still unclear as to what sort of Training she required anyway.

"You've still no inkling the vast array and true depth of your Powers, have you?"

Lightning flashed and wind howled in her ear before Elspeth even felt the blow to her temple that sent her careening toward a tree by the path. A staff, previously unnoticed, rested in Minestio's hand as he considered her with something she took as scorn.

"Pity."

With this he turned and quickly passed the space between them and the forest. His hulking back disappeared within the trees. Elspeth's head rang from the blow as she trotted to catch up. A tingle of unease crept down her spine.

"Shouldn't I have a weapon if I'm supposed to defend myself from flying objects?" Elspeth questioned.

"You must first learn to use the weapon you were created to be," Minestio replied tersely. He stopped abruptly and faced her, a mountain of might. "Your focus stops on the surface, Elspeth Ealiverel. This is dangerous for you … for all."

Never would Elspeth have imagined Minestio's voice could be so quiet, so serious, so foreboding.

"You've seen Maelphaeus only as he is; clothed in the warped, depraved features of his Evil. He will never appear to you in that form outside of dreams, Elspeth. He will cloak himself in a light more glorious than any you have seen. The Light of this world does not always shine forth; neither the Darkness.

"You judge on the surface. I saw your eyes pass judgement at first glimpse of me. Do not deny it. I see within, throughout your Heart—you do not trust that I am the One to whom you were sent. So be it, but you will discover the truth through your Training. And, regardless of which way you master it, you must learn to discern the Heart."

His voice thundered, "Let us begin!" He spun and marched off through the trees.

Elspeth's attention focused on keeping up with Minestio's massive strides and missed out as their surroundings morphed into somewhere else. Towering Lookout Oaks shrank themselves down into Wispy Shrubberies scattered with abandon across a vast plain.

She blinked, and the grasses became blinding desert sands. The sun bore down unmercifully, and her tongue scraped against her cheek. She opened her mouth, but Minestio was no longer in sight.

She stopped short. Sand rose and stuck in the fur of her mystically cool boots. Realizing her mistake at the distraction, she craned her neck in every direction. He was nowhere. Where was here anyway? Far, far in the distance a black form appeared. Could she have simply lagged behind?

Elspeth set her course for the figure even as it approached her. Before she could comprehend what her vision told her, a massive creature barreled down upon her. She glanced all around—in vain. No battlements appeared. All she had to defend herself was sand—sand as far as her eye could see.

Eyes!

The Beast was nearly upon her ... only two bounds more. Its eyes glowed uneven—yellowish-green and a glistening gold. Power billowed inside her. She saw her battle plan unfold in her mind and recalled the first night her eyes glowed.

Once, long ago, when she was but a child, Elspeth had set off on one of her nighttime wanders across the moors of home only to fall down a steep ravine. The night was pitch and she had no idea where she had woken up. She was far wiser and braver then, so she sat calmly upon a fallen limb and closed her eyes. At first she chanted, "Help will come. Help will come. Help will come." Then something within the depths of her being stirred. She ceased her chant and heard *anamaeus en mi pouramblaês.* She opened her eyes and said, "Help within I possess."

She felt her eyes glow then. It was kind Lailiana who had told her they colored red around the edges during those moments. She watched herself follow a hidden path out of the ravine and back through the woods she knew and loved, all the way to her own warm bed. With a blink to clear the fogginess of that first Sight, Elspeth stood up, dusted off her nightgowned bottom and did just what she'd already witnessed herself do.

Anamaeus en mi pouramblaês!

Her Vision cleared; she carried it out, as she had done long ago. Elspeth danced and twirled, gaining speed. As she moved, the sand followed until she possessed a vicious funnel of it. Amid the stinging grains, she sang forth in a voice simultaneously breathtaking and horrifying:

Shamaeleigh un mi san ye, san ye sun ma shey cam a mi caulderon. Fil en fleigh a destrass aell Kaftar ... neun!

Elspeth's power radiated through the sand cloud. She hovered above the Beast with its gnashing teeth and sharpened claws. Her entire body glowed red as the Ealiverel's power consumed her; arms upraised, she commanded the sand to form into shards of glass. With one vicious thrust she cast it all at the now-shrinking Kaftar, were-hyena hybrid of nightmares. The Beast roared with a ground-shaking howl and reached its fullest height. It cast out its front limbs to dispel the glass into rainwater before shedding its form and disappearing from Elspeth's sight as the moisture cascaded around her.

When the rain cleared, she found herself in a meadow. In the center, light shone upon something too bright to look upon. She crept toward this new trial, for that's what these must be. Her powers and abilities were being awakened, tested. She pressed through the beam of light, as thick as a shimmering curtain. Gasping, she dropped beside Eail. Life was leaving her.

Elspeth's forearm burned as her markings glowed in unison with those upon Eail's horn. Each breath the filly took went more quickly and came more slowly. Elspeth felt the glow in her eyes again. This time, a Vision arose from her worst nightmares. She witnessed once more the battlefield on which she had ridden Eail in their victorious conquest. Instead of a victor's charge atop Eail, she looked down upon barren earth beneath her feet. It ran red with the blood of Faeries, light creatures and innocent beings. She stood in the midst and cried in anger and pain toward the heavens. Eail did not appear.

"We are fated, you and I," Elspeth cried into the rainbow mane beneath her. "Without you, I fail. Whatever this great Calling on my life, I cannot claim victory without your power beneath me. I need you."

The filly shuddered beneath her, and Elspeth felt her fighting to respond. Rays of unspoken love drifted about her rounded shoulders. She opened her now-green eyes in time to catch a glimpse of the filly's—oddly mismatched—before Eail closed them and exhaled.

"I haven't even heard the melody of your voice yet, lovely Princess of Light, though I already love it … and you. Please. Don't leave me."

Panic seized Elspeth's heart; grief overtook her. She wept. Her arm burned as it never had before … and, finally, she understood.

Anamaeus en mi pouramblaês! she whispered and then chanted louder, Lumen-lina, de ana mi. Lêfta su. Dhae, gun ta mi toren ei lumen-lina, de ana mi. Eail! Eail, rêstah!

She passed her forearm along the unicorn's still body until it locked above Eail's crest, beneath her flowing mane of many colors. The glow intensified, its beam healing the invisible wound.

Eail arose then, alive and well. She shook neck and mane and soared into the light-beam still veiling them from the world beyond. In the haste of Eail's ascent, Elspeth couldn't even say goodbye. As her hoofed friend rose, Elspeth descended, not into the earth but into the depths of the ocean.

Sea creatures and serpents danced around her, caging her in and pressing her down. Deeper, deeper she went. No longer could she see the light above. Darkness consumed her, and she withdrew into it. Rage and malice shrouded her existence.

Her mind flooded with the drowning waves of her Trials. The Beast she defeated. The horrors of losing Eail. The battle with Maelphaeus back in the tunnel aeons thence. A final crashing of the surf within her pulled Elspeth beneath its swell. She clung to her dearest Arabel—the one human who fully knew her—as she clutched the memory of their goodbye to her shattering heart.

All was darkened from her sight. Hope drowned in this abyss of Evil. Daemons replaced dark creatures;

their movements grew ever wilder, more erratic and dangerous. Weapons of Eternal Flame and consuming Darkness lashed at her from all sides. Their burns and stings slashed at her soul. Further she descended until two lights came steadily toward her. Two glowing and uneven lamps. Yellow or green? Gold glinted in one, though only the eerie glow of flashing flames shed light.

Before she could further ponder the orbs of color, Elspeth gasped and recoiled as the owner of those eyes took shape in her sight.

Maelphaeus.

Maelphaeus, in his fullest might and power, surrounded by his Legions. His laughter churned the waters. The horrors his amusement contained chilled the marrow. Ocean depths swirled around them. Rising. Roiling. Climbing. A Whirlpool of Despair and Darkness.

It gripped Elspeth with vice-like strength.

Anamaeus en mi pouramblaês!

All her rage against what she'd lost or could lose or must face gathered in her heart like a billowing storm. She saw now only Maelphaeus—with mismatched eyes— breeder of Evil and Dark.

All her malice focused on him. Her glowing eyes latched on to a speck of fear she felt more than saw.

Elspeth's fury overflowed as Maelphaeus' grip weakened slightly. She took control of the whirlpool, filling it with Hope and Light from the visions of all the creatures and beings she loved, the moors she'd raced, the streams she'd tripped within, the forests her bare feet learned to trust more than most people.

As her heart overflowed with love and beauty and goodness, she shone forth with an ethereal light of purest white, blinding all the dark creatures observing from above, sending all the Daemons shrieking from its perfection, and causing Maelphaeus to stumble into the midst of the pool. She caught him in her glow and carried him upward with her, soaring through ages of ocean, now parted for her. They ascended in a capsizing spray of foam and salt.

Maelphaeus would not give up easily. He regained some footing, now in the air, as the two forms gripped one another's necks. They spun, dove and soared again in a mighty wrestling match. Their battle waged for all realms and regions of the Earth and all the people, creatures and beings within. This war as old as Time would not be decided in one battle, great though it may be. And so, Maelphaeus pressed back from Elspeth. Each one flew backward for miles with the force before regaining balance. Within her, Elspeth's rage boiled until she could contain it no longer, and her white light tinted dark green.

Elspeth dove to the ocean's surface, scooping water and fashioning it as she soared toward the Master of Filth. As she swooped from below the great monster his eyes widened with understanding. Stronger than any claymore and sharper than any armor-piercing lance, Elspeth's water sword was crafted with one intent—to murder with malice. She struck, and he dove beneath her but could not escape the wrath of her blade. The pain sank in as his blood spewed out of the wound which spanned from his temple, through his eye and down his neck. Elspeth watched his eyes.

In their pain and uneven coloring, she knew. Her Master and Trainer—scarred Minestio—bore the wounds of her unchecked fury.

Grief dispelled the rest of her rage as she caught his falling form and bore him toward land. Her tears bathed his wounds as they came to a halt in the glade where they began. The light and season had changed once more. Trees had grown. Time had passed.

Elspeth sank to earth with Minestio in his regular form. She used her forearm to close and heal the wound she had caused. The healing done to the best of her newfound ability, she wept again as his eyes met hers. In them she saw his Heart—one of Goodness, Love, and Light.

"*Emastêae*. Teacher. Forgive my reckless rage. I saw not the Heart."

Blindly, Elspeth had mistaken his concern for malice. She cast herself upon his heaving chest, bathing him in tears until times and seasons had turned and twisted round them again.

When weeping ceased and healing progressed, they rose and sat together on a fallen tree.

"You knew … before." Her subdued voice compared not at all with the one that commanded both elements and healing earlier.

"Before. After. Time is, and Time shall always be. What is ordained must come to pass."

"Then, did you know I would … heal you?"

Minestio replied with a slow-surfacing smile, "Many things are known. Many futures may be seen. The knowledge of which shall come to pass is not always given." He nodded at her. "Many futures you've seen already. Which shall be?"

"Can I know that?" she asked in wonder.

Minestio only gazed at her with a half-smile that shone in his eyes.

"It was you. Every time. It was you. I should have seen the first time, in the Kaftar."

"Your Training had to continue for all three Trials— the Triucible—to match the three points of your Powers. Come."

At Minestio's command, the woods parted to reveal the moss-covered stairs to the bright white Temple Elspeth entered earlier. She followed his lead, taking three steps for each of his. The immense red door opened. They entered and stepped not onto a cobbled patio but a marbled floor, their reflections cast beneath them.

Elspeth looked up in awe at the Temple's grandeur. The space was simple at first glance, a giant rectangle with walls so high she barely saw the ceiling. It appeared now as the waters of the ocean on a clear, calm day—a cheerful blue with tufts of waves breaking across its expanse. An occasional pod of porpoises swam across.

Woodwork hand-carved into creatures—both Light and Dark—adorned the walls. From top to bottom these carvings stood out, the craftsmanship so exquisite and precise the creatures seemed alive. A few times Elspeth swore a faun or centaur blinked at her from above or a banshee glared as she passed. Flecks of gold highlighted varying parts of each figure, causing shimmering light to produce an even greater sense of movement.

Elspeth followed Minestio across the marbled floor toward a pedestaled basin, miniscule in the cavernous hall. The Master stopped and stepped aside. Elspeth glanced at his stalwart gaze toward the basin and wondered what mysteries awaited.

She paused to glance back at Minestio whose eyes remained fixed. With a deep breath, Elspeth turned and bowed her head to see what lay within. Her reflection floated in what appeared simply as water. She grasped the sides and looked more carefully until she spied the ocean reflected behind her. As she watched, it rapidly darkened. The waves swelled. Her eyes then claimed her attention— the glowing red rims reappearing. Water in the basin surged, and the mirrored image she'd just witnessed became scenes of the past, scenes of the present and scenes of the future. Unlike the Pool of Future Light, this water held both truths and half-truths and devastating lies, all mixed together in a twisted timeline of uncertainty and despair.

Elspeth's heart burned at the horrors she saw and the Darkness she witnessed within her own soul. She gasped for air as she thought herself bonded to the basin, until … *Anamaeus en mi pouramblaês!*

With the strength in those words, Elspeth overcame the Magic's hold on her and released herself from its vicious grip. The scenes ceased flashing, and she stood upright with her hands back at her sides. Again the waters churned, gently now, as she heard a Voice from within speak to her in deeply rumbling, yet pleasant tones.

"Elspeth Ealiverel, your Training has now begun as you have first faced the fates that lie ahead and still stand tall. To your Master, Minestio Emastêae, hearken and heed all with which he teaches and guides you. You are the prophesied One of whom Dhae proclaimed:

Battles wage within the Warrior; Tenderness grows within the Shepherdess. She who trods unclad amongst thistles, Rustling not a blade of grass.

Elspeth recognized the final stanza of her own prophecy, recalling the Triucible and how it shed a new light on these lines.

"You host tremendous battles within, Shepherdess of the Fae," the Voice continued, for this was not an audible proclamation but a conversation inside Elspeth's own mind. "Your war has only now begun. You of callous, guarded heart have thrice learned to open up in love and compassion. This Tenderness will grow as you seek to use it wisely."

Thrice?

"Arabel. Eail. Minestio."

Minestio mentioned the three points of my Power. Would this Tenderness be one?

"You guess in part, Child of Light. Your Powers form a triangle for perfection within you—when each is wielded properly."

The Voice became foreboding with the final words, and Elspeth understood the gravity of the warning.

"At the base of this your Trialaeum reside your Power over Nature and your Power to Heal."

Elspeth's understanding grew. *I commanded the sand and the ocean. I healed Eail and Minestio. But … he I healed only after I had nearly killed him in my rage.*

"The Trials awakened your Senses, controlled by the Ealiverel. The apex of your Trialaeum must be your Power over Evil Within. Elspeth, you shall learn not only to use your first two Powers, you must learn to use them rightly. You should use the first to defeat your enemies and defend the defenseless, but do so without succumbing to hatred and malice in your attack. You also ought to learn to harness the Tenderness of your Power to Heal without allowing your compassion in grief to fester into a Darkness as dark as your love is Light. Connecting each point of this Trialaeum encapsulates the crux of your Training."

Elspeth turned from the Voice to Minestio. He looked now into her eyes.

"Are you ready, Elspeth Ealiverel?"

"I am."

"Step through the veil where your weapons await you."

SCIENCE FICTION

THE BLUE ROSE

By Audrey Driscoll

https://audreydriscoll.com/

Deon and Luna grew up together in their ancient, multi-level City, an outpost far from the Blasted Lands. Now Deon is a Fabricator with a grand ambition, and Luna is a member of the Guards, pledged to maintain the City's laws. When Deon is inspired to make a perilous journey, Luna must suspend her faith in order and search for her friend on the edge of Chaos.

Black. *Again.* Every bloom on the rose was black, grotesque, and necrotic. His latest formula had failed, just like all its predecessors.

Banging shut the glasshouse door with an oath, Deon whirled through his tiny laboratory and out into the courtyard, not bothering to stopper and put away the flasks on the workbench.

"All right, it's time."

Deon made for the canal-side street with only one thought in mind. Sylvius. He'd promised.

Fragrant blooms of the callimandra tree mingled their scent with the rankness of the black canal water. Waxy white petals floated on the turbid surface, accepted along with all the muck of the lower town.

Intent on his goal, Deon ignored the scents, both fetid and sweet, as he made for the East Funicular. Seeing a long queue of sweepers, runners and leaf-gatherers waiting to board, he ran the stairs instead. Only nine flights to Sylvius's house. Nine long, steep flights.

Deon retraced his steps to the canal and the First Stair, pausing when a callimandra bloom, spent and heavy with pollen, brushed his cheek and landed on the stones at his feet. He stooped and picked it up, remembering the old maxim, "Callimandra kiss brings luck to the daring." He needed luck, masses of it, if he was to make a blue rose for Aldona Magna.

Sniffing the musky fragrance of the flower, Deon remembered the Lady Aldona, tall in pleated sapphire silk, her straight dark brows beneath the crown of braided hair, serene eyes regarding the newly qualified Fabricators in the Academy's assembly hall. Her voice rang out like the noon chime of the Hour-Bell. Her eyes, whose color matched precisely the blue of her gown, rested on each of them in turn. "In my task of maintaining the life of our City, I may ask great things of you. I may demand of you an iron horse, a harp of crystal, a cloak of wind, or a ship of air. And from one of you"—here her glance fell on Deon where he stood at the end of the rearmost row— "from one of you I may require a blue rose."

She smiled then, making a bow of her lips, from which flew an invisible arrow into the heart of Deon. "My Lady," he murmured, in such a hushed tone that she could not possibly hear, "I will make for you a blue rose, and I will do it by the day of the Sun's Exaltation."

The memory lightened his feet, and he was at the top the Fourth Stair before the reality struck him like a bag full of grindstones—scarcely a month left before the Exaltation, and the rose he had injected with his latest elixir was a black and ugly mess.

Deon sank onto a stone bench under an ancient cypress whose lower limbs were supported by crutches fashioned by generations of tree-healers. The tiny red birds that lived in the cliffs made swooping arcs of scarlet through the air, uttering their high-pitched cries. From this height (only halfway to the Ninth Terrace where Sylvius lived), he looked across the river plain to where the green fields of grain and vegetables gave way to forests and scrub, and beyond them to misty, unguessed distances.

Sylvius knows. He was one of the Master Fabricators, who made colors and flavors, scents and textures.

Always when Deon asked him questions, he gave answers. Almost always.

You must open your heart.

Three weeks ago, Sylvius had taken him to a euphorium on the Second level, behind the brick houses of the district, its door half hidden under a swag of ivy. In the dimly lit interior, crowded with a motley assortment of folk, they drank a fiery red spirit from small crystal glasses, and Sylvius talked. Talked in a way most unlike himself, quick and nervous.

"As a Fabricator, you are aware that Making is merely rearranging the energies that flow through the world. But if you want—or need—to do something extraordinary, you must throw yourself into the work. Literally—mind, heart and body. You must open your heart and let your lifeblood flow upon the dead stones. I see you don't understand. But you will, when you experience a great need, a great desire."

"A great desire..." Deon murmured.

He leaned over the parapet, removing the spectacles he wore for close work. A fat, bruise-colored cloud lolled on the horizon, perhaps over the Blasted Lands. If the substance he needed didn't exist in the City, he would search elsewhere. He put the spectacles into a waistcoat pocket and continued on his way, rising stair by stair, as brick houses gave way to ones built of stone.

At the gate of the Ninth Terrace, Deon showed his copper token and muttered the password. The gate-guard admitted him with her usual silent stare and nod. A minute later he rang the bell of Sylvius's house.

There was no response for so long that Deon rang again, frowning. Where was Perrin? As if the second ring was the required element, the door opened, revealing Sylvius's butler, manservant and laboratory assistant, solid and familiar in his leather apron.

"Mr. Deon, sir! I'm sorry, but Master Sylvius is not at home."

"Hello, Perrin," he said. "When do you expect him back?"

"Not until late, I'm afraid, but Miss Luna is here. Oh, and Master Sylvius asked me to give you this." Perrin reached into his apron pocket and held out an envelope. "Deon" was written on it in Sylvius's handwriting.

The envelope contained something lumpy, but before Deon could open it, a door opened at the end of the hallway, and a girl ran down the hall toward them. No longer a girl, he saw as she came closer, but a young woman. Luna, Sylvius's niece.

She was still gawky—though past the age when gawkiness can be charming—and a bit plump. Her untidy long brown hair hung about her face, and she brushed it out of her eyes. "Deon! It's good to see you. It's been ages. Come along to the library."

She turned with such spirit that her skirts swirled about her legs. Still with the hem coming down, Deon noted with amusement. Some things never changed. He followed her because he could not think of anything better to do. Sylvius's study and library were the center of his world. Deon had spent many hours there. Perhaps the familiar place would reassure him he'd made the right decision.

Luna closed the door and gestured toward the envelope in his hand. "Well, open it!" she said. "Perrin wouldn't let me, since it's addressed to you." She picked up a penknife from Sylvius's desk and handed it to him.

He didn't remember Luna being so bossy, but then he hadn't seen her in months. "Rightly so. Perrin's a great one for correctness. What are you up to these days? You're just out of your Academy, right? Are you apprenticed to the Council of Matriarchs or something?"

"I've been in the Guards for the past six months," said Luna. "Aren't you going to open that envelope?" Deon slit it open and drew out a sheet of paper. Thrusting the envelope into a pocket, he unfolded the note and read.

It's now or never, and if you wait too long, it will be never. Remember what I told you the last time we met? The enclosed should help. Sylvius.

"And you? Still wasting time in coffee salons with those aspiring poets?"

Deon was too elated to be annoyed. "My friends, you mean? I'm a Fabricator now. I have a laboratory."

"Really? Where?"

Deon hesitated. "On the Lower, actually. Near the canal, but it suits me."

"What do you make there? Singing flowers? Or flying ones? As if birds didn't do those things already."

Deon frowned. "Just because you're making yourself into one of the pillars of the City doesn't mean you can make fun of us Fabricators. Someone has to create beauty. Didn't you listen to the Lady's speech last week?

Or were you too busy memorizing rules and marching in formation?"

Luna's face grew pink. She pressed her lips together.

"Never mind. So what's in that envelope from Uncle Syl? It felt lumpy."

"Never *you* mind. Since you think I'm just a frivolous idler, you can't possibly be interested. I came to ask Sylvius a question, but since he's out, there's no point in my being here. And he did answer it, in a way." Deon held up the note. He went over to one of the bookshelves that lined the room, pausing by the collection of travelers' writings. "Luna, do you know— has Sylvius ever left the City?"

Luna hesitated. "I don't think so. Hardly anyone does that anymore."

"Not now, maybe, but we used to. And Sylvius has nearly every book ever written by people who did." Deon pulled a heavy tome from one of the shelves. "*A Journey to the Southlands.* Griffon Descar. Everyone knows Descar's *Journey.* And then there's Alluna Pesca."

"Oh, Pesca! Everyone knows she made up all that stuff! A world of noise and smoke? Infernal machines? No one else ever saw any of it."

"That was in ancient times. What I'd like to see is a decent account of the Blasted Lands."

"There isn't one," said Luna, staring at him. "If anyone's ever gone there, they haven't lived to write about it."

"A few got close," said Deon. "Take Valery Nigill, for example. The trouble is, she never got closer than the edges and spent all her time painting pictures of plants." No blue roses, though, he thought.

"Sensible woman!" said Luna. "But then, women are sensible. Someone has to be."

"Oh, never mind!" Deon shoved the book back into its place, releasing a puff of dust. "Look, I've got to go now. Things to do, you know."

"I can imagine. I'll show you out."

Remembering the envelope in his pocket, Deon pulled it out. Inside were a bead of blue glass and a brass token. Good old Sylvius! He slid the envelope back into his pocket, an involuntary smile forming on his lips.

Luna closed the door of the library and Deon ran down the hall, startling Perrin, who emerged from the kitchen stairs.

"Sorry, Perrin, I've got to run." And run he did, to the funicular, making a list along the way. Home first, to get the necessities together. No time to go to his mother's Ministry; he would send her a message. *Going away for a few days.* No, it would be longer, a few weeks at least.

***

A week passed before anyone realized Deon was missing. Everyone assumed he was somewhere else. When his friends realized none of them had seen him for several days, a disorganized search was conducted. Soon after that, the Guard was informed, and an organized one ensued.

In Sylvius's study, Luna flopped into a chair. She wore her Guards uniform, wet with rain. "No sign of him anywhere," she said. "Uncle, I have to ask you something."

Sylvius finished writing a note and closed two books, carefully inserting bookmarks. Sliding his spectacles down his nose, he turned to Luna. "Ask away, my dear."

"Do you think Deon has left the City?"

"What gives you that idea?" Sylvius asked.

"The last time I saw him was here, just about a week ago, Perrin gave him an envelope. It was addressed to him, in your handwriting. He opened it right there and seemed pleased at what he saw."

Sylvius nodded but said nothing. He rested his elbows on the arms of his chair and pressed his fingertips together.

"He didn't tell me what was inside, but I saw something that looked like an exit token for the Outer Gates."

Sylvius nodded again, studying his fingers.

"Did you give him that token?"

Sylvius dropped his hands and raised his head, looking at Luna with his clear grey eyes. "I did."

Luna leaned forward. *"Why?"*

"Because he was ready."

"Ready for what? Deon was—*is*—the most unready person I've ever known. Why would he need, or even want, an exit token?"

"He needed to go on a voyage of discovery, what we Fabricators call 'making a journey,' and I thought he was ready. Mentally, anyway."

"But no one leaves the City. Not really."

"You know that's not true, my dear. Misfits and criminal elements often choose to leave. Exiles have scraped a living beyond the walls for thousands of years. They fish and hunt and grow crops. A few scavenge the Blasted Lands."

"What for?"

"Materials unobtainable here that are of interest to Fabricators. There's a kind of inn about a day's travel from the City, where transactions are carried out."

"Have you been there?"

Sylvius nodded. "Several times."

Luna rested her chin on a hand. "Why would Deon need such things?"

"For a grand and rather impractical project, to turn a red rose blue. That was his stated reason. But the true reason is to discover himself and his abilities and thereby inspire others."

Luna shook her head and slapped her palms on her thighs. "But going to the Blasted Lands! How could you sit here comfortably and encourage him to do something so stupid? He's probably dead."

"Oh, he has no reason to go to the Blasted Lands himself. I referred him to one of the more reliable groups of Exile scavengers. They'll keep him safe."

"Scavengers! They're unreliable and corrupt."

Sylvius raised an eyebrow. "The voice of experience? Unlike you, I've had dealings with Exiles. Just like us, they aren't all the same."

Luna drew a breath to protest, but Sylvius raised a hand. "Hear me out. You and I both know the history of our City, island of order and beauty in a chaotic world.

We know that is because of the rules laid down by our Foremothers. You are one who lives those rules every day. But beauty…"

Sylvius took off his spectacles and laid them on the desk. "Those who study birds know that in most species, it is the males that are brightly colored and ornamented. You might also say that of us. Women, from the High Lady to the army of Cultivators, and all the grades and degrees in between, keep the City alive and orderly. We men, to counter our inherently destructive impulses, have been called upon to create things of beauty. Our combined talents have maintained civilization here for thousands of years. But those who seek the ineffable are privileged to engage in what some regard as frivolities. And some choose to seek out chaos."

Sylvius picked up the spectacles and toyed with them. "True beauty is born of chaos. Actions such as Deon's journey, which he decided to undertake with my help and encouragement, may benefit all Citizens by inspiring a few."

For a long moment, Luna sat looking at her tightly clasped hands. When she spoke, her voice was tight. "I can't see what benefit to anyone can come of sending a soft, untrained boy anywhere near the Blasted Lands."

"We will see, when Deon comes back."

"*If* he comes back."

***

Summer came, and the City dreamed in warm air and sunlight. Birds nested and Climbers climbed to find eggs for those who could afford the exorbitant prices for

68

these strictly regulated delicacies. Fabricators tinkered with their creations. Bee-gardeners tended their plots on the edges of the vine-terraces. The Cultivators cultivated and in due course, harvested.

Luna found herself drawn to a small garden on the Seventh Level, near to the Temple of Music. Overgrown and unfrequented, it looked toward the empty country beyond the City's fields, and beyond that to the Blasted Lands.

The standard protocols regarding missing persons had been observed. Searchers had returned without result and there was deemed to be no reason to persist. Deon was of age and had left the City with the proper token. To travel with groups of Exiles, or for that matter, alone, was a choice available to any Citizen, although frowned upon and rarely made.

Through the winter, with its rains, frosts, icy winds and occasional snows, Luna continued to watch, fitting her vigils in the abandoned garden into her busy round of duties and responsibilities. She told no one about them, not even Sylvius. Every week or two, though, she spent an evening in his study, sitting on the rug before the fire, nursing a cup of steaming fruit brew and poring over travelers' tales. All her thoughts and speculations led to the same hard truths: Deon was gone into the wide world.

Maybe he would return, and maybe not.

***

Small owls spent the winters in the grottoes warmed by the steam escaping from the ductwork conveying volcanic heat to warm the City. Their presence was welcome because they fed upon rats that threatened stored foodstuffs. In Spring the owls flew away to the forests to build their nests of sticks and the beardlike lichens that draped the northern sides of ancient trees.

One morning, Luna saw long strings of geese and ducks flying inland, to the rumored lakes and marshes on the edges of the Blasted Lands. As their honks and cries died away with distance, she made up her mind.

That afternoon, she requested leave from her Captain and assembled equipment and foodstuffs. The evening before her departure, she knocked once more on Sylvius's door.

"I wasn't going to tell you," she began.

"But you thought you should give me a chance to argue with you," he said, smiling.

"Yes. Are you going to?"

"No," said Sylvius. "I know you're more than capable and ready. But I'll give you this." He went to a cabinet and returned with an object some two feet long, contained in a leather case.

"What is it?" Luna unfastened the clasps on the case.

"A fire-stick. An invention of mine. Perhaps you could test its effectiveness, should you find yourself in a tight spot."

He showed her how to use the device and gave her a supply of iron projectiles and explosive propellants. "Thank you, Uncle Syl," said Luna. "I can see why you didn't bring this to the attention of the Governing Council. But actually, I hope I won't need to use it." Sylvius nodded. "It may be that what made the Blasted

Lands began with something like this," he said, on his face a mixture of slyness and regret. "The Foremothers knew what they were doing when they wrote the laws. That's why I'm giving it to you."

***

It took three days for the City to vanish below the horizon. Luna let her mind drift, disengaging from the lifelong routines of the City while her body jogged along at the steady pace set by the Exiles. Sometimes she thought about her last conversation with Sylvius, feeling the weight of the firestick strapped to her knapsack. She thought how bleak the land seemed, flat and featureless compared to the heights and depths, the hollows and pinnacles of the City. She listened to the talk of the Exiles who were her guides and companions, noting the similarities and differences in speech and manner between them and the people of home. Otherwise, her mind traced the twenty years of her life, hovering over nameless summer days when two children had played in sunlit gardens or pursued intricate games in the cobbled streets and alleys of their ancient home.

Only once did anything occur that might have been described as a "tight spot." They met another group of travelers. Greetings and exchanges of news developed into an argument, which became a fight. Fists flew and knives were drawn. Standing apart from the fray, Luna readied the firestick for action as Sylvius had shown her.

Which of the struggling shapes deserved impaling by iron projectile? How would that improve the situation?

Luna shrugged and aimed the firestick at a large stone several yards away. The loud bang and shower of sparks ended the fight. Luna ran to stamp out a small fire that had started. The grass was damp and it didn't take long.

"I haven't seen such a thing before," said the caravan's leader, eyeing the firestick as Luna returned it to its case.

"Something one of our Fabricators gave me," she said.

"Well, it gave our folk something to think about besides fighting."

***

A week on the road, they entered low hills. The road dipped and rose, twisting this way and that, showing bits of itself and then hiding. On one of the still distant segments, a number of moving figures appeared. Humans, and some unfamiliar animal, the sight of which produced muttered remarks among Luna's companions. The next time the group appeared, she saw the humped beast clearly. Though she still did not recognize it, the sight stirred a memory of things she had read not long before her journey.

The third glimpse was a telling one. "Blasters," said a man walking at Luna's left.

"I know 'em," said another. "Barka's lot. They're not as bad as some. Rigged up some sort of outfits for protection, and don't go too far in."

"These people go into the Blasted Lands?" asked Luna.

"Said so, didn't I? Blasters. No one else has those humpalops. Capture them in the Lands, they do. Take a good look at those folk, young Citizen. I've heard they kill their worst cases soon's they're born."

The approaching group had vanished behind another hillock but soon emerged over its top. Beside the humpalops walked seven people. The one in front was a woman; it was hard to tell about the others. Luna didn't pay them much attention once she realized there was an eighth person riding on the beast's back.

There was a protocol, it seemed, for greeting Blasters. "Stay back a ways until I find out what's what," said Luna's caravan leader. "Looks like they've got someone sick there."

The two leaders approached one another, stopping several paces apart. Barka, the woman who led the Blasters, was a tall, robust type, like many in the Guard, except she had six fingers on one hand and three on the other. Her companions, who had looked normal at a distance, displayed more obvious signs of strangeness. Facial features oddly proportioned and distributed. A man with three legs, a woman with a tail. Hunched backs, rather like that of the humpalops. All had wrapped their heads with brightly colored cloths, except the one riding the beast. That figure's head was swathed in white, and so was most of its face.

The two leaders finished their palaver and approached Luna's group. "He wants to go back to the City," said Barka, pointing at the mounted figure. "We did what we could with him all winter, but…" She shook her head. "Ran off into the heart of the Zone, going after the Blue Shine, and we didn't see him again 'til the turn of the moon. Couple of my folk took the risk and fetched him. We know better than to touch the Blue Shine."

He. Him. The person being described did nothing, only sat placidly on the back of the humpalops, eyes closed. Luna stepped forward. The humpalops looked down at her, disdain clouding its eyes. Luna reached up to touch the bandaged hands that lay on the animal's back.

"Deon," she said, and the veiled head turned toward her.

***

Another cycle of the Sun, another year. On the day of the Sun's Exaltation, the Lady Aldona Magna, Matriarch of the City, climbed to the Pinnacle to greet its first rays. Later, in the plaza before the Temple of the Twelve, she received the gifts of the Fabricators. Clad in black robes trimmed in the colors peculiar to his craft, each one stepped up in turn to present his creation. Articles of beauty and ingenuity shone in the new sunlight.

Last came Sylvius, with two of his students bearing a vessel of the sort used to contain plants in courtyard gardens. A white cloth shrouded the occupant of the pot. The students placed the pot among the other offerings, and Sylvius whisked away the cloth.

The small shrub's twisted stems bore pointed buds of a dark, vivid blue. A single open flower, recognizable as a rose, glowed indigo and sapphire, with golden anthers.

Luna stood with the other Guards who had escorted the Fabricators to the Peak. She was glad the rose had opened its first flower on this day. The other plant, the one on Deon's grave, was already in full bloom.

A crowd of young Fabricators talked and laughed as they waited to follow their elders from the City's heights. Luna wondered how many of them had read a slender book with the title *A Fabricator's Travels in the Blasted Lands*. A one-eyed man can write nearly as well as any other, and when Deon's strength failed near the end, his friends took turns writing down what he dictated. One of them printed a dozen copies and another bound three of them in blue leather. Of these three, one reposed in Sylvius's library. Deon's mother had another, and the third had been presented to Aldona Magna, but not as an official gift. The other copies circulated in modest paper bindings.

Luna didn't need to read the book. Deon had told her his tale as she sat holding his hand or applied salves to comfort his ravaged skin. He had told her about finding the Blue Shine, a garbled account whose details didn't quite match from one evening to the next.

"The rocks sweated a blue ichor. It dried to a kind of crystal. The colors shifted, you know? From darkest indigo to purest sky blue. So beautiful." Deon closed his remaining eye and lay back on the pillows, smiling.

Deon had brought back a vial of the substance, and Sylvius had used a minute quantity of it to change an ordinary pink rose into the miracle of blueness he had unveiled today. But the two plants, grown from cuttings, were stunted and strange. Only their blue flowers gave them beauty. The remaining blue crystals were secured in a lead-lined vault, along with the ashes of the parent rose.

How many other young men would Deon's book inspire, Luna wondered. Inspire to make a journey, not merely to the inn where Citizens did business with Exiles, not only to the edges of the Blasted Lands, but into the Zone of Peril itself, seeking the Blue Shine.

Luna broke ranks as Sylvius passed by the Guards, his face pale and eyes downcast. She tugged at his robe. "Will you be home tonight, Uncle Syl? I have a proposal for you."

ELIXIR

By V. P. Grey

The world passes beneath my window, white cotton candy clouds slipping to pieces in the pure blue sky. I lean back in my seat and wish I could live up here, up in peaceful life above the chaos.

The gentle movement of the plane lulls me into a doze. I drift into dreams of her. Her warm smile and tiny hands, her small baby-fresh body against mine.

At some point, I come back to the blue sky, but it has lost its appeal. I roll my aching shoulders and reach to rub my sore neck. I stretch, as much as I can in the cramped seat. According to my phone, there's an hour left of the flight until I land and the adventure begins.

The corner of a photo peaks out from the pocket in the phone case, and I pull it out. It is creased with white lines marking the folds—scars from a life of pockets, and bags, and purses.

Ten years' worth.

As the plane descends, my nerves tingle. Anticipation of another new world, another step into the unknown, snakes through me.

***

He had called me in the middle of the night which wasn't unusual. I'd rolled out of bed, and pulled on my clothes, all while on the phone promising I'd be there as soon as I could.

It was a short drive from my tiny, half-empty apartment— nothing more than a bedroom and bathroom, really—to the basement where he conducted his business. I knocked and got the usual gruff reply of "come in."

I pushed open the paint-stripped wooden door and ignored the musty smell that greeted me. He sat at his desk, papers spread out before him, amongst them a map. My heart skipped a little—a new job?

I sat down in the chair opposite him. "What's up?" "I think we've found it." He didn't look up.

I swallowed against the palpitations hitting me like a jolt of electricity. "The elixir?"

"Yes. I have proof it exists, Evie. Irrefutable proof." He pushed a photo my way, and it glinted in the lamplight.

My quick eye passed over it, taking in a scene that looked like something out of an alien movie. But there in the corner, ringed in red marker, was a vial. "Is that it?"

"It is. That's just one part of it. My spies have found it, Evie. Now you have to retrieve it. But we are not the only ones who know of it. There are others. You will have to be the first."

He finally looked up, and his dark eyes met mine.

"Tell me what I have to do."

***

Midday sun brightens the vibrant, wild grass, grown long without man's hand to tame into uniformity. My feet ache from the hike here, but as I drink in the emerald light of this secret valley, I forget my pain.

Pale stones, carved and built by human hands, are all that's left of the building that once stood here. Its remains stand exactly where his maps said they would.

Uneven, rounded grass steps lead up to the yawning, dark archway that forms the building's entrance. The sun breaks through the clouds yet casts no shadow. I climb the steps, straining my ears for any whisper of life. He warned me there would be others chasing the prize I seek. There always have been.

The pale stones shimmer in the glaring light, as if they are laced with thousands of tiny diamonds. I stand beneath the arch on the precipice of entering the ancient building. A glimmer, a small sphere of magic, flickers in the darkness. It dances as if tiny butterfly wings move too fast to be seen, all jumbled up in beautiful chaos.

It grows, expanding to fill the passageway.

I take a step, then one more, and the light and dancing butterflies envelop me, wings fluttering against my skin in shivers of excitement and fear.

✳✳✳

I was weak when he found me, I hadn't eaten in days. All I could feel was the empty place in my heart that she had been torn from.

His shadow had frightened me as it came down the alley, and I hid as far back into the darkness as I could. He still found me. I suppose he was looking for me.

He crouched down, the lines on his face deeper in those shadows. "Evie, isn't it? I've come for you, Evie. I've come to help you."

I pulled the tattered remains of my coat around me, trying to hide in it. How did he know my name? Was he death, come to free me from the pain I couldn't end myself?

"I'm not death, Evie, and I can't end your pain. Not right now. But I can make you warm and comfortable, and I can offer you hope. If you'll trust me."

What could I have done? I could have turned him away, refused to take the hand he offered, but then I'd have died on the streets. I would never have spoken another word to another human ever again.

I would have starved in pain.

So I took his hand, and let him save me as much as he could.

***

Breath mists before my eyes, seeping into the gloom. I stand in a tunnel, walls close to my shoulders. Is this the place I'm meant to be?

My boots are heavy, echoing off the walls and dark ceiling. My torch casts a tiny light, just enough to see the next step.

The ground slopes down, leading me further into the earth, and then ends abruptly, forming into a wide cavern. In the center is the pillar, tall and ridged, reaching up into unending blackness.

I run my hands over it and mentally walk through his instructions. There—the symbol on the back. It's etched into a flat square of stone. My fingers hover over it, and time stands still as my mind races.

Decision made, there's no turning back now. The stone image presses in easily, as if it is eager for this moment it was made for.

The ground shakes and rumbles as the stone shifts and grinds, rearranging itself by some power I can't name. The back wall opens in a jigsaw of shapes, revealing a room that is too modern for my world.

A glass wall separates me from the apparatus beyond. There's a code pad on the right edge of the glass—there must be a hidden door!

A white table fills most of the sterile room. My mind recalls the stories he told me about this place. I shudder and push them from my thoughts.

I hold my phone up to the code pad. Beeps cycle, alternating faster than my ears can comprehend.

The code cracks, and the door slides open with a hiss, the glass to my right shrinking into itself.

Inside, the room is drenched in blinding, stark white light, and I am faced with machines I don't understand. My fingers itch to brush over their angles and smooth surfaces, to chance touching things from an alien world.

As my eyes wander, they catch on a set of glass vials.

My heart lurches. Have I found it? So easily?

I cross the room, drawn by the stark light glinting off the glass. Labels on each are written in a language that doesn't resemble any on earth. *The liquid will be clear*, he'd said—but two vials contain clear liquid. My hand vacillates between them, but I grab both, unable to choose. *Do not drink it*, he said, *you will be tempted, but do not drink it yet—we will save her together, remember?*

It's true. I can feel the temptation curling around my fingers and tongue. The ache to know the taste of this strange liquid—this elixir over which humanity has searched for millennia—runs deep … but not as deep as the ache to find out if he told me the truth, if this elixir will truly give me the power to save my daughter from those who took her from me.

I bite my lower lip, resisting as I shove the vials into my backpack. Out of sight. Deny the temptation. I glance around the room again, hoping I have the right thing— but the burning inside tells me I am right.

I make my way back out the way I came, shifting glass and stone back into place. As I walk back down the tunnel, the feather-light vials weigh heavily at my back and on my mind. *Don't drink. Don't.*

He said the portal would take me back, but where is it?

Tingling and itching creeps across my skin. I shiver and take another step. The butterfly-wing trembling spreads through me, shaking my lungs and breath. And then I am standing on the precipice of the building again, staring into emerald light.

I breathe in the warm air, the sun heating my skin.

Do not *drink.* His warning echoes. He's never guided me wrong, and I've always trusted him.

I should now.

I should.

But the burning inside, the ache … how can I keep denying it?

The barrier breaks, and I take my bag from my back, hands grasping for the vials. Which one? I am beyond caring. My mind screams at me, needing the elixir, needing her. I pull the top off and let the dropper spill onto my tongue. Satisfaction courses through me like a wave, cool after the heat of drought.

At the base of the steps, three figures appear. Men. Hats like cowboys of old. One holds a gun. "Give it over, girl. You know how this goes."

"No." I hold my hand up, and his gun disintegrates like sand in a breeze.

Their mouths drop open, staring.

"She has it!"

I can feel the power of the elixir flying through my body, boosting my mother's ancient blood. It curls my fingers in anger, and blood rushes in my ears. Static fades my vision.

Breathing grows more difficult with each passing moment, and I grasp at my chest. The men are reduced to moving shadows in a hazy world. My knees hit the ground. What is happening? The elixir … I have to take it back … take it back to him …

"Now's our chance." The man's voice echoes, his body a shadow looming over me.

I blink, trying hard to reach the surface of my thoughts, of my mind. I am drowning.

Her cry bleeds into the rushing in my ears. I reach, falling further into her voice, letting it take over me. A shadowed, grinning face fills what remains of my vision.

He has the vial, glinting silver in my dying emerald light.

He drinks.

And I smile even as the last breath slips from my body.

I chose the wrong vial.

VANISHED

By E. E. Rawls

http://www.rawlse.wordpress.com/

David has gone missing--and there are very few clues left as to why. Regardless, his sister Karin is determined to find him. Even if it leads her into the mysterious landscape of Ireland ... and the lair of the Fae ...

He had to be alive, somewhere out there. And she would find him. Determined, Karin finished packing her travel bag and hugged her parents.

"I don't want you to do this," her mother said. "What if we lose you, too?"

Karin rubbed her shoulder comfortingly. "You won't lose me, Mom. I promise. I'll find David, and bring him back home."

Dad gave her a stern look. "Don't take any risks. We're already prepared to mourn his loss, but not yours on top of it," he told her.

Karin shook her head, knowing there was no point in arguing. "I'll keep in touch and let you know what I find."

Karin hopped into the taxi, waving out the window as the vehicle carried her down the street and away from the comfortable suburbs. Time seemed to crawl by; she wanted to get to Ireland quickly, find out what had happened to David—where it was he was last seen. It felt like hours before she was finally seated on the plane and the aircraft began lifting off the runway. She tried to make her mind rest and her body reserve its strength as the plane crossed over the chilly waters of the Atlantic.

She woke from a half-sleep many hours later when the airplane's wheels hit the runaway.

The last time she'd spoken to David over the phone he'd told her he was readying for a hike through Killarney National Park. There hadn't been a word from him since that day, though she called and called in vain. Ireland's local Killarney police and international investigators combed through his hotel and planned hiking route, searching much of County Kerry, but nothing had come up—not even his missing backpack. It was as if he'd entered Killarney's woods and disappeared from this world.

Karin strode down the plane's off-ramp, luggage in tow, and then called her parents to let them know she'd arrived safely. There was a long drive to reach the destination of Muckross Park Hotel, the place where David was last seen. The view was scenic beyond the taxi's window: rolling landscape, the fresh shade of green that only constant rain could create, and a glistening blue loch. She tried to relax and let the view calm her nerves.

The hotel came into view, reminding her of a castle in small mansion form, complete with a miniature tower which rose before a groomed front garden and parking lot. The glass entrance doors were set at the base of the tower. She trotted under the overhang, and an usher opened one door for her. The hotel's interior was a lavish mix of Victorian and modern styles. She passed through cream tiled hallways, past ornate gilded mirrors and expensive paintings. White columns protruded from the walls, serving no purpose but for decoration. It felt like she'd stepped into a fairy tale castle.

Karin soon settled into her modernized Victorian room for the evening—a color palette of blue grays—and made her body rest in the queen-size fluffy bed to adjust to the new time difference.

She woke with the dawn and breakfasted in a dining room that resembled something plucked from Downton Abbey. Beyond the window beside her table, the perfectly trimmed trees filled her vision and beckoned her to wonder where David could have gone.

He was always such an adventurer, his spirit that of a restless traveler who had to see what lay beyond the next horizon. She could picture him here, ignoring the fancy interior and eating quickly so he could get back out into nature and follow the trails wherever they may lead...

The day was hot and bright, and Karin set about pouring over the many maps of trails, looking for the paths she suspected might have most appealed to David. She asked the hotel receptionist and a waiter who faintly remembered David's stay. The waiter, with slicked-back red hair, told her David had spent the first two days hiking through Killarney National Park and talked about his adventures over dinner. But the third day had been different: he'd eaten breakfast and left in a hurry, with no mention of his day's plan. He was never seen again.

Karin decided to start her search at the national park. Backpack on and hair in a high ponytail, she followed the park trail leading to Torc Waterfall. Moss ran up many of the old, tall trees making their bark fuzzy green. A stream babbled over moss-topped rocks and boulders, its murmur mingling with the calls of foreign songbirds.

The distant rushing thunder of water grew as she navigated down a series of rock steps set in the inclined dirt path. The humid air moistened across her bare arms. The waterfall's steepest drop came into view, and she lingered at the tourist platform and gazed at its cascading curtain of white. David might have been tempted to get a closer look, so she edged off the path and searched for footprints or any belongings along the bank.

The day ended with nothing found but discouragement as Karin hiked back to the hotel.

Sweaty and full of negative emotions, she put on her bathing suit and headed downstairs to the hotel's Vitality Pool: a wide, heated pool with stone islands and palm trees ringing its rim. Light slanted in through low windows, playing across the water as Karin slipped inside.

The warmth relaxed her back muscles, aching legs and throbbing headache. This warmth … it brought to mind the summer days when her family would visit the beaches in South Carolina. The sun would beat down on her older brother's back, burning his sensitive skin when he ignored Mom's call to use sunblock. Karin would laugh.

But David always got her back. One time he dug a deep hole in the sand, set a blanket over it, and called her over to see a shell he'd found. He made sure Karin had to cross the blanket to reach him, and she fell with a yelp down the hole, nothing but the top of her head visible as he laughed and laughed.

As children they were always pranking and teasing each other. Only a year apart, they had been like twins in appearance. Of course, growing up had made their genders too obvious and ended any "guess who I am" twin games.

Karin chuckled to herself, letting her head rest back against one of the stone islands.

As much as she and David had teased one another, they'd always had a strong bond. When they'd attended separate colleges, he kept in touch, checking in on her. His parting gift to her was a moleskin journal filled with encouraging quotes. She kept it with her wherever she went. Even tucked in the backpack she left in her hotel room.

Karin sighed and pulled herself out of the water before she dozed off.

***

"I don't know if he actually went there or not," the receptionist told Karin the next day. "But he mentioned how eerie Muchross Abbey looked from photos he saw online. Mayhaps he was curious about the place? Hope the info helps. I'm terribly sorry for your loss, miss."

Karin nodded in thanks. She looked up the abbey on her phone. It did seem like a mysterious place that would pique David's interest. It was worth a try checking out, anyway and was nearby.

Karin donned a blue fabric hat this time before setting off. Rolling gray clouds threatened rain, and she berated herself for not thinking to bring an umbrella.

Muchross Abbey was a grand old place, grayed and speckled with lichen and vines, a bushy plant with red flowers growing around it and about the adjacent cemetery. Headstones in the shape of Celtic crosses rose out of the ground like strange flowers, the darkening sky giving them a haunted glow.

Karen stepped inside the abbey's weathered walls. She could make out traces of Irish and Christian symbols and medieval stone window patterns. The heavy clouds hovered where the ceiling had long since vanished.

She came to the tower where one window remained intact, stone tracery creating six diamond shapes at its high, pointed arch. She approached and almost stumbled into several blocks of rock. She couldn't tell if they were markers, some kind of stone coffin, or simply surfaces to place things. One had a symbol carved into its side: the shape of a chalice with a coat-of-arms, twin horses and topped with some kind of animal she couldn't decipher.

She continued farther, making her way inside a passageway which broadened into an arcade and almost slipped on the slick stones. The vaulted ceiling, speckled in damp mold, formed four-point stars above her. This early in the day, there were few tourists around; the only sound was the rough scraping of the grit under her shoes.

From the arcade, she exited into a square courtyard and found, soaring high at its center, a grand yew tree.

She moved near, tilting her head back to admire the tree. David would have loved this. He would've been taking photos and rubbing the bark with his fingers to memorize its grandeur. Karin reached out her hand now to touch the bumpy bark. The sky was frightfully dark, the scent of rain heavy in the air. She closed her eyes, feeling the tree, breathing in the mist.

Mist?

The ground beneath her feet suddenly rumbled and sank. Her eyes flew open with a gasp, but before she could react, she dropped into darkness.

Karin couldn't recall landing but found herself lying flat on her back in dirt, surrounded by the high walls of a cavern. Light poured in through a fracture in the rocky ceiling. She panted rapidly and tried to collect herself, testing arms and legs, shifting to make sure nothing had broken. Her body seemed to be intact.

"Karin?"

Her heartbeat hitched.

She turned where the light slanted down upon a white structure in the cavern floor. In front of it, a tall figure with an unkempt beard stood bathed in light. Even with the beard, she recognized him.

"David!" She scrambled to her feet and half-ran, half-stumbled up the white steps, and they embraced.

"I can't believe you're here; you found me," David said, his voice weary and hoarse. But before Karin could ask any questions, he grabbed her arm and hurried her towards a tunnel in the mossy wall. "You must leave, now, before they find you."

"They? David, what are you talking about? I'm not leaving you!" Her brow furrowed. "Why is your hair bleached white? Have you been trapped down here all this time?"

"I shouldn't have done it, but I did. And it's my punishment to bear, not yours," David mumbled, pulling her along.

"Did what?"

The tunnel shook before they could reach it, and fear filled David's eyes. He drew Karin close and hid her behind his back as two beings materialized through the wall before them.

"You cannot leave here, David of Humankind," spoke one of the beings. His skin glowed like pearls in the dim light, his hair as white as David's.

Karin couldn't believe what she was seeing, and she struggled to keep back her panic. "Why?" was the only word she could get out of her throat.

The being's head angled to look at her. "He ate of the Fae Tree. Now, he can never return to the land of humans." A graceful hand swung out, indicating the tree bearing white fruit planted near the structure.

"Why does that matter?" Karin persisted. "It's just fruit!"

The being regarded her gravely. "Those who eat of the Fae Tree are no longer mortal, no longer human. They cannot be allowed to interfere with the human world or its balance between life and death."

Karin felt her face paling.

"But she can still leave," David insisted. "She hasn't eaten anything." Sweat beaded his brow.

The second being slowly nodded.

"I already told you, I'm not leaving you behind!" Karin said. "I don't understand what this is, or if I've simply hit my head and am dreaming, but I will not let you stay here, David. Mom and Dad think you're dead!"

"But, Karin—"

She turned to the fae-like beings. "There must be some way to undo this, some way for you to let him leave, yes?"

The beings shared a long look. "There is but one way," the first said, lifting his palm out. "A life for a life. Someone must take his place, or he cannot leave."

"Then I'll take his place," she said without thinking. She didn't let herself stop to consider what it could mean for her—she just wanted to save her brother.

"No, Karin!" David exclaimed. He tried to stop her, but she placed her hand in the palm of the fae's.

A white glow rose from David's skin, the white lifted out of his hair, and the gathered glow left him and floated towards Karin, settling around her. The being stepped back. Karin's skin glowed and her hair turned white. But David was back to normal.

"Go, David. Go home to Mom and Dad. Tell them I'm fine, that I'll find a way to come back." Karin hugged her brother, as anger and sadness battled across David's features. "This was my choice; don't blame yourself for it." She offered a smile.

The beings pulled David towards the tunnel. "The human lands lay on the other side," one told him, before forcing him into the archway. David turned back, meeting Karin's gaze one last time.

"I won't rest until you're free!" he promised.

She nodded and watched as he disappeared with the being into the dark tunnel. Then she fell to her knees, overcome and shaking. The reality of her situation began to set in. She was trapped, barred from the human world.

"Come, human. You must enter the land of the Fae, now." The second being forced her to stand, and motioned towards a different archway and tunnel, one lined with runes.

Karin drew in a deep breath, straightened her shoulders, and took her first steps toward another world.

THE BUSS STOP

By K. R. Ludlow

https://www.facebook.com/krludlow/

Jason didn't know what the series of green switches were for. He didn't know why there was a bright blue light shining in his eyes. He didn't recognize the gravelly voice that boomed through unseen speakers. He had never seen the tangle of wires hanging above his head, nor did he know what would happen if he were to press the big red button near his left elbow.

But there was one thing of which he was absolutely certain.

He definitely wasn't on the bus anymore.

Blinded by the light, he reached out and felt his fingertips brush against cool glass. He appeared to be standing in a tube no bigger than the broom closet in his shoebox of an apartment. But unlike his broom closet, there didn't seem to be a door. There was no way out. He was trapped.

On instinct, Jason reached for his mobile phone, fumbling at the screen with trembling fingers. He cursed under his breath. No signal.

When he had woken up this morning, his biggest worry had been getting to work on time. That and getting a high score on the popular mobile game, *Avians of a Fowl Disposition*. It all seemed so pathetic now that he was facing the prospect of starving to death—or even suffocating— right here in this glass coffin.

"Help!" he cried, slamming his fists against the glass. "Somebody, help!"

A heart-shaped face framed with silver hair appeared on the other side of the glass.

"Oh, thank goodness!" Jason cried. "Can you get me out of here?"

If the woman was surprised about seeing a strange man stuck in an even stranger contraption, she certainly didn't show it. In fact, she looked rather bored, as though this sort of thing happened every day. With her lips set in a straight line, she raised a finger and pointed to the red button near Jason's elbow. He slammed his palm across the button, probably a little harder than it needed, and a glass door slid open with a loud hiss. Cool, refreshing air gushed into the tube.

"Thank you," Jason gasped, stumbling forward into a long, metallic hallway lined with tubes similar to the one from which he had just escaped. "Where are we? What is that thing?"

The lady raised a dark eyebrow and, as Jason regarded her more fully, he realized her features were much younger than her silver hair implied.

"Ain't you ever ridden the Bagahnavian Universal Space Shuttle, before?"

Jason stared at her blankly. "The *what?*"

"You know, the Bagahnavian Universal Space Shuttle. B-U-S-S, the BUSS."

"I-I really don't know what you're talking about."

"What planet you been livin' on?"

Jason noted the suspicious expression on her face and quickly arranged his own face into what he hoped was a knowing look. "Oh yeah, the BUSS. Of course I know about the BUSS. Everyone knows about the BUSS. You'd have to be really stupid not to know about the BUSS."

The woman sneered. Even with her face crinkled up like that, she still looked pretty. "Whatever," she said before turning on her heel and stalking away.

Jason hesitated for only a moment before his natural instincts kicked in. No matter what the circumstance, no matter the time, location or weather, Jason Grier never let a pretty woman just walk away. He slicked back his hair and ran a hand through his tangled beard before jogging to catch up with her.

"My name's Jason, by the way. What's yours?" The woman blew a raspberry and continued walking.

"Excuse me?"

She blew another raspberry then said, "That's my name."

Jason grinned. She was a sassy one and no mistake. He opened his mouth to charm her with his best pick up line when she took something out of her jacket pocket. At first Jason thought it was some sort of smart phone, but it turned out to be a curious device covered in wires and tiny lights. She pressed a few buttons and flicked a couple of switches, then suddenly Jason's vision went blurry.

No, not his vision. He could see the tube-lined hallway perfectly fine. The blue lights running along the ceiling were in focus. It was the woman who had gone blurry. Then she refocused. But instead of a pretty woman with silver hair, there was now a squat little creature—vaguely resembling a potato in shape—with brown lumpy skin, four flabby arms, and two long stalks protruding from— for want of a better word—a head that looked like a squashed tomato. Attached to the stalks were two bulbous eyes.

Jason froze, watching the ugly little creature waddle down to the end of the hallway where it disappeared around the corner. He was dreaming. That had to be it. He had fallen asleep on the bus and was dreaming.

"All right, wake up, Jason," he told himself, slapping at his cheeks. "Time to wake up now, otherwise you'll miss your stop and be late for work. Again. You know what the boss is like. Can't have that now, can we. Time to wake up. Time. To. Wake ..."

Without realising it, his feet had taken him around the corner and into what looked like a massive underground terminal. The high rocky ceiling was dotted with bright fluorescent lights. Pipes and cables crisscrossed along the walls, connecting to metal doors, flickering monitors and strange contraptions Jason couldn't name, let alone comprehend. A glowing green substance covered the ground like radioactive moss. But by far the strangest sight was the swirling sea of little creatures covering the floor of the cavern. Some were in a hurry, using all four elbows to push their way through the bustling crowd. Some wandered past as though they had all the time in the world. Every now and then, a pair of eyes would periscope up from the swirling mass of brown bodies, swivel around for a moment as though searching for something, and then drop back down again.

Jason watched on as two tiny creatures ran up to a larger one that was carrying a suitcase. The larger one set the suitcase on the ground before wrapping its arms around the youngsters. It then picked them up and swung them around, all the while making a high-pitched whistling sound. They were soon joined by another creature—Jason suspected it to be a female—and together the little family wandered away, disappearing into the crowd. It would have been a sweet, heart-warming moment if Jason hadn't been out of his mind with panic.

This wasn't a dream. There was no way it could be a dream. The sights, the sounds, the slightly sticky feeling of alien bodies brushing past him, it all seemed far too real to simply be conjured up by his imagination.

He looked around and saw a bench not too far away. Its only other occupant was a creature holding some sort of cane, its brown skin nothing but a mass of wrinkles. Hurrying over to the bench, Jason sat down as far away from the elderly creature as he could. He put his head in his hands and tried to piece together what had happened.

He remembered leaving his apartment that morning to go to work. He remembered turning down a small street. Or was it an alley? To be honest he hadn't been paying much attention. He remembered lining up behind a group of people waiting for the bus. Well, he had assumed they were waiting for the bus. He had been too busy playing *Avians of a Fowl Disposition* to take much notice. He was still stuck on that one level—the one where the viridescent swine were hidden in a neat little castle made of glass, stone and wood. There were only five avians available in the level, and no matter what strategy he used, there would always be one swine left. One smug little swine sitting behind his wooden barricade, mocking Jason from the other side of the screen. But his days were numbered. Oh yes, they were. Jason was going to get him one way or another. It might take five more attempts, maybe fifty, but sooner or later he was going to do it.

Jason blinked and shook his head. Where was he? Oh yes, the bus stop. He remembered a bus pulling up, and he remembered getting onto it. He remembered the bus turning onto Main Street. He remembered reaching up to press the button that told the bus driver to stop. And then

… and then …

And then he found himself in that tube.

"'Scuse me, sir, can I have your BHIDD, please?"

Jason looked up to see a creature standing right in front of him, a little blue cap perched at a jaunty angle between his eye stalks.

"My what?" Jason asked wearily. He had given up trying to understand what was happening.

"Your Bagahnavian to Human Interplanetary Disguising Device." It held out a little collection box full of devices like the one the silver haired woman had been carrying. "You know, most people remove their disguise as soon as they arrive—a vanity thing, I guess. I mean, who in their right mind would want to go around looking like a human? But I can see why you've chosen to keep it on. That has got to be one of the most convincing human disguises I've seen for a while. A little on the ugly side, that's for sure, but then aren't all humans?" The creature gave a little bark that almost sounded like a laugh. "But come on, mate, time to take it off." He shoved the box underneath Jason's nose and gave it a shake.

"I-I don't have one of those … *things.*"

"None of that now, sir. Do I need to remind you that taking a BHIDD out of the Arrival Area is an Interplanetary offense? Anyway, if you were planning to steal it, you probably should have removed your disguise first. I mean, it's pretty obvious that you have a BHIDD on your person. Now come on, hand it over, otherwise I'll have to call security and neither of us would want that. The paperwork's a nightmare."

"I really don't have a … a *BHIDD.* I'm a real human."

The creature gave another bark. "Like I haven't heard *that* one before." He reached under his cap and withdrew a small, metal cylinder. "Now please hold still sir, this won't hurt a bit." He waved the cylinder in

Jason's general direction. Nothing happened. He inspected it, frowned, and then waved it again. And again.

"Well now, either my BHIDD detector is malfunctioning or—" His already large eyes somehow grew larger. "You're a human! A real live, honest to goodness, card-carrying human being! I don't believe it! A real human on Bagahnavia!" He glanced around and lowered his voice. "Quick, in here."

Jason followed him through a metal doorway into a small, empty room. The creature pressed a button on the wall and a heavy door came thudding down.

"Now, human," the capped little creature said in a hushed tone, "tell me the truth. How did you get here?"

Jason shrugged. "I've been trying to work that out myself. One minute I was playing a game on my phone on the bus, next minute I'm here."

The creature scratched what was presumably his chin. "Which button did you press? The yellow one? Or the purple?"

Jason hadn't taken much notice of the button. He was very well acquainted with public transport having ridden it most of his adult life. His hand had moved automatically to the button while his eyes and mind were on his phone, focused on destroying that one last viridescent swine.

"Alrighty then, what about the bus? Which bus did you get on?"

Jason stared slack-jawed. His eyes had been glued to his phone.

"Come on, mate, think back. What was on the front of the bus? Was it 'BUSS,' you know, with two esses? Or just the one?"

Jason shrugged.

"What about the bus stop? Surely you remember which stop you were waiting at."

Jason grimaced in thought and then shook his head. "There were a bunch of people waiting around, so I just sort of joined them. To be fair, it was a really tricky level.

It required all my concentration."

The creature massaged its temples. "Either that's one incredible game, or you're a bit of an idiot, no offense."

Although Jason wasn't sure how not to take offense at this comment, he had to agree. "So how do I get home?"

The creature adjusted his cap. "You'll need to go to the Departure Area and catch the BUSS."

"Oh, that sounds simple enough—"

"But no one can know you're a human."

"Oh."

"Cos, you know, it's a crime against the Intergalactic Federation for a human to be on Bagahnavia. If word got out you were here, you'd be thrown into prison."

"Oh."

"And then you'd probably be executed."

"Oh."

"And then I'd probably be thrown into prison as well on account of my associating with you. And then the BUSS Station would come under investigation. And then the media would get involved and it would be the scandal of the decade. And then there'd be the paperwork …." The alien closed its eyes and shuddered.

Jason would have sympathized with the creature if it wasn't for the threat of execution hanging over his own head. "So, what are we going to do?" he asked.

The creature's eyes popped open and he snapped his long fingers. "I've got it. Just follow my lead." He began to turn towards the door, but then stopped and turned back to Jason.

"By the way, my name's—" he gave what sounded like a loud burp.

Jason furrowed his brow. Unlike his old college buddies, he never could burp on cue. Not without drinking copious amounts of soda first. "Do you mind if I just call you 'Burp'?"

The creature wrinkled its snout. "If you absolutely have to, mate," he said, not at all sounding pleased with his new nickname. "And what should I call *you*?"

"My name's Jason." He held out his hand.

Burp shook it, his skin slimy against Jason's hand. "Nice to meet you, *Jitzum*."

"It's Jason."

"Joofen."

"Jason."

Burp looked Jason straight in the eye and very deliberately said, "Joshin."

Jason sighed. The alien was clearly playing silly games with him. "All right then, Burp. Where are we going?"

"This way."

Burp lead him out of the room and back into the busy terminal. Jason couldn't help but notice the pointing, staring and hushed conversation that followed them as they pushed through the crowd. He wondered how long it would take before someone called security.

Burp, however, didn't seem to notice. He was calling out to other aliens as they passed, as though it was just another day at the office. "Looking good, *bfffffpttt*. Love what you've done with your stalks. Lovely weather we've been having in the Biosphere, eh. Wotcha, *shbllllllllb*. How're the kids? Still teething? Hey, *blblblblblb*, long time no see! Yeah, things are going all right here. Can't complain. Ah, here we go," said Burp as they reached another metal door. "The back way."

On the other side of the door stretched a long, white corridor that finished in a set of double doors. As they approached the end, the doors flew open and out stepped a very fat alien who immediately let out a massive burp. Jason wasn't sure if the alien was greeting Burp, or if he had simply had a big lunch. Burp whistled in response.

"Whoa, dude," said the fat alien when it saw Jason. "That disguise is totally gnarly. So gross!"

"You'd think he was a real human, eh."

"I'll say. You guys takin' the service elevator?"

Burp nodded. "We're going to the Departure Area."

The fat alien pointed two pudgy hands at Jason. "You best get that disguise off, dude. *Shkshkcrecha* is in the lunchroom, and you know how pernickety he gets about BHIDD use."

"Oh monitors and meteors, not *Shkshkcrecha*. Thanks for the heads up, mate."

"No probs. Well later, dudes!" The fat alien plodded away down the corridor as Jason and Burp got on the service elevator. The doors slid close behind them, sealing them into a space barely big enough for the two of them. Feeling a little claustrophobic, Jason fidgeted nervously as Burp reached under his cap and pulled out a small card which he slid across a panel by the doors. Tinny music— that sounded like a bagpipe being thrown down the stairs—floated down from the elevator speaker.

"What did fatso mean about that—" Jason tried, and failed, to imitate the squawking noise the alien had made "—guy?"

"*Shkshkcrecha?*" said Burp as he fiddled with a series of buttons. "He's gonna be a bit of a problem. But don't you worry. I've got an idea. Here, hold this."

He handed Jason a BHIDD and then turned back to the panel. All of a sudden, there was a loud ding and Jason felt himself being pulled, not up or down, but sideways.

Above the door stretched a row of strange symbols that Jason guessed were alien numbers. A tiny blue light began to move slowly along the symbols.

Jason and Burp stared at the blue light in silence. The floor beneath their feet vibrated steadily as unseen machinery moved the elevator along. Jason subconsciously fiddled with the wires on the BHIDD. Burp causally scratched his side and then straightened his cap. The bagpipe music was starting to give Jason a headache. By now the blue light was almost halfway between the first two symbols.

"So why come to Earth?" Jason said at last, eager to break the uncomfortable silence.

"Don't you know? The Earth is the only planet in the known universe that can produce avocados."

"Avocados?"

"Yup. One of the rarest, most valuable resources in the galaxy. One ripe avocado can fetch up to a whopping one hundred *snarglegargles*. We send out workers on the BUSS to earn Earth dollars, which they use to get avocados, which they then bring back and trade for *snarglegargles*. It's a very lucrative business."

"I didn't realize aliens ate avocados."

Burp frowned at Jason. "Firstly, watch who you're calling 'alien,' pal. We're Bagahnavians. It is you, sir, who is the alien. And secondly, who ever said anything about *eating* avocados? I don't know what you do with avocados on Earth, but here on Bagahnavia we use them for fuel."

"Oh," said Jason, unable to come up with any sort of intelligent response.

Jason and Burp stared at the creeping blue light in silence. A screeching noise floated up from somewhere beneath the elevator. Jason pressed a couple of buttons on the BHIDD, but they didn't seem to do anything. Burp crossed all four of his arms and gave a small sigh. The bagpipe had been replaced by something that resembled a sitar. By the sound of it, it too was being thrown down the stairs.

"So if this is another planet, why are you all speaking English?" Jason tried again.

"We've been receiving and studying Earth's television transmissions for years now. It was quite simple to learn the various Earthian dialects. We are currently in the English-speaking terminal, the Japanese-speaking terminal is to the east, and the—"

"You've been watching TV?" asked Jason.

Burp nodded and shot him a sly grin. "I gotta say, that Lucy Ricardo's a real babe."

"Uh, yeah," Jason replied awkwardly.

Jason and Burp resumed staring at the blue light in silence. The light seemed to pause momentarily between two of the symbols, as though revaluating its life decisions, before once again resuming its long, lengthy journey to the other side. Jason put the BHIDD in his pocket then, thinking better of it, took it out again. Burp coughed. The bagpipe joined the sitar on its trip down the stairs.

At long last the elevator came to a shuddering stop. There was a loud ding and the doors flew open, revealing a small room with a checkerboard of black and white tiles covering the floor. The only occupant of the room was a red-eyed alien with a puckered scar running down its face. Its arms were much thicker—and more muscular—than any of the other aliens Jason had seen, and its face was twisted in a vicious scowl. In its hand it held a petrol can. It raised the can to its slash of a mouth and took a long drink.

"Let me do the talking," Burp whispered to Jason as they stepped out of the elevator. Then louder he said, "Hey, *Shkshkcrecha*. How's things?"

The alien ignored Burp, its red eyes focused on Jason. Very slowly, it lowered the petrol can and pointed at Jason with two accusatory fingers. "You there. What's your name?"

Jason glanced at Burp, unsure of how to respond. "It's, ah, it's J—"

Burp interrupted with a loud raspberry. "He's my cousin."

"Your cousin, eh? And can you tell me why dear cousin—" he blew a raspberry "—is currently using a BHIDD outside of the regulated areas?"

"It's malfunctioning," Burp said casually. "We're taking it to the tech department to get it fixed. And until its fixed, my poor cousin's stuck looking like this."

The other alien gave a sadistic laugh. "Out of all the disguises you could've got stuck in, you had to get stuck in that one."

Jason frowned. He was getting sick of all these disparaging remarks about his appearance. "I'll have you know that on Earth, I'm—this disguise—is a big hit with the ladies."

The alien narrowed his eyes and moved his stalks closer to Jason's face.

"T-the Earth ladies, I mean," Jason added, glancing nervously at the alien's bulging muscles. Had the alien seen through the lie? Was he going to be imprisoned and executed? He looked the alien in the eye and tried to smile.

Out of the corner of his eye he saw Burp take a tentative step toward the elevator.

The alien snorted. Jason flinched as the putrid blast of hot air from the creature's nostrils hit him full square in the face.

The alien then drew back and took another swig of petrol. "There's no accounting for taste, is there," he grunted.

"No. No there's not," said Burp, the relief audible in his voice. He wrapped a flabby arm around Jason's elbow and started to drag him towards the door at the other end of the room.

Jason's legs felt like they had turned to blocks of stone, and it took him a couple of seconds to regain control of them. Leaving the red-eyed alien to his petrol, Burp and Jason wandered down several empty corridors before emerging once more into a bustling terminal. The Departure Area was even larger than the Arrival Area, and it was full of aliens and humans alike. No, not humans, Jason reminded himself. Aliens. Aliens in disguise. Businessmen and women—pulling wheeled bags across the glowing green floor—walked side by side with their alien brethren. Quaint little cafes, shops and stalls lined the rocky walls and rising above it all, at the other end of the cavern, was a massive white edifice, reminiscent of some of ancient Greek temple one would find on Earth.

Burp swept two hands towards the colossus. "And there she is. The BUSS Stop. Come on, Jerkshon, let's get you on board."

He led Jason through the crowd, up a set of green stairs, and through a massive archway. The inside of the building was just as impressive as the outside. White pillars lined the hall and along one wall were a series of dark tunnels. They were so dark that Jason began to wonder if someone hadn't just splashed black paint on the walls. But no, a steady stream of human-aliens were entering these tunnels, only to disappear into the darkness.

Burp led Jason up to a marble desk behind which sat an alien wearing cat eyeglasses, precariously perched on her stalks.

"How can I help you?" drawled the alien, in a scratchy, nasally voice.

"One ticket to …" Burp looked to Jason.

"To Main Street, please," Jason finished.

The female alien simply stared at him, her already large eyes magnified by the glasses. "Which city? Which country?"

"Sydney, Australia."

"Return trip?"

Before Jason could answer, Burp interrupted. "One way. Definitely one way."

"That'll be ten *snarglegargles*." Burp paid the alien lady who handed Jason a small metal chip. "Step through the gateway on the far left, please."

"Well, mate," said Burp, as they reached the leftmost tunnel, "this is where I leave you."

Jason scratched the back of his head and looked down at his feet. He never was good at saying goodbye. "Thanks for all your help, Burp."

"It was nothing, honest. Just don't go blabbing to all your Earth friends about us, all right?" Jason nodded.

"And for goodness sake, next time you decide to catch public transport, make sure you pay attention to your surroundings."

"OK."

Burp tapped his chest with a closed fist and then held up two fingers. "Keep it real, Jason."

"You too, Burp," said Jason. Even though he had only known him for less than an hour, he was going to miss the little guy.

Burp turned around and began to waddle away. "Remember," he called over his shoulder, "the yellow button stops the BUSS. Make sure you press the *yellow* button this time!"

Jason turned towards the gaping hole that was the gateway. "Here goes …" He took a deep breath, stepped into the darkness and then—

—he found himself back on the bus. He blinked and rubbed his eyes. What just happened? Had he been asleep? He ran a hand through his beard and looked around blearily at the commuters around him, all wearing smart suits and glum expressions, engrossed by their smart phones or the view out the window.

Jason sighed. After all that, it had just been a dream. A bizarre dream that would soon fade from his memory.

He was about to turn towards the window when something caught his eye. A man holding an abnormally large bag of avocados. Jason stared at the bag. No, it couldn't be…

It was then that he became aware of the faint music coming from the bus driver's radio. It sounded like a very sad bagpipe. Snatches of hushed conversation floated to his ears, punctuated with raspberries, whistles and other strange noises. The sharp, acrid smell of petrol wafted through the confines of the bus as the woman sitting across the aisle from Jason took a swig from a bottle full of black liquid.

His mind whirring with confusion, Jason reached into his pocket for the security of his phone. His fingers wrapped around a metallic case, but when he pulled it from his pocket he found himself holding not his phone, but a curious device covered in lights and wires.

It was the BHIDD.

Jason took a deep breath, trying to calm his nerves. He looked around at the commuters again. Aliens. All going out undetected into the workforce. He turned his attention to cityscape whizzing past. Just how many aliens were out there, walking the streets? He thought of his coworkers. Were any of them secretly BHIDD carrying Bagahnavians? What about his boss? He glanced once more at the man with the avocados. What was it Burp had said? One ripe avocado could fetch up to one hundred *snai* … *sargl* … whatever it was the Bagahnavians used as currency. In spite of his initial panic, a small smile crept across Jason's face. Perhaps it was time for a career change. Quit his dull desk job and branch out into the avocado industry.

The bus turned into Main Street, quickly approaching Jason's stop. With his mind firmly focused on his new business venture, he reached out his hand like he did every day and pressed his palm against a button.

A purple button.

THE CAVE OF LEGIX

By David Jesson

https://fictioncanbefun.wordpress.com/

Deep in the jungles of Indonesia there is a cave, the Cave of Legix. Bill has made many mistakes in his life, and joining the expedition to explore the cave might be his latest. Can he find the answers to a 1700-year-old mystery in the cave, or will he just unearth more questions? More importantly, can he find himself?

For the fifth time that morning, Bill wondered what on earth he was doing here. People talked about the Indonesian paradise, of the unspoilt country, but he suspected that most of them hadn't stepped that far outside of the resort. It was designed to look rustic but had all the modern conveniences, including running water. The only running water here was the sweat forming on his forehead and dripping off his nose, or forming rivulets that ran into his beard. He'd grown the beard partly because he could, which he knew would annoy his brother, and partly for the cliched reason that it made him look older, which … well, there were all sorts of reasons why looking older was a good thing.

The heat and humidity squeezed him from every direction. A year or so ago he'd done a few sessions of Bikram yoga, going with a girl that he liked and was planning to ask out. The intensity of the workout in a room at 40°C and 40% relative humidity had been punishing, and he'd almost been glad when the girl had started going out with someone else. Here, though, there was no option; they were three days into the rainforest, and at best they would be three days getting out again. No one else would turn back, he was sure, which meant that three days would turn into never escaping this jungle.

Ah, yes. The jungle. It made him uneasy in ways he would never have expected. He'd heard people talk about the silence amongst the trees, but the next person who tried that line was asking for a biff on the nose. There was silence, from time to time, but never when he expected it. For three days he'd followed Lestari, her stonewashed denim hair a beacon in the shaded light under the encompassing canopy of the jungle. Sometimes they would be closer together, exchanging a few words with whatever spare energy they could muster, and sometimes further apart as Bill lagged a little whilst Lestari caught up with Adi. It was in those moments that Bill found himself assaulted by noise and silence. The noises came from all around: disquieting, eerie, aimless ... foreboding. Trees creaked, branches rustled, sticks on the ground broke (sometimes for no apparent reason), birds called to each other, animals ... Bill was more worried about the animals he couldn't hear. Insects chittered, and he would swear that he could hear them walking about. And then a patch of silence. He didn't notice at first, and then he came to realize that there was nothing on the air, nothing on the fetid breathing of the jungle that passed for a breeze, and he strained his ears as hard as he could to hear something, anything.

***

"Hey, Bill!"

"Hey, Lestari. Do you know if we're nearly there?"

"Hmmm." She cocked her head, trying to gauge the sun through the canopy. She gave it up as a bad job and looked at her watch instead. "Another few hours, we'll probably push on instead of breaking for lunch."

"Oh … I'm not sure if that's good news or bad!"

The pattern of the last few days had been an early start—there was nothing to hang around for, and the travelling was easier in the mornings—and a longish break for an early lunch.

"Oh, good news, for sure—we're going to see the cave, at last. What do you think it will be like?"

"Well, for all the song and dance the Prof's been making, it could be the Forty Thieves' lair with all its riches, but given that we're archaeologists … I'm going to go with damp or dusty … probably both in different places."

"Adi think's there's going to be a big black block of stone." She said this with her trademark giggle.

"That would be cool … but I think Adi watches too many sci-fi films."

***

The last half hour was agony, and even the Prof looked like she was flagging, the first sign of weakness that Bill had seen her display in, well, forever. It was Budi, late middle-aged and the oldest here, who had kept spirits up, lent a hand where needed, and kept them all moving. He'd probably walked twice as far as everyone else to get here today. He liked leading from the front, but he would come back and politely chivvy anyone who was lagging, help them with their packs, bring a bottle of water, whatever it took to keep people moving so that they could reach this spot.

They reached the cave shortly after 1 pm. By this time Budi was at the front again—a cynic might think that he'd planned to be in the lead when they arrived. He stood proprietarily on the ridge and exclaimed, "We're here!" in such a joyful way that everyone dug deep and pulled themselves up the last hill. They formed little knots: a group of post-docs here, a group of students there. The Prof stood next to Budi, hands on hips, drinking in the scene. Bill, shy and never really sure of his standing in the party, tried to stand as close to the Prof as possible, without making it obvious he was doing so.

The cave mouth itself was unprepossessing. There was nothing to mark it out as special, nothing to suggest that this cave, over all the others they had passed on the slopes of the mountain, was the cave.

"Right." The Prof's soft Scottish brough caused the 'r' to roll like a car going over a rumble strip. "Tell me what I'm looking at, Budi, please."

Bill was surprised. The Prof rarely used pleasantries, and everyone here knew she was the expert that Budi had moved Heaven and Earth to bring to this place. Perhaps some vestigial politeness acknowledged Budi as the host.

Budi pointed. "There is the cave itself, of course, but I defy you to find the cache of stores. My team spent months ferrying equipment and supplies to this place!"

"You didn't put it all in the cave?"

"I might not be famous—yet—but I am a professional."

"Actually, I suggested that." Adi, Budi's senior postdoc, had detached himself from the cluster of researchers and joined his mentor and the Prof. "I had an idea of marking out an area with a home-made stone-wall using the rocks lying around, but—"

"But I said it must remain untouched until it could be catalogued properly, with guidance on the world's greatest expert on these antiquities."

Professor Elsa Fitzallen either ignored the flattery or accepted it as her due. Her face didn't register the remark, and Bill didn't know her well enough to say which might be true.

The Prof shaded her eyes and scanned the cliff face. "There." She pointed. "I don't know how you could have stashed everything you said you've brought here, but that's the only place where you could put anything."

Bill stared, trying to see what she could see. This cave was even less alluring, barely more than a hollow under an outcropping of the rock. Budi looked at the Prof, clearly impressed that she'd spotted the feature, equally open about being pleased that she couldn't see how the trick was done.

"We had to have some protection for both the cache and the cave itself," Budi said. "There are prying eyes not too far away and the creatures that make their homes hereabout. So, I asked my grandfather for help."

"Your grandfather?" Bill blurted out, surprised. The Prof, Budi, and Adi all turned to look at him, and he tried to pretend he hadn't been ear-wigging the whole conversation.

"My grandfather was a rōmusha, a forced laborer, used by the Japanese to build their military infrastructure during the Second World War. He learned a lot from them, and he and his old cronies helped excavate a secret hidey-hole for me.

"It took six months from my grandfather visiting this site and designing the cache himself to us sealing the equipment in, ready for us today. I found an interesting site nearby we could use as cover." ***

The fairy-tale that would be told, in years to come, would be of Budi's own child, Arif, finding the red clay tablet, which obviously did not belong in Indonesia. In point of fact, it was one of his neighbor's children who had found the tile and traded it with the subtle Arif for a comic book and a mixed bag (as big as two fists) of kolak, klepon and other sweets. Arif didn't know what it was but was certain his father would be interested. (He was continuing to reap the goodwill of his father but was sensible enough to share with his friend).

The tablet bore the legend 'Legix.' Budi had tasked Arif and his friends with finding more such items, but softly, softly. Some things had come to light, enough that Budi was quietly confident that there was something worth looking for. He had enough evidence that he could send some things for analysis and others to Professor Elsa Fitzallen; if they were genuine, she would be able to tell at a glance. It had taken Budi two years, mainly because he had tried to ensure that no one realized quite how interested he was, but he'd tracked every artefact's journey across Indonesia and had pinned down the source to one island.

***

Initially, Elsa had been intrigued. Her attitude quickly turned rude when she'd realized where Budi was from and where he claimed the artefacts originated—there was no way these objects could have been found in Indonesia ... Budi must be a fraud. Somehow their professional relationship had survived this rocky start.

It had been difficult beyond belief to keep hidden the project from two sets of university authorities, but the situation was so incredible that authenticated evidence needed to be collected before funders could be approached for a full-scale investigation. Elsa and Budi had managed to swing a visiting post for Elsa—both institutions had been pleased with the connections being built—and Elsa had found some 'funny money' squirreled away from other projects to pay for her team to join her: Felix and Seren ostensibly for a conference and Bill hired for the duration as Elsa's research assistant, with the cover that he was helping her with her teaching and research commitments in her visiting post.

Elsa was desperate to get to the site, not that she would ever admit it to anyone. She had gone past thinking if *this is genuine* …. She knew there was something important here. They didn't give a Nobel Prize for Archaeology, but the discovery of this site would mean a rewriting of the history books. It wouldn't necessarily mean fortune, but there would certainly be glory.

***

The Cave of Legix: the cave of wonders as far as most here were concerned. The cave opening itself was surprisingly large—wide enough for two or three people to walk side-by-side and high enough that it was comfortably above even Bill's head—he didn't even flinch instinctively when he eventually walked in. They'd all had a peep in at some point in the afternoon.

They'd had lunch, pottered about, admired the secret stash—which none of them had been able to spot until Budi showed them how to find it. Budi had taken the Prof to see the cave first, of course. Then Adi had taken Lestari and Felix. Seren had gone a little later with Lutfi and Setiawan, and Bill had been in the last group, with Kadek, shown the sights by Adi, who seemed to project some sort of ownership. Not that there was much to see in the entrance of the cave itself, except for some very unusual carvings, carvings that had no place being on the cave of a wall in Indonesia.

Bill had noticed over the last few days that Adi seemed to be very cool toward him, and the introduction to the site was no different. Adi took great pains to show the various carvings to Kadek, and to opine on their significance, but somehow he managed to leave Bill out of it all. Bill wondered if Adi looked down on him because he wasn't post doc or PhD researcher. Somehow it seemed to go beyond that.

Bill knew he was lucky to be here, he knew that, but there was a part of him that wondered at his luck. He really was the low man on the pole here, a newly minted MSc amongst seasoned researchers. He'd inveigled his way into Professor Fitzallen's group, not through any particular malice or ambition, although he'd been aware of her reputation and had hung on her every word in lectures. Mainly, he'd hoped to get an opportunity to talk to a girl he liked. Bill was painfully shy and found it difficult to tell a girl exactly how he felt. Of course, by the time Bill was ready to ask her on a date, she'd gone off with someone else—a PhD student in another group where she'd decided to do her project after all. Whilst Bill, poor Bill, unlucky in love again, was committed to a project with the demanding, meticulous Elsa Fitzallen. But if Elsa was exacting as a supervisor, she was also a supportive one, taking the time to find out her students' strengths and weaknesses. She'd quickly uncovered Bill's interest in photography; he could be a professional if he put his mind to it. It wasn't only technical skill but also an instinctive talent for framing the shot and selecting the right settings.

Bill had pulled his weight in setting up the camp and in ferrying equipment to the cave, but he really wanted to get on with the photography. There was little else that he could do at this point, and he knew that his first objective was to get good photos of the carvings on the walls of the defile leading to the cave mouth. It was going to be tricky to get a good angle, and he wasn't sure whether there would be enough natural light or not. Certainly, there was no direct light at this time of the afternoon, but tomorrow in the late morning might be better. Or he could go with whatever artificial lighting could be mustered. He needed to look and consider angles. He was also wondering if there might be better opportunities looking down.

Bill pulled his climbing shoes and belt out of his backpack and opened his personal camera kit. Budi had arranged for a top-line photography kit to be on hand, including tripods, some battery-powered lights, a complete range of lenses, filters—everything that a photographer might want or need but probably couldn't afford if he was, essentially, a student. Still, there were some things that you wanted your own tools for, and Bill rummaged in his kit to find his trusty Pentax. It was a middle-of-the-range body, more expensive than most people would go for, less expensive than someone really serious might pay. He fitted a general-purpose lens, checked the battery, tucked some filters in a dedicated pouch on his belt, and set off.

If you didn't know the cave was here, there was a good chance that you would overlook it completely; whilst the cave itself was large enough, the fissure in the rock that you needed to clamber through was narrow and uneven. For all that, it was open to the sky. As he'd expected, it was tricky to get a clean view of the most impressive carving, but Bill had managed it with a macro, taken in less than ideal conditions, one handed whilst he held on to an outcrop of rock with the other hand. He took a couple of others from different positions. He was beginning to form a theory.

***

Budi seemed to have thought of everything, including some powerful software for producing 3D visualizations of spaces from photographs. Lestari was the acknowledged expert at using this software to best effect. Even though he had a legitimate reason for talking to her, Bill was still tempted to see what he could do on his own. In the end, Lestari had overheard him talking to Elsa and Budi and taken charge, finding a space to set up the laptop and chivvying Bill to make sure that the solar chargers were set up properly. The software was every bit as good as Bill had hoped, and Lestari was a generous teacher, explaining what she was doing at every stage. They fed his photographs into the software, rendered the wall of the fissure, and manipulated it so that it could be seen from different angles. One might have expected that the sweetspot would be either the mouth of the cave or the fissure itself; actually, it was some apparently random spot halfway between the carving and the mouth of the fissure. That point would need to be inspected more closely.

Elsa and Budi were impressed and made Lestari and Bill show their findings after dinner. Bill let Lestari do most of the talking, but she insisted on giving all the credit to Bill. Bill couldn't help noticing that Adi scowled hard at this.

The carving, which was *something*, had been carved in an unusual manner, taking into account perspective. There was only one point where it could be viewed properly, revealing a perfect Roman aquila, the spread wings of the eagle appearing to give benediction rather than warning.

But that was a tad too fanciful, surely.

***

The following morning, Bill was back at work early, before anyone else was up. He found the sweet-spot and took more photos, both with his own camera and with Budi's more expensive equipment. On a personal note, Bill was interested to see how much of a difference the equipment made.

He took some close-up photos of the carving itself, showing the bite of the chisel into the stone. There had clearly been some level of weathering, but equally, this fissure seemed quite well protected from the elements; these carvings were not new, but it was hard to tell how old they might be. Bill also surveyed the whole fissure from ground level and found a much cruder carving that looked like the Roman equivalent of a 'woz ere' piece of graffiti. He got a good shot of that too. He was packing up when Lestari found him, bringing a cup of coffee and the news that breakfast was ready.

Adi looked up as Lestari and Bill walked back together; again, a scowl imprinted his face. At breakfast Bill tried to ignore the dagger-eyes and showed Elsa and Budi his picture of the aquila, which confirmed that yesterday's computer model was correct. Both were pleased, but … not dismissive exactly; they'd already moved on. Neither had doubted that it was what it had appeared to be—although confirmation was good—but they couldn't agree what it meant, especially given the unusual trick with perspective, which Elsa had not seen done anywhere else. If you didn't know that they were influential academics, then you might almost think they were bickering.

They had agreed that the symbol had been placed there deliberately, but by whom? When? Why? It was clearly important, because there was no way that the symbol could have been carved without building some sort of platform. Was it a benediction? Or simply a reminder of the power of Rome? And what on earth was it doing here, where it had no right to be?

***

They reached what they later dubbed the 'Central Cave' a day and a half later. It was not that it was any great distance from the cave entrance, under five hundred meters, but that they had been meticulous in their examination of the floor, walls, and ceiling of the passage that led into the bowels of the mountain. Everyone was pleased that the cave was dry, although that begged its own questions. The search was justified and rewarded. More carvings, both large, obvious artistic bits, and the more surreptitiously obscene graffiti of the bored adolescent or rank-and-file soldier. More pottery fragments. Broken tools. The bits and pieces that warm the hearts of archaeologists.

Each item was photographed *in situ*, cleaned with a fine brush, cataloged, photographed again, and, if portable, removed to be packed for carting back to base camp, and ready for shipment to the University of Indonesia. Every member of the team was busy; every member of the team had a role to play. Budi had invested in all sorts of equipment to make their lives easier, including networked radios with throat mics. Everyone had their own channel, which was being recorded whilst they described the artefacts they were finding, and there was a general channel that they could use to coordinate activities; the most important of these, of course, was to notify everyone that meals were ready.

The passageway led downward at a relatively shallow incline but angled steep enough to be uncomfortable if one tried to move too quickly. When they had finally traversed it, they found that it led to a ledge which looked out over the central cave. The passageway sloped so that they couldn't see the cavern until they stepped out onto the ledge. And then they got the full effect.

The ledge was about halfway up the side of the cavern wall, which meant that it was a five- or six-meter drop to the cavern floor, and the roof of the cavern was about the same distance again above their heads. The floor of the cavern was an irregular circle, around one hundred meters across, and on the far side small openings led off, presumably passageways like this one. There were at least a dozen of these openings, but who knew if all of them were visible from this angle? Some were at ground level, and some were set further up the wall of the cavern. These appeared to have steps leading down to the cavern floor. When they got over the shock, they looked for steps down from the ledge.

Shock. Everyone was in shock. For a start, the cave was more brightly lit than the passageway, although it was not possible to tell where this light was coming from. But it was the object that was lit up that was more shocking: a Roman Triumphal Arch, some three layers in height, with the bottom half forming the arch itself, and then the top half forming two stories of smaller arches. It nearly reached the top of the cavern, and whilst it was not possible to see the top from the ledge, it appeared that there was at least enough room to stand up if there was a way of reaching the top.

Bill recovered first, and started snapping pictures of the arch and the cavern. The sound of the shutter whirring closed and open, closed and open, was enough to bring the others round.

***

Everyone wanted to rush over and inspect the arch. Who wouldn't? But Budi and Elsa exerted their authority, and the explorations continued in a rigorous manner. This took another two days. First, they had to find and assess the steps down. Then they explored the entire periphery, establishing that the passageway leading to the outside world was the only one on their side and that the other passageways lay exactly within an 45° arc.

At this point, Budi and Elsa were not prepared to explore the passages, but there was equipment in the cache that could be used to carry out a limited survey from the cavern. This was brought down. It was at the end of the first day's exploration when they realized that within the cavern there was no dust of any kind. Anywhere.

***

Seren and Lutfi, who'd become good friends over the last few days, were on cooking duty, and they called over the radio to say that the evening meal was ready. The team in the cavern assembled on the ledge, and it was then that they noticed that Lestari was missing. They were trying to work out a plan for trying to find her when Bill spotted her near the top of the arch.

Elsa and Budi had only just allowed them to start looking at the arch itself that afternoon, and they'd found that there were steps leading up on both sides of the arch, in the inside, but that had been as far as they'd allowed anyone to go. Lestari's patience had finally given way.

Budi, Adi, Elsa and Bill flew down from the ledge and raced across the open ground to the arch. Bill's long legs gave him an advantage, coupled with the vim and vigor of his youth. He reached the steps and hesitated a perceptible fraction of a second before heading inside the arch. Taking the steps two at a time, he reached the first land of the structure. The next staircase opened onto the second level of the arch, and now there were outer steps leading up to the third level.

Here he was more cautious; there was no kind of rail to prevent a drop of seven meters or so. He reached the top and found the same again. He heard Adi reach the top of the first flight of stairs, and an audible in-drawing of breath. He carried on and reached the top. He almost didn't see Lestari.

At the top he found something that none of them could ever have predicted. In a precise circle, five meters across, were the standards of a legion. The four most important were not aligned with the geometry of the structure in any way, which made Bill wonder what the significance was—they'd already established that the arch was aligned with magnetic North. The next thing he realized was that the standards were not completely vertical, they were bending inward, into the center of the circle.

He saw Lestari, who beckoned him over to the most important standard, the Aquila: this bore the inscription Legio IX Hispania. The Eagle of the Ninth Legion. The cursed Ninth, supposedly lost in the heather of Scotland.

Bill uncapped his Pentax and started taking pictures, forgetting that he had come to find Lestari. Adi appeared at the top of the arch, trying to shout but out of breath. Adi half ran, half stumbled, still trying to shout.

Bill looked up and saw Lestari looking back, he thought—at first—at him, but then he realized that she was looking rather coyly at Adi. Her dyed hair, shining in the bright, ethereal light, flicked as she turned her attention back to the circle. She said something which he didn't catch as she stepped across the threshold in the instant that Adi grabbed hold of her arm. They both vanished just as Elsa reached the top.

***

Back home, a month later, Bill looked over the paperwork for his PhD, supervised by Elsa. For the hundredth time, he hit play on the audio file of Lestari's last words before she disappeared. No one else had heard this—not even Elsa: he'd spent a lot of time cleaning up the recording. Budi's precautions in mic'ing everyone up and recording the discussions around the archaeological dig had paid off.

"My God, it's full of stars!"

It was the giggle at the end, like she knew what was coming, that had him vacillating about this opportunity. Suddenly, he picked up the pen and dashed off his signature.

A MYSTERY WRAPPED IN A RIDDLE

By Deb Whittam

https://debwhittam.allauthor.com/

Secrets are harbored in a small town that will influence the fate of all.

Nursing a chronic hangover, Jeff winced as the door slammed. He paused his half-hearted raking and glanced up without looking at the offender of his temporary peace, especially since he'd come out into the garden to escape her perpetual hangdog expression. As she shuffled into his field of vision, he looked off to the left toward the church, grimacing as a merciless stab of sunlight pierced through his useless sunglasses. Squinting, he noticed how a hunched figure hidden beneath a trailing cape scurried up the church path.

Jeff half-smiled. Everyone who walked that way had a secret, and this visitor was no different; her secret was blatantly apparent to all who cared to look. As the sneaky figure reached the doorway and paused, Jeff frowned. They should be grateful for what they had. It could be stolen from them in an instant. Even as the thought crossed his mind, it dawned on him that something seemed wrong with the picture this stranger presented, but before he could determine what, she disappeared inside the church.

"Jeff?" Her voice clawed back his attention, interrupting his speculation. "Are you coming in yet?"

His lips tightened as he turned to gaze at the palefaced woman. "Soon."

***

No one ever believed him ... he was just the kid who didn't talk. What they didn't realize was that he watched...watched and took photographs.

Edging forward, he glanced toward Mr. Todd and then dismissed him out of hand. Mr. Todd's drinking problem was common knowledge, and he wasn't a fitting choice for his latest discovery. He wanted to talk to Father Ryan who always listened—well, pretended to—and, anyway, he'd raced through the woods to show the Father what he had witnessed.

What he hadn't anticipated was their presence, and as Randall eyed the shadowy personage creeping into the church, his brow wrinkled in confusion. His camera might speak the truth, but now he had to find someone willing to see it.

***

Lisa paused, blinking back tears as she reapplied her lipstick, aware that her hand trembled ever so slightly. When she had left the clinic, she'd believed she had accepted the outcome of his decision, but now she felt numbed, even as she berated her reflection. "Stop this, Lisa girl, you knew what he planned—anyway you're way too young to have a kid, it's for the best."

As her voice echoed within the church, she flushed, aware that in this holiest of houses her actions would be condemned, that she might not be able to ask for forgiveness this time. But habit had led her here, for Father Ryan always listened. He had never judged her despite the rashness of her actions, despite the contempt of others.

She bit back a curse at the sound of footsteps. She couldn't face Father Ryan; she couldn't bear to see the condemnation in his eyes, and desperate, she sought the refuge of the antechamber only to catch a glimpse of a figure hurrying past.

"Been there, done that," she muttered.

***

It was always the same: dust this, mop that, and don't forget to empty the bins. Marg's smile faltered for a moment as she recalled the not-too-distant past. Then she shrugged away the ghosts. She had been doing this for years, but the way the Father went on you would think she was going senile.

Marg paused and stared at the bin secreted beside the altar. Damn fool place to put a bin, and as the door creaked she bent over to seize the offending item.

Endeavoring to straighten, she felt it—a sickening crack.

"Damn," Marg muttered. Her back had gone again.

Engulfed in agony, she closed her eyes.

***

Father Ryan paused and acknowledged his unworthiness. He had sinned, yet he felt no guilt. It was a crime he fell victim to every time, and though he swore that each occasion would be the last, he always succumbed.

Standing at the top of the bell tower's steps he hung his head, and then he tucked the offending item back into its place of concealment. Priests didn't have time to read comic books. He had parishioners to tend to, and he forced his feet to take the first step only to pause when a glorious influx of color bathed the staircase.

"Oh my," he murmured, seconds before a scream rent the silence, and his typically dignified stride transformed into a panicked run.

***

A mesmerizing kaleidoscope of dancing colors assailed Lisa as she stepped into the foyer. She stood in a trancelike state as the inner church door was flung open to reveal a slim figure hidden beneath a voluptuous cape.

The other drew to a halt, and Lisa paled, her eyes widening as she recognized the changes that had occurred in a moment, her hand drifting to touch her stomach involuntarily.

For a moment, silence, and then this apparition reached out and touched her cheek with hands as cold as death. Lisa trembled, exhausted as if she had just …

Her thoughts dissipated like mist in the sun when the cloaked stranger slipped past and outside, but Lisa's eyes were drawn to the trail left in their wake.

Lisa frowned. It wasn't blood, was it? It couldn't be for it was the wrong shade.

***

Irritation scored Jeff's features as Mabel's droning voice once again penetrated his thoughts.

"Just come inside and …" Her voice faded, and Jeff looked at her, one eyebrow raised in question. "Blimey, what's that?" she asked, her eyes wide.

He turned to peer where she stared, his eyes squinting at the blinding light streaming through the church's windows.

Wincing, he averted his gaze, catching sight of a slight figure emerging from the door.

"Hey you!" he shouted, overwhelmed by a sense of urgency. "Wait here, Mabel."

***

As the hunched cloak-wearer fled the church and headed in his direction, Randall's lips compressed, the other was now decidedly slimmer which in his mind suggested only one thing, and his anger flared.

All his life he had been alone, abandoned by his parents at birth, ostracized by all he met. And now this one was committing the same crime, if the evidence before his eyes was any indication. He scowled as the stranger paused before him, his remembered pain almost unbearable as she tilted her head and then stretched out a hand.

They sought the evidence his camera had recorded, and amused, he bit out a sharp laugh.

It was the first sound to ever pass his lips.

***

She didn't notice it at first, but as the pain subsided she recalled the noise and identified it in an instant. It was a breathing pattern she recognized with ease, for she had borne four children of her own; it was a swift intake, followed by a very slow labored exhale, and it prompted action on her part. Ignoring the pain in her back, Marg gritted her teeth, forcing herself upright.

The first thing she noticed was the unnatural glow which hung over the room, the second was the heavy silence, and the third was the swinging of the door.

"Well I never," she muttered, gingerly passing the altar, her heartbeat quickening as she spied the bundle upon the floor.

"Oh no." She hurried towards it, and as she lifted it the blanket fell away, exposing a cold pale blue limb. "Please no."

For a moment she hesitated, recognizing the truth, and then Marg pushed the shock aside to yell. "Father! Father Ryan!"

Frozen, her gaze stayed fixed upon how weak its movements were. Death beckoned.

It needed help—now—regardless of what it was.

***

The low pitch of Mr. Todd's voice startled Randall from his staring contest with the stranger, and as he looked over to meet Mr. Todd's eyes, he felt his stomach contract.

"Let it go, boy. Give her the camera."

Randall saw something reflected in the depths of this hollow man's eyes which held him spellbound—a sternness that invoked new emotions.

He may have held the evidence of this one's sins, but as Mr. Todd laid a hand upon his shoulder he felt all of his animosity toward the dark stranger evaporate.

United they stood before the stranger.

"Give it to her, mate," Mr. Todd said in a gentle, coaxing tone. "No good will come of it, Randall, you have to trust me. She's doing this for a good reason." He sounded different, and Randall looked up to find Mr. Todd considering him. "It's ok—we'll look after him."

He wanted to relinquish the pain, the hardship which was his existence, and as the stranger reached out he let the camera slip from his grasp.

The other was already disappearing into the woods as Mr. Todd's hand tightened on his shoulder, a presence gone but not forgotten.

***

Father Ryan rushed through the doorway as the second cry sounded only to come to a halt when he spied Lisa standing silent and still.

"Lisa?"

His eyes slipped over her, struggling to assimilate the glaring alteration in her appearance. Though she had chosen to openly flaunt her sins, she had remained a regular visitor to the church, and he knew beneath her flashy exterior and inexcusable behavior she felt herself unworthy. He hadn't accepted this truth, for he believed her pure of spirit, but now, in the wake of these changes he was forced to reassess his opinion, even though at this moment he was transfixed.

She radiated an inner light which transformed her from beautiful to breathtaking.

***

The dull thunder of running footsteps broke the brief silence, and Jeff turned to see Mabel rushing toward them, her features resolute.

"Jeff! Jeff, are you alright?"

It was there before him and he had never noticed: the fear, the pain, the need for reassurance. He had failed her out of a feeling of guilt, but she had stayed … regardless of the loss they had endured.

He struggled to articulate his feelings, but as Randall shifted beneath his hands the words trapped in his throat found voice. "Things have to change, Mabel. We can't grieve any longer. Our baby was stillborn—his life lost…but ours isn't."

Mabel stilled. He saw her swallow and knew she had waited for him to accept.

"No more blame, no more escaping." Tears welled in his wife's eyes, and he looked down at the boy before him—a child who had never known a parent's love.

"And as for you, mate, it's time you had a home. And we could sure do with a son."

***

It was gone—the pain, the joy, the heartache and feeling bereft. Lisa looked up, only to meet Father Ryan's puzzled gaze.

"She's gone," she muttered as tears streamed down her face.

Father Ryan met her eyes, and then he looked toward the outer door, noticing the trail of blood for the first time. "Oh no."

When he turned toward the inner doors Lisa reached out, declaring with certainty, "You'll need me."

His hesitation was forestalled as Marg called out, "Father, bring a towel."

***

In silence, Father Ryan looked at each of them in turn, aware that only he knew their secrets. And though it was his duty to keep them, he couldn't help but consider each in light of current circumstances.

Looking into Marg's weathered features, it was impossible to envisage her as anything other than a loving grandmother. Few knew that she had been addicted to painkillers and that this had led to her dismissal from the local school. If he hadn't provided another option, her slide into the abyss would have been complete.

Then there was Jeff and Mabel, who had lost more than a child. They had lost their faith. Mabel had blamed the alcohol she had secretly consumed throughout her pregnancy, while Jeff thought it was judgment for a lifetime of sins. Non-communication had only widened the breach, which had seemed impossible to span.

Each of them may have committed a minor transgression, but it was Lisa whose latest atrocity spoke for itself. Pregnant to another woman's husband, she had flaunted her sin with no thought for those within her sphere. While this brazenness had tarnished her reputation, if it became known that she had terminated her pregnancy in the last trimester, no forgiveness would have been possible, for it was a moral sin.

Even Randall had his secrets, Father Ryan thought as he eyed the boy who hung back. Though he couldn't speak, Randall did spread tales and perhaps in this case he had one to tell, but regardless they were bound now, with a burden they would share forever.

"We will call him Jason," Father Ryan announced as the adults nodded their agreement, but as he met Randall's eyes he glanced away, unwilling to recognize the mute appeal in their depths. The boy would be fine; he would accept the outcome in time. Jeff and Mabel would ensure he did, since they were family now. Randall would understand that it was sanctioned by God, for it had unfolded beneath his roof.

As a small, scaled arm sneaked from the blanket's folds, Father Ryan pushed aside his reservations, even as his gaze returned to Lisa. An unfamiliar wave of longing swept over him.

***

As he closed the front door Father Ryan smiled. The change in Randall since the adoption had been finalized was amazing. But the sense of disquiet returned as he walked back into the sitting room recalling yet again that he had never seen Randall touch Jason. The boy refused to, only watching the baby in a studious manner. Father Ryan sighed, sometimes when he let his imagination run rampant he understood why.

"They seem happy."

At Lisa's comment, he pushed his reservations aside to focus on the woman who nursed Jason with a contented smile. There had been gossip and censure when he took single-mother Lisa into his home, but Marg's presence had stopped tongues wagging. Though he would freely admit they had just cause.

"You were pretty quiet this evening," Lisa prompted.

He turned to the fireplace and leaned against it. "It's been six months," he murmured, "and I was just considering all the changes that brief timespan had witnessed." Sometimes he questioned their actions that night, whether their acceptance was prompted by a miracle or the desire to witness one. "Shall I make a cup of tea?"

Inwardly he acknowledged his desire to escape scrutiny, for in these dark moments what he tried to forget resurfaced.

The last few nights a scratching had emanated from Jason's room, and though he had taken his time in responding—pausing before opening the door—he had still seen it. What they had all seen in those first few moments. What they had all chosen to ignore.

It had left him questioning exactly what they had invited into their lives.

It had left him wondering what had been reborn.

"Tea would be lovely wouldn't it, Jason?"

Turning at Lisa's words he met Jason's unnatural, knowing gaze and a plethora of proverbs sprung to mind—a wolf in sheep's clothing; evil in the guise of an angel; be careful who you trust; the devil was once an angel.

He shivered. It was a mystery wrapped in a riddle, and he didn't have the courage to solve it today.

A JOURNEY WITH DEATH

By Briar Shea

https://fictionfanaddict.wordpress.com

The bells are ringing like crazy throughout my castle, and I'm about to go crazy. There was a bus crash in Norfolk, Virginia, along with an earthquake in Marseille, France, and people just keep showing up! Apparently, they can't understand that despite who I am, I have a life too. I'll never be able to keep up with how many people I've sent off, and it's only 11:28 AM.

"Your most grim eminence, sir, there is a new group coming through the gates in the back," Drogman, one of my lackeys, says with a note of annoyance in his otherwise bland voice.

"Ugh, if one more bloody person comes through that gate, I won't even look at their files; I'll just flip a four-sided coin!" Drogman whimpers, and I let out an exasperated sigh. "Fine. What are their stories?"

He pulls out twelve folders and hands them to me. I open the first. "Margie—kid's doctor—that's good enough." I flip through the rest of the files quickly. "Send them all to the west sector except that Chris guy; he was a puppy abuser, and that's just not right. Send him South." "Yes, sir. Thank you, sir." Just like that he's gone. Finally! I can relax, maybe eat my breakfast, even though it's probably cold since it was made five hours ago. I sniff my bagel, and my tongue instantly waters. My jaw opens wide as I bring the bagel to my lips—

"Sorry, sir, it is me again." Drogman says without a hint of remorse.

My expelled breath deflates my chest like a leaky bagpipe. I scowl into the circle of my bagel and count to five in my head.

"Um, there are five others, sir," he says with some hesitation.

Before I have time to process my thoughts, I growl and throw the bagel at his head, and then lower my voice because it always seems to scare Drogman.

"I have had enough! I want to kill something, but killing something means I have to take care of it! Fine, I will send off these five people, but then I am done! Now show me their files, then I am taking a break and going to the city."

He yelps a little and hands me the files.

"Christy goes to the North sector, Wesley to the West." I squint down at the numbers on the next one. "That guy killed three—no—eight people …? Hmm, well puppy abuser was sent South so this guy can join him."

I finish and hand the files to Drogman, pressing them to his chest as I stride by. He stays close behind me as I walk toward my gates so I can leave.

"Sir, I don't mean to be, um…to be demanding at all … but you can't really leave."

"Why? Because I don't have any vacation days left? Oh right! I don't get vacation days!" I continue my march toward the gates.

"Sir, I am truly sorry, but um … you can't leave because … well, because."

I roll my eyes and turn around, holding my black cloaks around my shadowy figure. "Because why? Because I'm … Death?" I smirk, motioning to my body of shadows. "Yes, dinghead, I know that, but I've been thinking. All I do, day after day, is look at files and then decide whether or not to send people to Paradise—North—or Hell—South—or in between." I motion to each the west, east, south and north sectors leaving the castle. "It's not that hard. I'm sure you can take care of it for a few weeks." I wink and pivot back around and walk toward the gates. "Oh and, Drogman?" I let myself hover in the air using shadows. "Don't eat my bagels." With that sentence, my robes surround me, suffocating all the light from my body while I shed the shadow of death from my persona.

My manly form isn't anything special, but it isn't supposed to be since it's a disguise from my true character. I can never fully be rid of the essence of Death, but the pale man with brown hair covering his head and chin suggests I am a friendly guy instead of someone who could kill you with the snap of his fingers.

Double checking that I'm ready to go, I set off on the path leading from my somber castle to the city.

***

After a day of traveling, people envelop me, and I'm already feeling the regrets of leaving my solitude. Without thinking of anything other than the fact that I need to escape the clutches of the city people emerging from every corner in sight, I start off toward a hill that seems to shine a little brighter than the rest. Awhile back I expropriated some man's sunglasses when he wasn't looking. After being enclosed in my aphotic realm for the past two hundred seventy-three years, my eyes could not take seeing a bright sun for more than an hour. When I reach the hill, I realize the reason few people are around here is because it is a temple, a very intense, white, annoying temple. I glare at this behemoth of a hill and out of curiosity, my hand reaches toward the temple's fluorescent glow to— "What are you doing?"

If I was anyone other than Death that would have scared me. When I turn I see a woman perched on one of the steps to the temple, her aura tells me she's an explorer who is around twenty-seven. She glares at me like she was just shown a picture of trash. Very reassuring.

"I asked, what are you doing? Why were you about to touch the temple—my temple?"

Of course this lady has a temple. I roll my eyes. I do not feel like dealing with this right now. If there weren't people to cause a scene, I would just kill her, but that isn't an option.

"Well you see, miss, I was just so fascinated by the aura!" She huffs at my sarcasm. "Okay, fine, I was just wondering why it's here. Compared to the rest of this dull town, it is quite out of place atop this hill." She looks at me like I'm speaking a different language.

"I'm an explorer and quite successful. This is where I do my studies." She squints her eyes at me while saying that. "And everyone knows best not to bother me, especially now!"

I cannot take her anymore, she is way too bossy. "Well why is it 'especially now?'"

"You know absolutely nothing do you?" She crosses her arms and blows the hair out of her eyes in annoyance. "Even if you're a tourist, everyone has heard that I am off to slay Death. I discovered a path to his castle, and I will be the person that helps everyone escape death once and for all."

I don't know whether to flinch or chuckle.

"No way. I'm actually going that direction!" I do my best to show a charming smile. "I pass his castle every time I travel home. The first couple times it's rather creepy, but I'm used to it by now."

She gapes at me. "So you're telling me you have been to Death's castle?"

I shrug. "I mean I've been to the gates a couple times, but never inside."

"You have to come with me on my mission! You probably know shortcuts and passages beyond any of my knowledge."

"Of course I do! I would absolutely love to help you." I try to suppress the smirk that creeps up. How entertaining. Now all I have to do is carry out a plan to get us away from the swarms of people. That way I can kill her, go back to my castle, and forget that I ever took this break.

***

The windy trails leading away from the city are annoyingly uneven, and my human body aches from the work. I forgot how much I enjoyed having a figure constructed completely of shadows. The woman who I soon learned has the name Crystal Knowles has a careful step that helps her maneuver between the cracks.

I wonder how much could have possibly gone wrong at the castle in the last forty-eight hours I've been gone. Drogman may be the smartest out of all my lackeys, but he definitely has his faults. I just got so caught up in the workload that I couldn't take the strain of it. Now I know that taking a break probably wasn't the best way to handle that situation.

A shrill cry for help brings my attention back to the present, and I see Crystal fall. I rush to her side and drape her collapsed body across my knee. That's when the glint of metal catches my eye.

An archer strings his bow carefully and aims it directly at my head.

Quickly checking to make sure Crystal is unconscious, I yell. "Hey you, yes you with the bow! I suggest you put it down." I hear a soft chuckle, but he doesn't lower the bow, instead steadying his aim. "Wow, you're a fool." I wink, focusing my powers toward his heart, and that's when I hear the ever-so-familiar final

150

thud of a last heartbeat, followed by the thump of his body hitting the ground.

Crystal mutters something, which is when I notice the blood seeping through her clothes.

"Crap, humans are so delicate." I realize however that this is the perfect moment to kill her. But I think twice. Instead of killing her, I'll just let her bleed out. Perfect. Laying her gently on the ground, I notice her blood is on my jeans. That's fine, I'm used to blood. Her compass falls to the ground when I stand up, and I think her fingers must have loosened their grip upon it.

I walk away, down the path toward my castle, but I can't get the phantom feeling of her blood against my leg to dissipate. The pinch of guilt in my chest confuses me. I shouldn't be bothered by a random, silly woman's blood. Especially not when she was off to slay Death. AKA me. Even so, my feet turn and take me back to the woman.

All I can think when I place my hands on her hip—where the arrow sticks out—is why am I healing her? I don't care if she is dying, and I certainly don't care whether I let her or not. Somehow, this thought is not a statement but a sentence trying to convince me of it. My hands pull the arrow out. I cannot believe I'm doing this.

My power works its way through her body, and I watch as her wound mends itself. As soon as she's healed, I stride away to my castle. I barely get five feet from her when I hear it.

"Where ... are you going?" Great, she's awake.

"Um, I was just going to…"

"Leave me here to die. Wait … there was an arrow and blood … and … what did you do?" She gawks at me. "I didn't do anything. I simply came over, and the arrow must have hit something metal because you were completely fine." Swiftly, before she can say anything else, I spin and start back on my path. My speed isn't enough to get rid of her because Crystal's footsteps fall quick behind me.

"Hey! Hey!" She calls after me. "Hello? I am talking to you!"

I roll my eyes, annoyed at her irritating character, never minding her own business. I rotate so that I am walking backwards.

"What do you want with me? Sorry, but I don't feel like helping you anymore, so leave me alone!" She gives me a death stare.

"You can't back out of this. Do you even know who I am? My family disowned me when they found out I wanted to be an explorer, and it pushed me to work harder. People are counting on me to complete this mission, and I know you can help me!"

"You have the wrong image of me, Crystal. I suggest you turn the other way." Why am I warning her? Why do I keep trying to protect her? This is not who I am.

"Well, all I see is a selfish, ignorant fool who still hasn't told me his name."

"My name is De-Derek."

"Well, Derek, watch out."

"What?" Then, because of my backward steps, I run into a boulder and lose my footing.

She comes to stand over me with a look I swear I've seen before and says, "Told you so."

I stand, brushing the dirt off of my newly ripped jeans and tower over her. Only inches apart now, I lower my voice.

"You listen here. I did not sign up for this, and I will not have some woman who wants to do the stupidest things just to impress people getting in my way. Do not mess with me, because I mean it when I say you do not understand anything about me." She doesn't say anything.

"Fine." I growl and turn back, now extremely bothered by her stubbornness. "But—"

Not again. The unsaid words rumble low in my throat. I keep walking but she follows.

"When I first saw you, I knew you were trouble," she says, her tone accusing. "I had never seen you before, and then all of a sudden, here you are. I thought maybe it was a sign that this mission would be successful, but now I see that you are just a cold-hearted, headstrong jerk."

She puts her hand on my arm, and a shiver runs down my spine. I stumble to a halt. This feeling is foreign to me, and I don't know what to make of it. Nothing ever makes me flinch, and certainly nothing ever gives me shivers.

"You can still help, though." Her tone is softer, cajoling. "Come with me, and as soon as we reach the castle you can leave."

My lips purse as I actually consider her offer. "Okay, I'll come." The words slur out of my mouth, and it's like I'm not even in control of my own body anymore.

She smiles a slight joyful smile and takes her hand off of my arm. I notice my skin is turning back to shadows where she touched me. That is definitely strange.

***

My eyes trail to the back of Crystal's head as she walks in front of me. What am I going to do? I certainly cannot let this woman who somehow messes with my mind distract me from what I need to do. She needs to die before she even gets a look at my castle. All it would take is one thought, one concentrated thought, and I can stop her heart. Yet every time I focus, all I hear is the strangely familiar thrum of her heartbeat, and I can't bring myself to stop it. She glances back at me with a smile on her face, and I avert my eyes to stare at the passing trees. My cheeks flush, and I can feel how hot they are. Why does she make me feel this way? Is she some type of manipulator? No, that's ridiculous; I would be able to sense that.

"Hey, Derek?"

"Yeah?"

She slows down until she is walking beside me. My human form has a heart, and I can feel it speed up.

"So I was thinking, we are probably close to reaching the castle. What is the plan once we get there?"

"You're the great explorer. Don't you have all this figured out?"

"Actually ... yes." She pulls her pack off of her shoulders and reaches into the front pocket. "I have done my research and gone on many journeys to get to this point. I discovered a very rare gem known as librolite, which has the power to weaken Death."

I chuckle. "Nothing has the power to weaken Death, sweetheart." I look up and see the shadows circling the tip of castle.

"Actually, it does. My research showed me that death's true form is a makeup of shadows, which is why it is impossible to kill him, since he has no true heart. Librolite, however, destroys shadows. It's a slow process but it does."

Words cannot escape my mouth. This can't possibly be true. Then I remember how when she touched me earlier my flesh weakened and turned to shadows. We reach my castle and stop directly in front of the gates.

"Um, wow, Crystal ... that is very interesting. Where is the librolite?"

My voice shakes as she reaches in the bag's front pocket and pulls out a baseball sized rock with an appearance of coal, speckled in yellow gems. As soon as it is out in the open, my body feels like it is being ripped apart. My screams blare across the open paths, and I collapse to the ground, grasping at anything to stabilize me.

"Derek? How is this harming you? It can only harm... Death. No, you can't be..." Quickly she backs up. Her eyes are so wide the whites of them consume all color.

My human form dissipates until I return to my shadowy figure. She shrieks. I can feel the shadows evaporating and every second is agony. I spot Drogman running out of the castle. When he sees what is happening to me he lets out a roar.

"You foolish girl!" His voice seems rougher, and he stares directly at Crystal. "I had a good thing going for me, and then you show up with your fancy librolite to ruin everything!" His thunderous voice booms around me.

"Drogman?" I croak his name, and my lackey's form shifts from his small, weak figure and grows into a tenfoot-tall silhouette of darkness. He isn't even made of shadows; he is just a figure of pure darkness.

"You were such an ignorant little puppet," Drogman says with resigned disappointment. "I wish our system could have lasted longer. Sadly, I must kill both of you now."

Crystal looks at me with an awed expression.

"What?" I exclaim.

"Y-your figure." The awe in her voice jolts through me. "Marcus? Is it really you?"

I look down, and all I see is the body of a teenage boy. The figure reminds me of something, like a fading memory.

"SHUT IT!" Drogman's voice thunders around us.

"Drogman?" I mutter, confusion suppressing my fear.

"My name is not Drogman, you fool. I am the real Death." He taps my head and I'm thrown backward as memories flash before my eyes. The most intense memory shows Crystal pushing me on a swing. I am telling her to push me higher. "Sister! Sister! Higher! Haha!" Crystal is my sister? Then the memories fade, and I am left crumpled on the ground, hot droplets of water streaming down my cheeks. I was never actually Death. I only died and Drogman took me over …"

Crystal runs over and wraps her arms around me. Relief floods my body.

"I thought you were dead! When you died … I-I knew I saw something. He took you!" She points to Drogman— I mean Death. "Our parents said I was crazy. I became an explorer to avenge you. How …? Oh, Marcus!" Her sobs block out any other emotion I'm feeling as I remember my past life.

"How dare you just stand there. I am *DEATH*. I deserve respect!"

Crystal glares daggers at the dark figure and then swiftly looks at me.

"Marcus, I love you so much, but we might not make it through this." Her voice shakes from her cries. "I did this all for you."

Death hovers over us, and the darkness is so intense that I feel all the light draining from my body. This is it. This is what true death feels like.

All of a sudden, a blinding light surrounds Crystal and I until we are completely consumed. When the light fades we are back inside the temple, and a woman is primly standing before us.

"Hello, she says with a voice like warm honey.

"Who are you?" My sister questions her with confidence.

"Oh, pardon me. Let me introduce myself." I flash Crystal a befuddled glance.

"My name," she says with a beaming smile, "is Life, and I have a job for you."

THE PATHS WE CHOOSE

By R. J. Llewellyn

writingwritingandmorewritinginspiteofcomputers.home.blog

They stood in contemplative silence, hidden in the one dark alcove, neither one ready to enter the light. Both fearful in their own way to take the next step.

She leaned her face against his back and enclosed him in her arms, drinking deeply of the memories of tender and of wild times, of laughter, of quiet celebrations of love. She indulged in the protection afforded by his strong, lean body and his steady breathing. He would ever be her warm, trusty castle.

Yet his heart raced at a pace known to the hare running from the dogs. Save they had nowhere to run. They had walked willingly into this place. Their choice had been made and was forged into a vow.

Vows are all well and good when taken in the flush of determination and necessity. But this is almost always only in the far away, when all are heady with belief and made comfortable by the surroundings. Yet even the best vow is prone to corrosions brought on by a journey fraught with the deluge of nature and her unrelenting fervour. Between the early spring weathers, lands cut by swift rivers—deceptive in their irregular depths—through high, stony places, home to keen winds and tumbling rocks, and woodlands thick and defiant, their vow was continually tested.

But nothing tested it so tenaciously as the pursuit of foes. Each small victory never could make up for the loss of good companions, either through accident or battle with Duke Dracansa's relentless cavalry.

Now, supported by shreds of their previous hope, they moved out into the pale steady glow from the ruins. They trod with care, apprehensive of the reality behind the speculations of this sacred place. The ordeals of their combined experience gave sufficient appreciation of the fact that there would be no simple solutions revealed.

So, before the cave wall they stood, each studying in their own way the neat, artistic, flowing words carved into the rock.

Opvern ran his calloused fingers along the grooves. "Whichever of the seven hard routes you took, the trail was but a preparation for the circumstance which now awaits you. To step back rewards you only with the bitterness of defeat and the knowledge of what you should have done. To step forward demands of you the sacrifice of all your love, for the charge which you are to bear requires you have no other in your life. To have come this far, for whatever reason, marks your desperation as one requiring this final act. Enter the Temple Forlorn and accept your Fate.'" He clenched his fist against the wall. "No," he said as if by the effort of his will he could change the pronouncement.

After all they had been through and witnessed Petehvina could only say, "It seems simple enough to me, my love." Her tone wavered though she tried to sound sure and decisive. "Within those ruins lies The Sword of Decision. A weapon none can prevail against." She rested her hand over his balled fist. "All wars require something beyond ordinary resolve in their prosecution. After all the horror Dracansa has brought upon the peninsula, we cannot have doubts now."

Opvern managed a brief sliver of a smile and, taking her gently by her shoulders, brushed her head with the whisper of a kiss. "Oh, my dear Petehvina. Still so simple in belief even after all we have been through." He gestured angrily to the ancient script, the flowing letters interspersed with runes. "I had hoped for some justice only to find this taunts me!" He jabbed a finger at one rune then another.

"See! See! Each of these bears the hidden meaning. This is no simple, pious warning of the sacrifice of comfort or acceptance of hardships beyond those already suffered. These indicate, in callous tones I would add, there must be a blood price paid for the Sword!"

Petehvina studied the account. She had a strong grasp of the script but not the runes, so she took Opvern's explanation at face value. Not surprising, to gain something as portentous as The Sword of Decision would not come without a cost.

When one seeks out a blade which will not be dulled, can cut through any substance, has the ability to guide the wielder's hand with speed and exceptional skill, and whose thunder blue sheen causes dread amongst foes and inspiration amongst one's own ... no ... simply finding and grasping such a sword would not do. No, the originators would expect exceptional resolution in the heart of anyone attempting to wield such power.

Petehvina understood. Her studies of histories, legends, religious and ethical works had all led her to conclude there must come a time in a crisis when one would be obliged to make a firm—even painful—decision to attain victory. This was simply the way of the world. Yes, she had every right not to be comfy much less happy with the situation, but who was she to insist the tides and storms of the world change just to suit her?

Opvern paced and fretted, running his hands through his hair and muttering his exasperation. Petehvina smiled gently, not that he noticed. Giving him a chance to settle, she turned her attention toward the circle of ruined pillars and their beckoning, pale glow, within which the faint outline of a raised altar or table could be made out.

She stepped in the way of Opvern's agitated progress, this time to grasp him about the waist, and rested her head against his chest.

"Your heart thunders," she said, managing to sound light. But she looked away; she did not want him to see her face, for this would only make matters worse. "You do not have to discuss anything. You do not have to say a word, Opvern. Just take my hand and let us walk together, for you know as well as I do what must transpire."

He tried to speak but tears fell, and he shook his head. But still, he took hold of her hands and let her lead him along the cracked stone pathway. A silent couple, he in anguish, she unflinching. Even if this would be her last walk with him, there would be no return for Lady Petehvina.

Just three steps of white stone, fractured and chipped by the visits of time, stood between them and destiny. For Opvern they may as well have been each a mountain. For Petehvina each small rise held another interlude to steel her resolve as she led her love before the dais and the darker altar, devoid of carvings.

Thereupon the surface lay the sword, a rather simple weapon save for its luster, indeed reminiscent of storm clouds. Both hilt and blade seemed inlaid into the altar surface, set into the very stone. The light which betrayed no source suggested a sheen on top of the display. Despite a warning gasp from Opvern, Petehvina reached out and lightly set fingers to the surface only to feel a cold, smooth hardness which stopped her touching either weapon or altar. Now she could understand why blood was to be spilled; it was the ultimate action to prove readiness to the cause, the very warmth of Life flowing to melt the barrier and rouse the sword. She had no need of runes to signify Fate, not when all was so clearly laid out.

"This must be, my love," she said, unbuttoning her jack, and then the topmost buttons of her shirt before arching back her head. "Be swift and be sure. Then pour me out over this waiting landscape. For there is no going back."

Opvern, despite more tears and sounds of dismay, did manage to draw forth his knife, but beyond holding it aloft he could do no more. Petehvina smiled sadly, reached up and gently eased the steel from his grip to take the hilt firmly in her right hand.

"No other course, my beloved Opvern. No other course," she intoned.

Dropping the blade towards her chest, in one smooth and swift dynamic, she twisted her wrist and drove the blade upwards into Opvern's throat. Thence to push the surprised man backward, rotating him so most of the red stream fell over the full length of the surface, which in turn hissed and cracked.

Upon him she lay, forcing his twitching form to stay in place; she hoped the surprise mixed with the fearful damage of the wound would have been enough to stun him into confusion and dull his realization of being slain by his beloved.

A short time ago she had held him tight for comfort while now she could feel his life seeping away. And this would be the only chance she would have to weep and suffer the depths of anguish, for once she walked away from both the ruins of a construct and of their love she would only be able to stride forward, remorseless, with no room for doubts or regrets.

The long-ago folk had fought invading nightmarish creatures to defend lands for Humanity. There had been no place for reasoned conversation or ethical discourse, thus they were forced to make iron choices and weighty decisions. Sacrifices accepted. Single lives given up for hundreds—thousands—to live, and so up the grim ladder to victory. As history had proved time and again, other great threats would arise. In consequence, they had put one weapon aside for times maybe not as deadly as theirs but bad enough for folk to journey hard lands and make harder decisions.

The Duke Dracansa was a pale imitation of the threats this folk had met. Even so, he had plowed a horrid furrow across the land. From local lordling he had risen through lies, duplicitous maneuvers, coercion, and if all else failed, slaying. His reputation cowed many while attracting all manner of brutal and opportunistic folk to his ranks. Once his army was large enough he had torn through the peninsula's patchwork of independent cities and pastoral regions, bringing devastation to the weaker in order to intimidate those who might have been able to fight back. There had been those willing to stand but outnumbered and disorganized. One by one they had been crushed.

Bitter in her weeping, Petehvina clung to Opvern as he shuddered out his last piece of life. No more would they be locked as one, sharing breath, sighing and drinking the movement of one against another. All was done. Dear Lord Opvern was dead and would be a legend. Tough and firm in battle but generous to the defeated, ever willing to let someone have another chance, and never the first to raise a sword. Never one to walk this hard path.

All were characteristics which Dracansa had taken advantage of with treaties broken, false words, and a whole bag of vile tricks. The sheer weight of his army had been beyond anything Opvern had managed to marshal. No matter how many victories in the field, losses could not be replaced, which had led to no more than a ragged band of followers seeking out in desperation a sliver of hope.

And what of Lady Petehvina, his wife? Ever at his side, ever constant, able to wield a reasonable sword, possessed of her own gentle strength. She was dead too. A new woman rising in her place. Petehvina the …?

She would leave the Naming to the imaginations of others. Time to take the stage and play a brutal trickster at his own game.

She drew upon the last anguish and grief to the best effect. She staggered back down the passage with tears cutting clear channels through Opvern's blood where it dried on her face and dragged the sword, for its weight would take some getting used to. The taunting echoes of her sobs bounced off the uncaring stone.

Loyal Thaner, at his anxious watch, stood transfixed by the weeping, stumbling, bloodied figure with one crimson-stained and clenching hand outstretched.

"My lady!"

Petehvina cut him off with a groan as she fell against a cavern wall. "Oh, my poor Opvern! My brave, poor Opvern! The price he paid!"

Thaner steadied her, his questions spilling out in concert with Petehvina's tears. This flood shook her to the core, being one of rage at the long-ago folk for their choice of an impassive path. Soon she rallied—she had to—for time was precious and much was to be done.

"This blade …" She brandished the weapon, noticing even now how much easier it was to wield.

The lies had to come next; she forced them out. "It demanded a price! A blood price!" Opvern rested beyond suffering while her torment was only beginning, the excruciating price exacted. "I …" she began, then shook her head. "But before I could speak further, he had slashed open great wounds on himself. He fell, washing the altar with his life. The sword released from its bonds, and he gave it to me, Thaner! To me! Told me I should bear this Sword of Decision. He said his time was done! Here was his last act!"

Thaner, ever loyal, always ready at their sides, remained mute with eyes wide in disbelief. He waivered, caught between helping his lady out of this horrid place or rushing to his lord. He could not move.

Petehvina dried out of true weeping for her love and fell into playing the part with sword gripped tightly in one hand. She waited a measure; she knew what had to come … what stood to reason.

A scrambling, a loud, frightened voice. "A column of cavalry is riding hard towards us!"

Now stalwart be, she thought. *Put to its bed Nobility. Meet like with like.*

Petehvina stood up, stiffened, and stepped away from Thaner.

"We cannot wait! Our hundred cannot make a stand here against Dracansa's. Not even with the advantage of high ground can we beat off odds of six to one. There is no time for grief, dear Thaner."

And leaving him to follow shaken and bewildered, she rushed out to the last, the most loyal, the most determined of Opvern's folk. The embers of his cause.

She looked upon their expressions of confusion, alarm and disbelief greeting her as she, a bloodied slight figure, raised the sword high.

"Our lord Opvern is dead!" Her voice rang clear and strong. "Shed his own blood to release this sword! Bade me—yes me, his simple wife—to carry on his work! Ask not, dear friends, for me to explain the reasons or the justifications for why he did forge this selfless act. His graciousness and valor transcended our dull senses. He read something in runes beyond my perceptions, thus courageous and selfless as ever, and made his warrior's choice!" She shook the blade in true anger at the circumstance. "Noble unto the end!" she screamed. "Let not his name be erased! Let not our cause die here! We will not stand in this lonely, unknown place in a pointless slaughter and sport for these base creatures! I bid you all now scatter to your own villages and towns. Spread the word of the great sacrifice done this day. Let all know it is by this solemn oath I swear to you!" She paused, lowered the sword, and kissed the blade as the last taste of her dear love, then threw back her head. Her voice ringing out, she cried, "Dracansa's bane begins here this day! All of true heart shall gather yet again, in greater numbers, a'fired with the Legend of Opvern of the Ages!"

She was content there were no rousing cheers; to hear those would have been too much to bear, for she was bending beneath the weight of her duplicity and jarring with stern resolve. The air of grim purpose and determination was a relief, for this would be the way from now on.

The followers gathered to their horses and sent out in small parties, scattering at a pace. Some would be caught, but many would get through to spread the Legend. It was the first part done—the easy part.

Of course, Thaner stayed. He, in his unwavering loyalty, would not leave her alone, bidding her to be swift as they too must ride.

"Aye we must." She placed one hand on his shoulder. "But scatter first. I can ride as swift and as devious as any, loyal Thaner, and we shall meet at the last ford we crossed. Stealthy, of course, lest there be outriders. We shall wait for each other under the moonlight!" This said, she did not wait but was to her horse, there was so little time. "Away!" she cried. "Set a pace! If you ever loved your lord, away!"

She glanced back. Dear, stalwart, ever loyal Thaner rode off into the wooded places, probably even daring some of the duke's men to follow him. She wished him farewell. Then once certain he was out of sight she rode back to the cave's entrance.

There she paused to gather her breath and wits. The new Petehvina coveted the time of a few extra breaths to take her place upon the stage, to become the one who wielded this Sword of Decision. A new vow usurped the old: she would bring downfall to Dracansa and his whole crew.

Here would come the epoch of this Petehvina: the beginning of a saga about a woman who in desperation to save herself purchased, through the murder of her own husband, an ominous and treacherous blade and set herself in an unholy alliance with the merciless Dracansa.

She who would then reveal her true nature, and by her own cunning and deviousness—and, aye, her body—spread dissension and confusion within his ranks. She would set one against another in bloody rivalry, always shifting the blame upon Dracansa until the time would be right for her to heap upon him humiliation before his death.

And so by acclamation, she would become a Leader his villainous host could understand. By which time there would be a growing revitalized and united folk who were nurtured from youth on the accounts of survivors from Opvern's last ride. But more importantly, they would be incensed by the tales of the treachery of his wife Petehvina, which she would ensure were spread as the scattering seeds of retribution.

To which she would respond by ensuring her army was led to disaster, and she captured to face humiliation and vengeance.

If the peninsula was to recover from this dread interlude and thrive, there had to be this dramatic shift of fortunes leading to the complete destruction of all which was Dracansa's. Thenceforth, the people must be ever vigilant against foes from without and within to ensure there could no longer be complacency.

The best of stories. Legend. Betrayal. Treachery. Downfall. Victory. Her reputation, her ultimate fate, and vilification in the histories would be a small price to pay. Dear Opvern could not imagine the strategies and tactics she had in mind.

The long-ago folk would understand and approve. Opvern had read words and runes but had failed to grasp the underlying meaning. Against such as Dracansa only total victory would do.

She supposed the blade would survive, though. After all, there would be other times and circumstances, which, truth be known, were not her concern. No doubt the longago folk had made provisions.

As the column of riders grew closer she stood upright, blade point into the stony ground and hands set upon the pommel. Dried blood smeared her face, hands and hair with stiffened strands whipping in the wind.

There was some unease as the outriders approached the unmoving, stained figure who stared intently through hooded eyes.

"You took your time," she said, "but by good fortune for you, I have done all the hard work. Opvern is dead, his followers scattered." She paused and raised the blade, crafting a triumphant smirk on her face. "And look what I bring to Duke Dracansa's cause."

She watched the expressions of confusion, turning in some to awe and others concern, but more importantly upon some into appreciation.

She had them. By Opvern's Blood, she had them.

DADDY FORGOT WATER

By Barb Taub

https://barbtaub.com/

In this science fiction dystopian future, life on earth has become a daily battle against a silent killer.

"We could hit him on the head with a rock."

The words shimmered, meaningless across waves of pain. Formless shadows hovered beyond Ross' intermittent vision.

"He looks big. Could he be … Daddy?"

"Nah. Daddy has hair on his face but not on his head, remember?"

"I can't remember."

"It's okay."

Ross let the soft voices float away, sliding back into the dark waiting beneath the agony. He preferred the dark.

Marla was there, swinging Peetie and singing "Somewhere Over the Rainbow." But then somehow Peetie— Peetie?—was whispering, "I don't want to. It looks yucky." And another voice replied, "Pretend it's bread.

Really nice soft bread that will fill your tummy. Yum." He heard the sounds of children throwing up.

Ross had no sense of time. Had moments passed? Weeks? Somehow he knew he had to swim up. The pain waves tossed him, trying to swamp him back to the darkness. But they were old enemies, and he'd defeated them before. *Concentrate. Move fingers first. Good. Toes? Feet, hands, arms, legs? Check. Okay, now the eyes.*

Ross slitted open his eyes, blurry and swollen. Across the campfire four little faces stared back. *Water?* He tried to say it, but all that came out was a groan.

The four children looked at each other, and the biggest one sighed. "I'll go. Watch him."

She handed what looked like a baseball bat to a smaller boy, and slipped away from the firelight. Ross closed his eyes again and fought the waves.

"Here."

He managed to open one eye. He lay propped up against his pack, but he'd have to lift his head to drink. *Don't think about it. Sit up and you can have water. You can.* The world heaved and spun in a whirl of flames and pain, but his arms held long enough for him to come up on one elbow. In the flickering light he saw a plastic bottle with a faint Diet Pepsi logo. The water was cool but not cold. He had a flash of memory—crossing the dry grass meadow to reach the green promise of a small hill where wrecked machinery guarded a pond. Then ... nothing.

"Maybe not drink too much?" Her soft voice was so young, just like Peetie's had been. Before Peetie …

Ross leaned to the side, stomach heaving. There wasn't much to come up. Finally, he wiped a sleeve across his mouth and raised the bottle again. *Small sips. Slow.*

That's it. Panting, he slumped back as the darkness welcomed him.

When he could open his eyes again, he saw the largest child had her arms around the others, piled together asleep around the fire. They must have a stash of wood, because flames danced and he could see more pieces of what looked like old dining room chairs waiting just outside the fire's circle.

The oldest girl brought more water, but they didn't seem to have anything to eat. She kept the others back, but they all watched him. *No, that's not right. They're waiting for me to … what?* The children's concentrated intensity stirred a flash of memory—Peetie, focused on the television. He shook his head, welcoming the visionsplintering pain that banished the memory. *They probably don't know what they're waiting for either.*

By the second day, Ross still had a raging headache— they wouldn't tell him what happened to him, but his money was on that baseball bat—but his hunger got him on his feet. He was stunned to find that his slingshot was still in his pack.

Stopping by the pond to splash water over his head and grab some small rocks, he was heading through late afternoon shadows for the meadow beyond when the first shots shattered the stillness. Rocks pinged and splintered as bullets hit boulders behind him. But though he was in plain sight, none of the shots came near him. Crouched behind one of the larger boulders, he waited until long after the random shots stopped and small evening noises resumed in the meadow beyond.

That night as he roasted a pair of rabbits under the avid eyes of the children, he tried to figure them out. He vaguely wondered if he should be ashamed of himself, but he traded the food for information. The tallest girl, Alice, said she was eight. She hesitated for a moment, watching the cooking meat, and added a burst of words in her near whisper. "I dint have a birthday anymore, so maybe I'm staying eight." She pointed to the others. "William and Sara are six."

Ross eyed the skinny children and found he couldn't tell William apart from Sara. All were dressed in what looked like men's t-shirts. There was a pile of them near the back of the group of boulders that formed their little shelter. Earlier that afternoon he'd heard Alice tell the others it was "bath time," and they had all solemnly waded at the edge of the pond, naked, while she swirled their discarded shirts in the water and spread them in the sun. She produced a comb and dragged it through each head of chin-length tangled hair. They grabbed dry shirts from the pile, and lined up for Alice to tie the hems up in a knot to shorten them.

But Alice was still talking and gestured to the fourth child. "When we found the little one, alls he could say was 'bunny,' so we call him that."

Ross hadn't heard even that much from the silent child, who he pegged at around four.

He divided up the meat and handed it around. The children inhaled every scrap, sucked the bones, and licked their fingers. They retreated to the far side of the fire and fell asleep in a pile, each one clutching some part of Alice.

The next day he dragged back a small deer that other predators had brought down—wolves or maybe dogs that had gone feral. They'd been driven off when the shooting started again. This time the target seemed to be a tree standing alone against the edge of the meadow.

Before he would give them the cooked meat, Ross tried to get more from Alice. "How long have you been here?"

She stared at the meat and swallowed. "Since Daddy took Mama away." When Ross made no move toward the food, all four children gave an almost soundless moan. "Daddy said stay here and he'd be watching for us, but Mama got the Sick and he might get sick too." The cooking meat spat and sizzled, and Alice turned to watch it. "Daddy brought food for a long time, but I think he forgot how to do that. He shots stuff with his gun still, but I think he forgot what rocks and water and food is. So mostly we look to see what else might be dead and we eat that." She shrugged. "William and Sara throw up lots but Bunny and me do okay."

After they all ate, Ross wrapped the remaining meat in leaves and put it on his side of the campfire. He thought the children were asleep in their pile, but he heard whispering.

"Are you our daddy now?" Alice's little voice had no emotion.

"No. I'm someone else's daddy." There was silence from the kid pileup. "His name was Peetie, but he got the Sick along with his mama." *And everyone else,* he thought bleakly. He didn't know how far he'd walked, always heading south, to get to this warm valley, but the few who were left in an empty world were afraid of everyone else, afraid they brought the Sick.

The next day the kids were stripping off their t-shirts for bath time when the shooting started. Water flew up as bullets slapped into the pond. Sara jolted forward, red blossoming across her little back. Ross was already racing to the pond, screaming at the frozen children to run. He snatched up Sara and Bunny, herding William and Alice ahead of him toward their shelter. They'd almost made it when the bullet hit his leg.

As he laid the tiny girl down, she shuddered once and was still.

"DADDY!" Alice, still naked, ran to the edge of the shelter. "You *forgot,* Daddy." Her scream echoed against the surrounding rock face. "You forgot what Sara is."

From the rocks above, there was an answering scream, followed by a single shot. Ross grabbed Alice and pulled her inside, but he was pretty sure she'd already seen the body plunging off the rocks.

Ross tied the tourniquet around his leg, but the pain was a tsunami, pulling him under. Occasionally he'd see the three children watching him. *No ... not watching. Waiting.* He drifted in and out, at one point waking up long enough to somehow dig a shallow little grave for Sara. But then the fever took him and he heard Peetie giggling and Marla singing, "Somewhere Over the

Rainbow." He opened his eyes once and told Alice, "I'm so sorry. But sometimes daddies need to forget."

He was already running through the dark to catch up to Peetie and Marla when he heard the little voices whispering above him. "Pretend it's bread. Really nice soft bread that will fill your tummy. Yum."

But he never heard the children throwing up.

RESTORE

By Angie Thompson

https://www.quietwaterspress.com

Abandoned and alone--or are they?

After Marick's ship is wrecked on a barren planet, companionship is the least of his worries. But when he rescues a strange girl from a watery death, their lives will change in ways neither could have predicted. As unseen dangers threaten, the two must band together for survival, and in the process, uncover the secrets hidden in the forbidden world--and each other.

A gust of wind whistled between the cliffs, and Marick shivered. The girl's tight-fitting suit seemed to repel the murky salt water much better than his own clothes, which felt as though they had spent a week in the frigid Martian desert back home. At least that was one good thing about this rock—the temperatures were bearable without a thermal unit. Or they had been until he'd dived into the vast salt lake after the strange Venusian ship.

"You should never have saved me."

The soft, expressionless, almost robotic voice brought Marick to a stop in front of the low tunnel, and he turned to look back. Only the edge of the orbital star was visible above the cliffs, and he could barely trace the girl's slender outline in the image from his visor. He lifted a hand to his temple and adjusted the dial to the nocturnal setting.

The shades of gray shifted into blurry focus again, and she stood with her head bowed, her light hair falling in dripping curtains over her face. It reminded Marick of the way he had stood as a child when caught with a stolen sugarnut in his pocket. Why hadn't she wanted him to save her? Was she angry? Afraid? Ashamed? Her voice gave him no clue.

"Why not?"

"I will be no help to you." She didn't raise her eyes to his. "I am worth nothing."

The same strange monotone. Was the girl incapable of feeling or just masterful at hiding it? Marick clenched his jaw to keep his teeth from rattling and felt a sharp twinge in his leg. His wound needed more careful tending than the thick strips of water-grass he had wrapped around it. Although if he didn't replenish his body warmth soon, the wound wouldn't matter.

"Come inside."

Marick ducked into the low opening, wondering what he would do if the girl didn't follow, and then asked himself why it should matter. He had been alone except for teachers and overseers since his fifth planetary year, or his tenth by standard measure. He'd learned long ago how to dull the strange ache in his chest that always accompanied the memory of his childhood classmates. Certainly, the solitary training and private laboratory had been a privilege, and he never longed for the close quarters of the laboring sectors. So why did the sound of boots on stone behind him give him such relief?

The narrow passage turned a corner and opened into a large chamber, empty except for the few supplies he'd managed to save from his own ship. Marick lifted the lid of the unopened case and dug through it until he recognized the large white cross of the medical kit. Beneath it was a second emergency blanket, and Marick held it out toward the girl, who stood at the entrance to the cavern and didn't reach to take it.

"Are you all right?" He unfolded the blanket and draped it over her shoulders, and then wrapped himself tightly in his own.

"Can you see in this?" Her head moved uncertainly, as though searching for light.

Of course. Venus must have been spared the strange plague that had left the fifth generation of Mars colonists and all their descendants with no natural eyesight. Maybe the visor wasn't the curse he'd always considered it.

"Keep the wall at your back and slide to the floor." Marick watched as she followed his instructions before turning his attention to the smaller case. His fingers traced the deep gash in its side, and his mind flashed back to the desperate dive, the blinding explosion, the shower of jagged rock and metal. They hadn't expected him to find the flaw in the code—at least, not so quickly. He should have been in the ship—should have been left a charred pile of ashes on the rocks. He shook his head to clear the image and focused on the case again. Taking two tablets from a pouch, he pressed one into the girl's hand.

"What is this?"

Still the same vacant tone. Was she curious? Fearful? Suspicious? Though her voice told him nothing, her softly outlined face swam with motion. The thin lines on her forehead bent downward, her mouth formed a tight circle, and she turned her large eyes in his direction. It suddenly struck Marick that her face told a story, if he could only read it, and he wondered if she would find his face as cold and unreadable as he found her voice.

She brushed the tablet hesitantly with a fingertip, and Marick pulled his attention back to the question.

"Nutrition tablet. Standard IEA kit. It won't hurt you."

The faint lines in her face smoothed, and the corners of her lips seemed to twitch upward. Marick placed his own tablet under his tongue and silently thanked the longdefunct Interplanetary Emergency Association for regulating the reserve supplies required on all spacecraft. Tasteless as the standardized rations were, he wasn't sure what effect a hearty Martian meal powder would have had on the slender Venusian girl.

As the last of the tablet dissolved, Marick reached for the small black box with the stark white cross and pulled it nearer, running his fingers over the textured bottles until he found a cleansing solution. He had hoped for something stronger, but this would have to do. Stretching his leg in front of him, he carefully unwrapped the long, thick leaves. The girl gasped, and

Marick turned toward her, glad to take his gaze off the jagged cut.

"Can you see it?"

"My eyes must be adjusting." She lifted her eyes toward a deep crack in the ceiling, then leaned closer to study his leg. "How did it happen?"

She must not have noticed it on the sand. Of course, she had been stunned and dazed; he didn't blame her.

"I cut it on a sharp rock."

"In this cave?" Her eyes swept the floor.

"No. In the salt lake."

Her head jerked up, and her face changed in an instant. "While coming after me?" There was the slightest hint of a tremor in her voice.

"Yes."

The large eyes suddenly blurred and swam, and the girl's next words were haunting in their softness.

"I am worth nothing. You should never have saved me."

"Why do you say that?" Marick clenched his teeth together as he poured the cleansing solution over his cut. The sting was not as painful as he had feared, and he let out a sigh of relief.

"I was not worthy to live."

Somehow, the quiet, impassive words stirred him more than the deepest cry of pain.

"Why?" He turned on her almost savagely, and her head drooped lower.

"I fell asleep at the controls. I drifted from the authorized lanes. My conduct has been unsatisfactory too many times. I was not worth further disciplinary action." She sounded as though she were passing judgment on a complete stranger.

"They fired on you."

"It should have killed me, only I woke and tried to correct my course. The blast hit the thruster regulators." Her shoulders lifted in a helpless gesture that needed no explanation. "The ship spun out of control. I landed here."

"Villains." Marick ground the word out through his teeth, and the girl looked up, her eyes round and staring.

"I was not—"

"Stop." The word came out too harsh, and the girl flinched. Marick sighed and softened his tone. "I know— what your people thought of you … whatever you did— you did not deserve that."

His shivering worsened with each passing second. Hands shaking, Marick wrapped a length of gauze around his leg and retreated into the folds of the blanket.

"I was also betrayed. Sabotaged. Sentenced to death— either by fire or on this barren rock of a planet." His throat was dry, and he reached for the canteen, then handed it to the girl. Her face pulled into a shape he recognized, and he surprised himself with a chuckle. "Water. And they were wrong. Your people and mine. I think—I think that's why I came after you."

A hint of warmth seemed to be returning to his body, and his head was suddenly as heavy as a pair of weighted exploration boots. Marick stretched himself on the ground and pulled the blanket closer around his shoulders.

He lifted a hand to his temple, but a soft voice interrupted him.

"Before you sleep—" The girl paused and seemed to hesitate. "What is your name?"

"Marick." His chest warmed. There had been nothing in her tone to show it, but the question seemed to speak trust. "And yours?"

Silence stretched for a long moment, but as Marick pressed the dial and the world fell to black, a whispered word made its way through the dark. "Amaea."

***

The flames of the burning ship engulfed him, roaring in his head, clawing at his leg. They had betrayed him. They had killed him. He was dying—dying of heat, of thirst, of pain.

"Marick." A voice filtered through the stifling fog. The girl. She was alive. They hadn't killed her. He tried to call her, to urge her to run, but his dry throat shriveled the words into a rasping cough. Someone lifted his head, and a stream of water flooded his mouth.

The dream image vanished, leaving only darkness, warmth, and pain. Marick lifted a shaking hand to his visor and felt for the dial. The girl's face wavered into cloudy focus above him—her eyes pinched and narrow, the lines above them deep and slanted, her mouth pressed into a thin line that lowered at the corners. She laid a hand on his head, and the touch chilled him to the bone. He pulled away, moaning in protest.

"Marick, lie still. You're hurt. You're too hot. I'm trying to help you."

Too hot? How was that possible when he was shaking from head to toe? But in the next instant, another burning wave rolled over him, leaving him gasping for a breath of cool air. Some kind of sickness—his wound—the fire in his leg. Something cold and wet was laid on his forehead, and this time he welcomed it. The rough, stony ceiling of the cavern swam and tilted above him, and he gasped at the sickening sensation.

"Marick, what is it?"

How could that impassive voice be so soothing? Marick forced a deep breath and tried to answer.

"My visor—the signals—won't process—"

"Turn it off." The girl's hand gently stroked the damp hair back from his forehead. "It won't help you. You should rest."

Rest. He craved it more than anything. But darkness—even the thought made panic rise in his chest. It was the reason he had worked himself to exhaustion every night, the dread that had fueled his uncompromising service to the council, the fear that had consumed him since his third-year teacher had punished some infraction by removing his visor for a day. To sit helpless and alone in darkness and silence—but the thought suddenly stilled him.

He wasn't alone. Not now. If the girl—what had she said her name was? Mara? May? The images blurred and rocked more violently, spinning his head and churning his stomach.

"Maira?"

He thought the corners of her lips twitched up as she bent nearer.

"Amaea."

"You'll stay?"

"Yes." Her hand touched his, and he drew a deep breath.

"The dial—on the left. Press it—hard."

He felt her cool hand against his temple and the wavering image dropped to black. ***

Marick awoke at last to a clear head and a pleasant coolness. Had it been hours he had lain there? Days? Weeks? The memories seemed to swirl together in a jumbled mass of heat, pain, and darkness. And through it all ran the thread of a quiet, expressionless voice speaking words he could not remember.

He lifted a hand to the dial on his visor and raised himself on his elbow, surprised to find that his body trembled at the effort.

"Marick." The girl's face took shape in front of him as she drew his shoulders to the wall and helped him lean against it. "Take it slowly. You're very weak."

"How—" His throat no longer burned, but it was dry, and the word ended in a cough.

The girl held the canteen to his lips, and he wondered how many times she had done it while he lay helpless. He raised his hands to take it, but they shook violently and would have dropped it if she had not kept her hold. Tepid water spilled over his lips and down the front of his shirt. He lifted a hand to wipe it away and found that the stubble on his chin had grown into a full beard—several days' growth at least.

The girl ignored his clumsy efforts and finally managed to get the water inside his mouth. Marick swallowed gratefully and drew a deep breath.

"How long?"

"Standard measure? It's nearing the end of the fifth day. And this planet's measure seems nearly the same." She turned to one of the open cases, then slipped a nutrition tablet between his lips. Marick watched her as it dissolved beneath his tongue. What would he have done if she hadn't stayed near him? Five days without food, without water—he could never have lived through it.

What was her name again? She'd told him twice, but his brain had been so clouded. Araya? Amara? No, it was softer. Gentler.

"Aramae?" he tried at last, and the corners of her lips turned up.

"Amaea."

That was it. So different. Flowing. Like a song. Now he was thinking like a poet. What had this sickness done to his mind? The image of her face blurred slightly, and he leaned back against the wall again.

"I owe you my life."

Her eyes dropped, then slowly lifted. "As I owe you mine. But it was the creature who helped most."

"Creature?" Marick leaned forward, but the image slipped and rocked, and a wave of dizziness swept over him.

"Marick." Her arm slid under his elbow, supporting him even as she drew him to the ground. "You should rest again. You've talked too long."

"No, I—" Marick fought the whirling of his head, trying to collect his thoughts. Something was wrong. Was the sickness returning? Could he be only tired? His visor had never—

He lifted a hand, but as he reached for the dial, the image went dark. Before he even had time to gasp, the light returned, wavering, flickering, and dimmer than ever. An icy fear shot through his chest.

"No." He ground out the word through clenched teeth. Amaea pressed a hand to his temple, and the image melted to black. Marick pounded his fist on the ground. "No! Leave me. Go!"

"What is it?" The same calm, emotionless voice. For a brief second, he wondered what her face would show if he could read it. Now he would never learn.

"Leave me. I'm no good to you. You should have let me die." As hard as he tried to stop it, his voice trembled at the thought of the dark chasm stretching ahead of him. A hand touched his arm, and he felt himself shaking. "I'm blind. Completely blind. I've been ten days without a charging signal, and my visor is failing. I can't help you.

Take the supplies and go."

"Leave you without supplies? How will you live?"

"Amaea, I'm useless. Worthless. I can give you nothing. Now go."

There was silence for a long moment, then Amaea's voice, very low. "You lied, then?"

"What?" Marick pushed himself up on his elbows, regardless of his spinning head, but Amaea pressed him back again.

"You said that I was not worthless—that my people were wrong. But now that you are weak, you say I should condemn you to die."

The words pierced him like a knife. This was different. Couldn't she see that? Of course she was not worthless; she had proved it in caring for him. But what help could he be to anyone now?

"I'm blind, Amaea." His voice caught on the words.

A cool hand brushed the hair from his forehead, gently tracing the edge of his visor.

"Sleep, Marick. And when you wake, I will be your eyes."

"Why won't you leave me?"

The long sleep had refreshed Marick more than he thought possible, and he had woken clear-headed, ravenously hungry, and filled with a lingering, unshakable dread. He swallowed the last of a frustratingly bland nutrition tablet and turned in the direction where he had last heard Amaea's voice.

"Drink." She placed the canteen in his hands, and he obeyed. Something rattled and thumped to the floor, and Marick cocked his head.

"What are you doing?"

"Examining your supplies."

"Examining them or destroying them?"

Something slapped his arm lightly as she took the canteen away.

"How long will this last?" Her voice moved away from him slightly, and something scraped against the floor.

"The water? As long as the atmosphere doesn't change. On Mars, one person could live on it with careful rationing. Here, the supply seems almost endless."

"Your flask creates water from the air?"

"Harvests the existing water vapor. I suppose, for a barren, worthless rock, we could have fared worse."

"Why do you call it that?"

Was she objecting or only curious?

Marick grunted. "It's the way the history books describe it."

"You don't mean—the Wasteland?"

"If that's the Venusian name for the planet the galactic ancestors abandoned at the time of the Expansion, then yes. Where did you think we were?"

"I hadn't stopped to think. I've been a bit busy since I landed here."

Had she just made a joke? Her words held humor, if her tone was flat, and Marick chuckled.

"And what do you think now that you know?"

"I'm—surprised."

"Why?"

"Perhaps things are easier on your planet." He could hear her rummaging through the supplies as she continued. "But on mine, we would not have lasted a minute outside the shields. Not without refrigeration tanks and breathing masks and the heaviest anti-corrosive suits."

"When I was forced down here, I expected to die the minute the shell cracked, but after I realized I could breathe, I didn't think much about it. And no, on Mars, no one can leave the domes without a thermal unit and a ventilator." Marick attempted to rub his chin, but his fingers caught in the scruffy beard. He sighed. "Why couldn't I have salvaged just one shaving blade?"

"I like it. It makes you look—strong."

Was it his imagination, or had her hand brushed close to his cheek? Marick started at the warmth that flooded his chest as her voice continued.

"And this planet may be abandoned, but it cannot be completely barren."

"What makes you say that?" Marick jolted upright.

"There is life here."

"What kind?"

"More than one."

How had he found that soft monotone comforting? At the moment, it was maddening. "Tell me."

"Let me see your leg."

"Amaea!"

"Let me see your leg, and I will tell you."

How could he argue with a machine? Marick groaned and stretched out his leg in the direction of her voice.

"I thought you would die." The words were so quiet he almost missed them. "Your wound was like fire. The water and the salve from the medical box did nothing. Then on the evening of the fourth day, I heard a noise in the passage—it goes on beyond this cave—and found a small creature caught in a hole. It had crushed leaves tied around its leg, and when I lifted them, I saw a small wound. When I took it to the cliffs to free it, I found the same leaves lying near the entrance, held down by a rock. I crushed them and applied them to your wound, and you know the rest."

Marick's heart pounded against his chest as though trying to force its way through his ribs. He had explored for miles along the barren face of the cliffs without spotting any sign of life beyond the thick water-grass.

"Amaea. This—creature. What was it like?"

She placed her hands over his and drew them to about a foot's length apart.

"No bigger than this. It was covered in thick hair, very short and much softer than yours. It shook all over, and its nose moved in every direction."

"Its ears?"

"Very long. On the top of its head, only they were flattened back."

The description was familiar—too familiar. There were animals of that kind in laboratories all over Mars, and none of them had the capacity—

"Its hands, Amaea."

"Hands?"

"Could it have—have held something in them—in one of them? Or were they more like—like feet? Paws?"

"Yes."

Was she purposely driving him to distraction? "Yes to which?"

She seemed to hesitate.

"I don't think it could hold things. Not the way—"

Not the way you or I can."

"Yes." Her voice still showed no trace of alarm.

Marick pushed himself to his feet, and Amaea caught his arm.

"What are you doing?"

"This isn't right. You said the leaves were tied? Like you've tied this?" He gestured to the unseen bandage. "Yes."

"Not caught. Not twisted. But tied. Neatly. Deliberately."

"I—I think so."

Marick took a step forward, and the girl blocked his way.

"Where are you going?"

He opened his mouth to answer, and then sank back to the floor with a groan, burying his head in his hands.

"Marick?"

"I told you to leave me. Why won't you leave me?"

"Are you afraid?" Her hand touched his shoulder. "The creature was not vicious."

"Of course it wasn't." Was she incredibly dense, or was his conclusion more difficult than he imagined? "Amaea, every intelligent being fled this planet centuries ago. You know that."

"Yes."

"But something tied the leaves on your creature's leg. Something with hands that can grip and hold. Something capable of finding and applying a remedy— beyond the instinct to ease its own suffering. Something— someone—that knows where we are and what we're doing."

"You think … it was sent here on purpose?" Marick swallowed hard.

"I do."

"Then you think … there is life here? Intelligent life?"

"There shouldn't be. But I can't think of another explanation. We need—you need—to leave here. Now."

"To go where? And do what?" The blunt question halted his churning thoughts, and Marick fumbled for an answer.

"To—find a safer place."

"Such as the open ground which is covered by water at night? My ship sunk in the salt lake? Or yours—the charred ruin on the rocks?"

Was she mocking him? Marick longed to reach out and shake her, but his hand touched empty air.

"Marick." She gently tipped his chin up. "Whoever they are, they have not harmed us. They have even helped us. Why should we fear them?"

Marick wrestled with the question for a moment before answering.

"They should not be here."

"Neither should we. But I think you are right. We should find out what is beyond these cliffs."

"You should find out." Marick leaned against the wall again, trembling with the strain and the fading tension. "You won't gain anything from the help of a blind man." If you do not leave here, I will not, and we will never know. Rest today and tomorrow we will try. But eat something now. You need to regain your strength."

"Is it truly eating when the food tastes like sand?" He took the tablet she offered and slid it under his tongue with a sigh.

"Is complaining a favorite Martian pastime?" His laugh slipped out before he realized it.

"Are all Venusians this insufferable?"

He was rewarded with a slap on his arm that nearly made him choke, and he leaned forward, coughing and gasping.

"Marick?" Amaea's voice sounded pained.

Marick was finally able to draw a breath and swallow the last of the tablet.

"Never mind—not insufferable—just murderers," he managed between gasps.

"Are you all right?" Amaea laid a hand on his shoulder.

He playfully turned his head away, and it struck hard against the invisible rock wall. Marick buried his face in his knees with a cry of pain.

"Marick. Let me see." Amaea gently forced his hands away from his head. She lifted his visor, and he groaned and raised a hand to stop her. "Please. Just let me look. It does you no good now."

She was right. Why was she always right? Reluctantly, Marick loosened his grasp. Amaea pulled the visor away from his tightly closed eyes and sighed in relief.

"Only a small mark. This took most of the blow. Are you all right?"

"Beginning to regret that I wasn't killed on impact."

A soft sound came from Amaea's direction, as though she wanted to laugh but wasn't sure how.

"If I am a murderer, I am not a very good one."

"Keep practicing. You'll accomplish it one of these days." Marick squeezed his eyes more tightly shut and winced.

"Do they hurt?" Amaea's touch was gentle and cool against the hot, aching skin.

"The atmosphere, probably. They haven't been exposed to it for years."

Without a word, she drew his shoulders to the ground, and a moment later, something wet and cool was laid across his eyes. Drowsiness mingled with a strange contentment, and Marick drifted into sleep.

When he woke again, he lay still, staring into the dark void and listening to the small sounds in the vast cavern as Amaea worked. Packing the supplies back into the cases, he suspected. Maybe he could manage to carry one of them for her. How did she intend to guide him through the maze of unknown passageways beyond the cavern? He should refuse to let her. But how could he do that when she was at least as stubborn as he was?

Marick sighed and turned his head, listening as Amaea moved back and forth like a shadow against the wall. A thin sliver of light from a deep crack in the ceiling landed on the long, light hair that fell over her face as she bent over the cases. She shook it back with an impatient gesture, revealing her lightly furrowed forehead and her mouth bent up at one corner. The sight nearly brought forth a chuckle, but it was stifled by a gasp.

"Marick?" Amaea glanced back over her shoulder.

Her shoulder. Her face. Her eyes. Had she repaired…? He lifted a hand to his temple. The visor was gone. It couldn't be possible.

"Marick?" She left the cases and knelt next to him, her eyes searching his face. "What is it?"

"I can see you." The words caught in his throat, and his eyes burned with moisture.

Her eyes rounded, and she lifted a hand, slowly moving it above his head. He caught it, held it, kissed it.

"Amaea, I can see!" It wasn't completely true; the hot liquid in his eyes blurred his vision for a moment, but when he wiped it away, the image remained.

"Oh, Marick." Her voice was still quiet, impassive, unreadable, but he needed no training to understand the glow on her face.

He turned his own face to the wall and let the water flow from his eyes and with it, the fear and pain of a lifetime. Amaea rubbed a hand against his shaking shoulders and gently stroked his hair.

After a few moments, the storm of emotion passed, and Marick would have started their journey immediately, but Amaea insisted he rest a while longer while she carefully folded the blankets, finished packing the supplies, and tended his leg again. At last, she consented, and they began carefully making their way along the passage that led into the deeper recesses beyond the cavern.

The walk down the unfamiliar tunnel was more tiring than Marick had anticipated, and they stopped often to rest his leg or to allow his eyes to adjust to the light that increased as the passage neared its end. When they finally stepped beyond the walls of the tunnel, Marick caught his breath in wonder.

A flock of small, winged animals with coverings of more brilliant colors than he had ever imagined hopped about on a sloping stone terrace covered in green. He stepped closer, and they rose into the air with musical shrieks that seemed to echo in his heart. As they danced above him in an ecstasy of color and sound, he glanced back at Amaea—and froze.

The girl who had been his rock, his shield, cowered in a heap on the ground, her hands pressed against her ears, her whole body trembling. Marick knelt next to her and carefully lifted her chin.

"What is it, Amaea?"

No answer. She likely couldn't hear him. He reached for her hand and gently tugged it loose. She stiffened, and he saw for the first time the tiny silver cylinder hidden in her ear. The surrounding noise quieted, and Amaea relaxed. Marick gestured to her ear, wrinkling his forehead in the same way he had seen her do. Her answer was soft, but her voice trembled.

"It is the only way I can hear you."

Marick's gaze lifted to the clear sky, then dropped again to take in the lush vegetation, the chorus of small winged creatures, and, beyond them, something he hadn't noticed before. Turning back to Amaea, he gently cupped his hand around her ear.

"Let me take it."

Her eyes rounded, and she shook her head back and forth. Marick felt her fear.

"Look around you, Amaea. The end to a lie we've believed for centuries. A planet made for life. My blindness, the blindness of generations, gone. This can't be an accident. Let me take it."

Her eyes blinked hard, but she slowly bowed her head.

Marick carefully drew the cylinder from each ear and waited breathlessly.

"Amaea?"

She didn't move.

"Amaea?"

Her eyes lifted to his, round, wet, and shining.

"Has the word 'silence' been removed from all Martian dictionaries or only yours?"

Her voice was hesitant, timid, uncertain, as if she was hearing it for the first time. Marick cast another look over his shoulder to where an imposing white structure, untarnished by the dust of time, towered above the green, stony path. The open door was free of brush and vines, and in its shadow a bit of cloth, like the edge of a garment, fluttered in the breeze. With a deep breath, Marick reached for Amaea's hand.

"Someday, I'll tell you how I feel about Venusians. But come with me now. I think we're expected."

THE KNIGHT ERRANT

(AN ANACHRONISTIC TALE)

By Sha'Tara

https://www.shatara46.wordpress.com

Dubbed an anachronistic tale, "The Knight Errant" begins in those wonderful mystical, pseudo-historical days of the lone wandering knights always on some quest to perform noble deeds. Hm, yes, well, be that as it may, this mysterious knight is on a quest that must cross time ... to our time, circa 1970. But even knights have perplexing dilemmas.

Ahead lie the beautiful plains of the march. Streams flow from the hills and a sluggish river meanders through, where deep green grasses undulate in the wind like the waves of the sea stirred by a steady gentle breeze. Behind, purple mountains etched sharply against their indigo backdrop seem to coax the weary traveler to return to the safety of their majesty. In the cloudless sky, the sun relentlessly describes his systematic arc over the plains, and as if exhausted by his earlier effort to reach so high, increases his tired pace towards the western end of this green ocean marked by a low pall of blue-brown haze ...   Out of a black cleft formed beneath two towering peaks emerges a tired knight on a plodding steed. His lance is laid carelessly against the saddle on the inside of his knee; its lackadaisical aim pointing at the ground some eight yards distant from his horse. His helmet hangs and sways on the pommel of the tarnished saddle. Without breaking his even pace, the horse periodically stretches his nose to pull at the grass beside the trail, munching contentedly with every successful reach of his great neck.

Eyes half closed, the knight peers over the shimmering distant plain, slowly shifting his head to the right, and then to the left. He looks up at the slanting sun before settling his gaze on the trail ahead of him.

Having satisfied himself that everything is as it should be, our knight prompts his steed to a faster walk and continues due west. The lumbered pounding of the mighty war horse echoes through the foothills, sometimes frightening small nondescript birds from their late afternoon torpor, setting up a short-lived series of peeps and calls reminiscent of the dewy morning.

The knight daydreams in the sultry oppressive heat, the pollen-laden air, the insect-filled vibration of the green shrubbery protecting the rounded hills. Every so often he raises his arm listlessly to ward off an arching branch drooping over the trail in front of him. As the tree line recedes behind him and the vista opens up he begins to discern the playful movements caused by the wind further in the valley. He longs for the ride in the evening breeze across the plains in the blaze of glory from the setting sun and for the cool crossing of the ford…soon now…soon…. He sighs and wipes the sweat from his eyes.

Suddenly, the great horse lifts his head and gives a loud snort—quickly answered from somewhere nearby. The knight's sluggish faculties refuse to consider the possibility of danger, yet he looks this way and that, straining his ears to pick up any sound which might indicate what could be lurking in some nearby glade.

The answer to his search is not long in coming. From a willow thicket comes a crashing and a clattering of hooves. An imposing knight, in gleaming white armor, astride a white steed and fully dressed for combat, lance at the ready, emerges with the inevitable challenge.

"Ah, this is better," mutters our dusty and sweaty knight. "At least now I know what I face … I think!" To the newcomer he cries, "What is the reason for this challenge?"

"I do not need to give a reason!" returns the challenger. "Prepare yourself to die!" The voice is deep and rumbling, meant to intimidate.

"I have been prepared to die more times than I care to remember," mumbles the tired knight. "I am prepared!" he says, returning the challenge. With a casual gesture he replaces the heavy helmet over his head. Unhurried, he raises and adjusts the lance, and then, his eager steed already at full charging pace, he meets the challenger.

The first encounter is short. Our knight shatters his well-used shaft while unseating his opponent and sending him clattering and clanking to the ground in a cloud of choking dust. While his horse performs a difficult u-turn around a clump of blackberry bushes, he pulls out his cumbersome two-handed, double-edged sword and charges the dismounted challenger now standing and waiting with his own sword and shield at the ready.

Somewhat awakened from the lethargic idleness of this long day's ride, his mind begins to function independently of his trained reaction and his emotions. He considers the fact that he is about to run down an opponent with a heavy war-horse whose killer instinct is also awakened, and he shakes his head (no small feat considering the weight of the helmet), pondering the situation.

Letting virtue triumph over common sense, with the deep awareness of duty imprinted in his mind by his protector and mentor, the sorceress Lucida (the same one who had sent him on his current quest), our knight chivalrously dismounts some ten yards from his unknown assailant.

"Sir knight, why do you insist on continuing this combat? My mission is elsewhere and urgent, and I have no wish to do you harm. Will you not let me pass?"

At this, the other's exposed face flushes red as blood rushes to his head, and giving a wild yell, he charges the traveler. His speed is hindered only by his heavy armor.

"Coward!" he cries as he throws himself at the other, attempting to topple him with the sheer weight of steel and man. "You dare violate this valley where no knight has ever passed unscathed and ask leave to go? You shall die here, as have all who have come before you. This place is sacred, and you have defiled it by your vile presence!"

Our knight, still uncertain about the reasoning behind this ludicrous challenge, is no longer uncertain as to his fate. This is no midday dream brought on by the faeries of the glens. He is facing what appears to be a madman, and the madman is real enough! All proper codes of conduct of chivalry considered, he turns his entire attention to defense and, as the situation leaves no other choice, to full offense.

Fortunately —or unfortunately— for the combatants, the sun still reigns the skies, and soon the two resemble steel kettles swaying slowly over a hot fire, steam escaping from the fissures of their respective armor. The blows ring less sharply and frequently. Eventually, experience and endurance developed from years of living the demanding and austere life of the knight errant proves more than a match for the skills of the challenger. He is brought down in a heap of dented steel, tinted here and there with crimson.

Some lucky armor maker would soon have himself a week-long job from this encounter! ("Your pain, my gain, sir!" he will say jokingly, keeping well out of reach of the blow which the angry gauntleted knight will aim at his head.)

Using the tip of his sword (professional knights always do it that way, you know), our knight undoes his opponent's helmet and sends it rolling down the trail in little puffs of dust. He places the sword at the defeated knight's throat.

"Yield ye, sir knight, or never shall ye defend this ground from intruders!"

"I do not know how to yield me. This is the first time I have been defeated. Would you tell me your name, bold sir, before I die at your hand?"

"My name is mine, as yours is yours. What do names matter? Give me the right of passage in your land, and you shall live and keep your name."

"Since I am at your mercy, and that is your will, the answer is yes. I have done my duty, as I know it, and you have done yours. May you find whatever it is you are looking for with such zeal, bold knight!"

With these words, the two antagonists part company. The challenger slowly rises to his feet and begins to remove his armor in order to attend to his many cuts and bruises. Our knight, equally slowly, staggers to a nearby stump, stands on it and calling his steed, mounts and faces west once again. Already his mind is back on his quest and the palpable dangers that he knows lie ahead.

In the fading light, Sir Nonchalant (I'm sure you have guessed his name by now, so I may as well write it down, for the record, and in case there's a sequel and we need to find him again) broods over his coming predicament. His next task has all the certainly to be the most difficult one of his career as a knight errant, and try as he might, he can think of no solution to what lies ahead.

He must meet with Morgrealin the witch and bring back a message from her to the king. If he fails, Lucida would die as she had been (falsely of course, and I might add, out of sheer jealousy and vindictiveness) implicated in a plot to substitute the king's favorite hawk for a pigeon …. (Well, that's another story … for another rainy day.)

Sir Nonchalant knows that the tower where Morgrealin works (she is now a famous independent advisor and counselor with her own office—and TWO secretaries!) is right downtown, in the very center of the banking area of the city. Her office is, predictably, room 1313 on the thirteenth floor.

He could ride up to the tower, that wasn't the problem, but he possesses no coins (his world didn't have such fancy means of trading) for the parking meters outside the building, and he would never be able to fit his steed inside the elevator. Knight errants were no longer welcome in the city.

The people have pompously entered what they call 'an age of progress' and they despise the 'silly' old ways. All war horses left outside the main entrance to any business and not properly and legally parked are immediately towed away by order of the mayor who is a firm believer in progress.

Sir Nonchalant has never been separated from his horse since it was bequeathed to him by his father on his dying bed. (I must point out here that it was the father who was dying, not the bed.) He could not just abandon him (the horse, not his father) outside the limits of the city to fend for himself. Certain he would then be of having the great horse stolen, along with his armor, his identity, the means to return to his own age and to Lucida!

As the sun fades over the horizon, he shifts uncomfortably in his saddle. What might he do? Dragons he had slain. Damsels in distress he had saved. Savage beasts he had beaten back. Witches and magicians he had fooled and foiled. Knights he had defeated in single combat. Armies he had confronted and fought against, but ...

Parking Meters?

What chance has chivalry against technology?

THE GOD STRAIN

By Gary Jefferies

https://www.fictionisfood.com

Smithy duplicity from his parents, adding his own signature just for good measure. On the one hand, he worked in a state-of-the-art research facility combating rare viral diseases and on the other he was where he was now. Messed up. The equivalent of Frankenstein's monster. The real deal Jekyll or Hyde. Take your pick while the world watches on. Buy your front row ticket now while you still can. Shops will be closing and not reopening any time soon.

The lab was high security, need-to-know and dealing with virulent flu strains that seemed intent on defeating anything Smithy's team threw at them. One in particular was almost showing signs of sentience, mutating before the vaccine even went live. Like it knew the coding sequence necessary to turn things 'round and undo months of work. Smithy had dwelt long on this one. He called it God Flu: a self-adapting sub-strain of a SARS-like flu bug, except it dealt in death—not just sometimes, every damn time.

They'd picked it up a month previous, after the strain somehow piggybacked on another plaque. Within days God Flu had wiped out the surrounding competition and sat staring back through the isolation booth. A red agar eye studying them studying it. Smithy now considered that was when things should have been incinerated.

Animal testing delivered consistently poor prognoses. Forty-eight-hour incubation, and then system wide collapse. Game over within three days, no variation. The end-of-day's contagion where judgement is passed.

Time and again he shook his head on this one, pushing up his spectacles and rubbing tired eyes. If it ever got out, the damn thing was indiscriminate. That it would infect humans he had no doubt, and the result of that he refused to think about. Sanity was fragile and too much ruminating over morals of his employ would lead to a breakdown.

Aside from God Flu aside, all was well in his world. That was until he began reading King's *The Stand* a week ago. A revelation of conscience began to eat into what remained of a mind that ... well maybe Oppenheimer felt the same when the nuclear bomb went off. *"I am become death, the destroyer of worlds."*

But for a roll of the dice, civilization could already be a dead wasteland, and what he was doing now would never have mattered.

He could feel self-justification eroding away as he read the opening gambit. A mistake and poof, society goes to hell, everyone panics and almost everyone dies.

Either which way it would mark the end of days or, for those that survived, a new Dark Age. Hell, there were already loads of TV series and films showcasing it. Books like the one he was reading. How many warnings did folk like him need for Christ's sake?

What's it feel like to grow the God Flu?

Smithy looked up from the book and frowned before shaking his head and stared out of the windshield at a carpark basking in full sun. A lunch break from the rat race … and the unknown contagion. God Flu.

Well, you ready to do this, Smithy?

This time he felt the spittle evaporate from his mouth and hairs rise on his neck. He listened, fearing his subconscious was tripping on the moral debate that haunted his nightmares. Job versus animal testing. Playing with viruses that could cause mayhem if containment failed or someone did something real stupid.

What, like make the God Virus?

"Yup, I guess so."

Secure is it? Deep in your bunker of death.

He thought of Oppenheimer. Atoms and viruses, both very small and yet capable of so much.

"Clearly," he said to an empty car. Wasn't talking to yourself a sign of madness?

You do know you're outside the building, right?

The book lay open at chapter twenty-three: the magician, man in black, all hail the Crimson King.

Coincidence? Maybe, but that was fiction.

"Yes, and what of it?"

What if you've got forty-eight hours left with life as you know it?

Anxiety threaded its way through his veins.

"Not possible," he said. "It's isolated and the lab would lock down."

It's God Flu, Smithy. You don't even know how it got there.

"And you do, I suppose?"

He scrutinized the greying hairs reflecting back from the vanity mirror. Dark rings under slung his eyes while fingers drummed on the steering wheel. The book now rested on the passenger seat. Who was the runner in there again? Campion. That was it. He worked in a military germ warfare lab where things went wrong. The similarities struck him as perverse. Safe while it's safe, but when it's not safe … well, people are people. They run, and what runs with them … *"I am become death."*

He shook his head. Who the hell was he talking to anyway? It must have been his own conscience drip feeding the worst-case scenario. There were safeguards for that, hermetic seals, positive air pressure, microfiltration systems and people suited and booted with respirators. Any breach and everything closed automatically. If you were in you were in. Simple. Infected or not infected, you weren't going anywhere until the all clear was given.

He needed air. A quick stroll down the sea front ought to do the trick. Waves were calming. The soft wash as they broke, the sound of gulls and smell of sea spray.

A long-haired youth rested on his elbows over the hood of a beat-up Ford. He eyed the breakers. "No good man, no good at all."

Smithy paused. "You talking to me?"

"Anyone who's listening, dude. No rides here." He looked glum as a hand touched the underside of the board resting on a roof rack.

Shall we send him to where the breakers never stop?

Smithy ignored the inner voice. Breakers were in one of King's books too. The nuance was fitting. Breakers for a breaking world. "... *the destroyer of worlds.*" He shook his head trying to dislodge the distraction.

"Ever tried Australia?" he asked. Where'd that thought come from?

The youth stood up, hair blowing in the wind as a smile crossed his face. "Idea! I could be in Melbourne tomorrow and riding waves by nightfall."

Smithy noticed a vacancy drift across the kid's face between him standing up and speaking. Must be on something, he thought.

Like God Flu, interjected the voice.

Smithy ignored it. "You serious?"

"Why not?" replied the youth. "Life's short and the world could end next week."

"What makes you say that?"

"God Flu, man. If it hits, then everyone dies, and I'm going out on a wave."

Smithy just stared as the surfer cast him a nod, turned, climbed into his car and headed off down the sea front.

Mental calculations trickled through his mind. Fortyeight hours, two airports and a million other encounters in London alone. He felt hot. How did the surfer know about God Flu, and was that sheer coincidence? The odds were staggering.

Not really, Smithy. Not from where I sit.

He stared out across the ocean, fearing his mind was breaking like the waves pounding the shoreline. "You're not real and I've got to get back to work."

As real as the plague that watched you staring in disbelief.

He turned and found himself walking to the bus station but not knowing why. "Do you blame me? It shouldn't be possible. New strains like that can't just appear spontaneously." But his retort lacked conviction because this one had. Just like that, the red eye looking at him looking at it.

God Flu, man. The voice mimicked the surfer.

Smithy started. "No!"

It takes less than a minute to upload.

"Upload?" He entered the terminal. Twenty or so passengers milled about either waiting for a bus to somewhere, pondering timetables or buying tickets. A few pensioners smiled at him as he walked past. Smithy joined a queue not knowing why. A child, holding her mother's hand looked up at him wide eyed and scared.

Twenty-meter radius, Smithy. How many you walked past already? How many has the hippy found, and how many have 'the found' themselves found?

The queue dismantled and he stood at the kiosk staring vacantly at the woman behind the counter.

"Where to?" she asked.

Smithy didn't even know why he was here in the first place and not back in the lab staring at the circle of red.

Frowning, he blinked and heard himself say, "Sorry, not today, I've changed my mind."

With that he watched the bus station drift away— distant, detached, as if watching a film— as he walked back into the sunshine. Pushed to the back, no longer in the moment. His own thoughts felt fuzzy.

His mind spoke up. *Are you saying it can infect people merely by being near them without any physical contact or aerosols? No carrier vectors at all?*

This time the answer came from his own mouth. "You catch on, Smithy, smarter than the average bear." There was an underlying sarcasm bleeding from the words.

His throat felt dry and hot like something had clutched his vocal chords and begun to squeeze. But that's…

"Impossible," the God Flu finished. "Yes, from your biological viewpoint." Meaning?

"You still don't know where I came from do you?"

Don't tell me … outer space. He could still feel pain, and the headache rearing up was becoming a red giant.

"Guess you just answered the big question all by yourself."

Which is? Smithy felt sick, his vision distorted and the outside world was far, far away.

"You're not alone."

The sledgehammer hit home and the headache disappeared. He was left in a dark, silent place. Interred in his own mind unable to reach out. Viruses wrest control of cells and use them to replicate. That was in the basic textbooks on virology. God Flu took over the body, taking it places with the sole purpose of infecting others, uploading like some computer virus. One purpose, one motive. On and on until there was nothing left to infect.

Why?

"We need a new home, Smithy, and this house is occupied. Call it an eviction notice and it's just been served."

***

Patrick Wakeman had a past that created the future. Most do, unless the past dominates the future and merely existing overrides living. The past is dead, long live the past kind of thing. Patrick's was hard only in one aspect. His parents were wealthy, too damn well off if you so please. At school he was the "Yes Man." Not because he sucked up, but because his dad was a big fan of the band and his name had been influenced, as Patrick found around the age of eleven, by a certain Rick Wakeman. A time when music became the "in thing," nicknames dropped Pat and evolved him into the keyboard maestro of the aforementioned group. By sixteen the 'p' had returned and for the next three years he became known as Prick. Not that he minded too much, because being of wealthy stock, he could afford to be laid back about most things.

Nurture was not just educational peer review. Back home his dad knocked around in political circles and was influential in flu pandemic planning. Given recent scares with influenza strains mutating and bird flu kicking up a storm, there was a fair amount of head rubbing deep inside government circles playing the "what if" game. As a sixth form teen doing the three sciences, Patrick had been involved in more than one ethical debate with his father about the merits of cordoning off affected areas in a way not too disparate from the handling of foot and mouth outbreaks in cattle. Movement exclusions and funeral pyres. Shoot to kill enforcement and damage limitation. Politicos nicely bunkered up in sterile safe zones with enough dried food and water to last until things has calmed down, burnt out or a viable vaccine found. Mix in the right circles, book your ticket and off we go. It reminded Patrick of Vault Tech in the Fallout series that had occupied him for many a long night of gaming.

Ethics and morals flipped over in his mind time and again. Was it right for the very people supposedly safeguarding countries to get free passes just because they slipped up and dropped the ball? Hell, they couldn't even fix roads properly.

By nineteen this had festered enough to turn him against the establishment, decide vegetarianism supported his outlook and take up riding the waves on a board at every opportunity. Life was good, parental ties were strained, but not severed, university beckoned after a gap year and both Wakeman seniors had concluded it was a phase that would pass once that year was up. Whereupon a politics, philosophy and law degree at King's College in London would sort him out.

Unbeknown to them, Patrick had decided university was not for him and touring as many beaches as possible was the immediate ambition, maybe the odd inspirational smoke and what would be would be.

All these things ran through his mind as he peered across a beach leaning on the bonnet of his rough-looking Ford sedan. A mild onshore breeze slew his hair backwards as he bemoaned an absence of decent waves.

That was when the weird bespectacled man dropped by and a moment when his brain tripped out before he'd subconsciously decided on selling his motor to go surfing in Australia. His last words before driving off had been deep, so deep he felt quite pleased about things and got one up on his old man at the same time.

"God Flu man. If it hits then everyone dies and I'm going out on a wave."

That was an hour ago, and while Smithy, the man whose name he didn't know, was passing things on and losing his body in a bus station, Patrick was munching a burger in a well-known fast food chain.

Nice is it, Rick?

He sat staring out of the window. The local high street going about its business, cars waiting at a pedestrian crossing whilst a woman with a pushchair crossed towards the market on the other side. A man leaning off a scaffold frame where the local council was restoring tired masonry on a listed building, below which dwelt an unlisted supermarket. It was through this revelry of film reel watching through his eyes that his mind rode breakers over sun glazed beaches overseas.

The subconscious voice stirred him up. It felt cold and emotionless.

"What the hell?" He blinked and looked at the half burger. The first words reaching through his head were when, what, why? He remembered heading off towards his flat to pick up some stuff, *what was it?* The next minute he was here drifting through burgers when he was a vegetarian. How did that happen?

Easy, surfer boy, I brought you here to mingle.

"Say what?"

He dropped the burger into its wrapper. Wasn't bad though...*but meat man...think of the morals and killing for food.*

Disgust rippled through him. It was tasty though.

You like to mingle don't you, Patrick?

"Just a bit, yes … but crowds no, can't be doing with crowds. It's why the surf's there. To escape and be free with the spray and sea air all around. Such a high man, such a high."

Why he was talking under his breath escaped him. It seemed logical, essential even.

I ain't no man, Patrick. They are under a countdown.

"Countdown?"

You said it yourself, to Smithy. "Who the hell is he?" *God Flu, man.*

He found himself walking along the pavement not quite remembering leaving the burger joint. "That vacantlooking egg head at the sea front?" *The very same. Patient zero.*

"Not following man."

He turned into the train station for no apparent reason and continued walking.

Your old man worked on flu pandemic planning yes. Not a question more a statement. *Mix in the right circles and Vault Tech Overseer.*

Patrick's mind was feeling hemmed in. The view from his eyes drawing further away and part blurred. Like he was coming down with something. "Too right, everyone's expendable except those with the golden tickets." His voice sounded duller, more internalised.

Doesn't have to be, dude, doesn't have to be. The voice was using his own phrases. "How do you mean?"

Give your mum a call.

He felt his forehead crease into a frown. *Why would I do that?*

"To say hi, tell her you love her before it's too late."

Too late for what, though? He was aware things had changed. His connection with the world was shutting down. Somewhere in the distance he heard a conversation that he wasn't having.

"Hey mum, how's it hanging?" There was a pause.

"Good, I just wanted to say I love you. Heading away for a few days so thought I'd upload a few thoughts before I left."

Upload? I don't say upload, he thought from deep inside his head. It was dark now and, if he had access to anything other than a mind tomb, about now he'd be entering anxiety bordering on serious insanity.

"Sweet," he heard, "say hi to Dad and just go to that party, mingle a bit and you'll feel a lot better. Laters."

It went quiet. The sounds of the station disappeared and he heard the street noises; cars, buses, chatter of unseen pedestrians, the wail of a disgruntled toddler.

The absence of physical chemistry did not placate the panic now settling in.

What are you?

"I'm the God Flu, Rick. You familiar with viruses?" *Only computer ones, and what the hell is God Flu?*

"Yes, your memories tell the tale, gave me an idea that solved your Vault Tech ticket conundrum."

There was a pause as a door shut and road noise turned into an air conditioning fan.

"Can I help you Sir?" Patrick heard an outsider's voice, male and not too old by the sound of it.

"Yeah man, an hour should be about enough time."

"Very good, sir. Take your pick, and for a fiver you can have a coffee too."

"Cool, I'll be by the window."

There was some shuffling and the sound of a chair scraping back.

Vault tech conundrum ... what's that mean?

"Bit of an upload realisation dude, free range is twenty metres. The phone network reaches wider. Your vaults have just been compromised."

Mum? Please, what's going on, I just wanted to ride some waves, maybe in Australia.

"Your species has a strong sense of fear Rick, very strong. Not to worry, though. By tomorrow we'll be surfing almost everywhere, and a few days after that no one will care anymore."

There were tapping noises in the distance, a keyboard entered his trapped mind and then an image of a cafe and streams of people walking past the window his possessed body sat at. All pausing briefly with a vacant stare before moving on.

What did you do to mum?

"Same as the lab geek, just passing on some tech. Countdowns rolling so just enjoy the ride, or … you're a surfer, right? Just not quite waves we're riding now, dude. With this button we get to surf the whole world."

Patrick was allowed a visual link to see his own finger hit enter on a keyboard. Above it the graphic user interface went black before strings of ones and zeros flew down the screen. Inside a minute, things went back to normal, good as new.

What did you just do?

"I just went viral."

He heard himself laughing, not just any old laugh but a real gut buster.

LOST AND FOUND

By Victoria Lynn

https://www.rufflesandgrace.com

Carson knew of her presence by the icy prickles on his skin that trailed like cold fingers down his spine. He would see her when he turned, her beautiful blonde hair now looking more of white than of honey, softly drifting in an unfelt breeze. He would seek to embrace her, but she would step back with a pained, lost look on her face. She never said anything, but her presence was enough to set him reeling.

His heart throbbed with the painful intensity of being broken. People said broken hearts heal …. They were wrong. His had refused. It had only rankled until the pain was even worse than it had been in that moment when he found out his wife had taken her own life.

Busy. He had been so busy, consumed in his own life, his job, his routine. Even the time he spent with his wife was scheduled. So much so that he had failed to see the trouble that grew in her spirit day by day until it was too late. His life had been well ordered, like a puzzle with all of its pieces fitting perfectly together. Her death had shattered that illusion and the puzzle had exploded, sending the pieces flying too far away to gather back.

Hands in his pockets, he sauntered casually, with one destination in mind. His family had begged him to get his act back together, to reinstate some level of normalcy. But he had lived with too much normal. He now floated through life—alone—without purpose or plan. He had fallen into the trap of order before, but he never would again. He had sworn so as he stood over his wife's grave and the first shovelful of dirt landed with a sickening thud atop the lid. The sound had jerked at his nerves, but he had somehow relished the pain. He'd failed to see her pain—it was only fair that he now experienced some of that, if only a little in comparison.

Everything he once held dear had vanished from his grasp. His job, his home, his routine. All because he had not been able to help the one person that mattered the most.

She now visited him. Her presence mocking him, begging him, pleading with him to open his eyes. To soak in the moment and realize what was going on. But now it was too late. While she was there—seemingly within reach—he could never fix it. She was the constant reminder that he had failed at what should have come first.

He walked into the wind, his coat held tight against the cold that seemed to slice right through his clothes and straight to his bones. He knew by the strange looks he was getting from people in the passing cars that he was crazy for walking on the bridge today. But he actually relished the discomfort. The physical pain cut ome of the emotional torment. It gave him a means to express and feel it.

He thought that when he reached the actual moment he wouldn't be able to gather up enough courage to go through with it. That he would be scared, nervous, shaky. But none of those emotions manifested themselves. He was as calm as if he were merely out for a stroll. There was a steadiness, an unnatural tranquility. A numbness. He almost wanted to be a little scared. He wished it was harder. Seeing her always there but always out of reach had finally brought him to this point. He had failed. He accepted it, and now, perhaps, he could join her.

Carson stopped precisely in the middle of the bridge. He leaned against the rail and looked over the edge at the swirling black water below. It was oddly poetic. It looked like what his soul was experiencing must feel.

Sensing a presence behind him, he turned. A man in a black wool coat and blue scarf stood there, his hands in his pockets and the wind playfully twirling his thick, blond hair. He looked middle-aged, maybe fifteen or twenty years older than Carson himself.

Carson caught his breath. Awkward seconds of unbroken silence and staring into each other's eyes distracted Carson from his self-appointed mission. He shook himself and turned back to the rail. If the man wanted to stop him, it was too late. His mind was made up. But something in the blue eyes unsettled him and doubt crept in.

"I have a proposition for you."

Carson turned. The man had not moved, those piercing eyes still staring deep into his. They almost pierced his soul.

"Why would I want to help you?" Carson asked, annoyed that this man was interrupting his planned escape.

"I never said it was to help me."

Carson stared at the man. Something within compelled him to help. It would be heroic. One last act of kindness before he ended it all.

"Help with what?"

"Are you willing to do it?"

"I don't even know what it is."

The man's crystalline eyes stared into his. A long pause stood between them like a waiting presence. Carson warred within himself, edgier by the second. He wanted to get it over with. Jumping over the bridge was seeming harder and harder as time went on. And this was only an excuse. He worried he wouldn't be able to go through with it if he waited too much longer. He gathered himself. If he just turned and lunged over the rail, all of this would be over. The decision would be made, and he could forever be rid of the guilt and shame that ate at him. His adrenaline spiked and his muscles tensed in preparation.

The man held out his hand, a stormy intensity radiating from him. Carson paused. Something tugged within him, pulling him from behind, wooing him and dragging him away from the offered hand. He swallowed against the bitterness in the back of his throat.

Something else compelled him to reach for the man's hand. Something inexplicable and undeniable.

The pull on him to jump was stronger than ever. To for one moment be suspended over the black expanse of water, to have it all over within seconds. But with one last effort he grasped the man's hand. Strength flowed through him as the man gripped him so hard it hurt.

Darkness closed in around him, and in the blink of an eye he was somewhere else entirely. Strange. He always thought that if you were teleported somewhere, you would feel a rush in your body, but he felt nothing.

This surreal somewhere welcomed him with shimmering green grass waving in the warm breeze that wafted over him. Carson closed his eyes and basked for a brief, unhindered moment in the warmth touching his heart as it did his skin. It almost felt as though they were in a cavern, the light falling just so across the space.

An abandoned white building stood upon a precipice, its design reminding him of old Roman architecture. It was a contradiction, out of place but at home at the same time. Its marble was discolored with dirt and time, and the grand arches were full of cracks. It looked as though it could fall down at any time and was holding itself up by sheer willpower.

Carson squinted. Someone stood on the precipice. It was a girl. Her long, brown hair blew in the wind and he gasped. She looked as though she was contemplating throwing herself off the edge. His heart constricted and his breathing grew shallow. There was no way she could survive a jump from that height. The sharp rocks below would make sure of that.

His vision intensified and he could see her features. Her face was young and pale. Fear clouded her eyes, but there was a darkness behind them. A despair that emanated from her face and her drooped shoulders. An overwhelming need to stop her came over him. He looked over at the stranger, panic quickening the blood in his veins. He didn't know what to ask, but a question was on the tip of his tongue.

The man's blue eyes intensified in color and instead of speaking, he took Carson's hand. "Look" was all he said.

Confused, Carson looked back at the girl and saw her life flash before his eyes. The family that would mourn her death. The despair she felt. The unloving spirit that constantly mocked her and dragged her down into the pit of despondency, whispering lies in her ear. He saw the friends that loved her. The young man who wished to marry her. He also saw her blindness to it all. Everyone loved her so much, but she never saw it. All she could see was the utter loneliness that had been whispered would be hers for eternity.

The visions made his brain whirl, and he fell to his knees beneath the weight of the knowledge. The stranger's hand slipped from his grasp as he fell.

The vision dimmed, and he was no longer able to see the girl's life. He knelt there, gasping, the lack of the vision making his pounding heart slow. He needed to stop her.

She shouldn't die. She had so much to live for.

The familiar icy sensation trailed down his spine, and goose bumps stood out on his arms. He shivered and looked up into the silver eyes of his wife. Her eyes used to be green. Like grass, and so beautiful. He stood and stared into her eyes.

"You can save her, Carson."

It was the first time he had heard her speak since her death. It set him reeling.

How could he save the girl?

All he knew was that he needed to do it.

But if he had failed his wife, how could he save this young woman?

"Then you will know the truth and the truth will set you free."

The verse felt far away like an echo receding into the distance. It had been a long time since he had recalled any scripture or indeed anything to do with the Bible. God had allowed Carson's wife to die; who was He to help in this situation?

Conviction stirred in his soul. God's word was the truth. He knew it. He didn't want to believe it, but it had been so ingrained in his life that he couldn't help but believe it, even when his heart desperately wanted to deny it.

"Hey!" he shouted, starting to run toward the precipice. The girl's head moved a bit, but she showed no other sign of having heard him. It took a few more shouts before he caught her attention.

She looked up from the drop below, and he could tell she was having a hard time focusing, her eyes glazed over and unfocused.

"Don't do it." He gasped for breath, pulling himself to a stop at the bottom of the drop off. She was so high up that it hurt his neck to keep her in sight.

She stared at him. Her blue eyes almost looked like shattered glass and her dark brown hair—nearly black, but with roots of a lighter color—splayed across her shoulders and blew across her face in the wind. His heart lurched into his throat. The dry eyes, the lost look ... it was the same face his wife had worn for months before her death.

The look of the living dead.

"You can't do this."

A bit of life came back into her eyes as she realized what he was saying. She shook her head in a despondent way. "You don't understand."

"No, you don't understand. I know what you're going through. I—" Carson gulped against the tightness in his throat. He knew exactly how she felt. Truth whispered into his soul. He fought it ... but how could he deny the truth while trying to force it on someone else? Did he believe it? Or didn't he?

"God, I know you can hear me. Why did you take her? How could you? Don't you dare say that you love me when this—" His voice broke. "When this happens. This doesn't feel good ... this doesn't feel like love." The anger spewed out of him. He had forced it down so long, it now burned as it worked its way up his throat.

A voice whispered in his soul—more like a conviction than a voice—giving him the answer. *"This wasn't Me. I am all that My Word says I AM. The enemy has come to steal, kill and destroy. But My Word is life and My law is kindness."* Then, just like that, he saw the curtain peeled back on his own life just as it had been for the girl. He saw the enemy twisting lies and forming them into arrows that pierced the heart of his most beloved one. He saw her fall prey to their poison. He saw himself listening to those same lies. He saw how he had heard them and shut his ears and eyes to the messages from His heavenly Father. God had never left. Carson had merely shut his heart to Him and pretended He wasn't there.

With the realization, a love like heat burned through his heart and soul. Shaking, he fell to his knees, the rocks piercing through his jeans and cutting the skin. But the pain didn't bother him. The truth flowed through his soul like cool water on a forest fire. The raging lies fell back and faltered under the steady stream of God's truth.

And now he knew. He couldn't share truth with someone until he believed it himself. He had not been at fault for his wife's death, but he now knew that the anger he harbored toward himself, at God, and at his wife, was misdirected. He should only burn with one kind of anger. A righteous one that the enemy could not stand against.

With the growl of a warrior deep in his throat, he stood. "You will not have her!" The words from his Bible that he had learned so long ago came flooding back. "For God so loved the world that he gave his one and only Son, that whoever believes in him shall not perish but have eternal life." He spoke the words as they came to mind and the veil between this life and the spiritual one lifted and he saw the darkness within the girl quake and shrink away in fear.

"See what great love the Father has lavished on us, that we should be called children of God!"

The girl shook and took an unsteady step away from the edge, pain blazing across her features and wrenching a strangled cry from her throat.

The conflict in her raged, but he could see the darkness cowering and pulling away. Her blue eyes became clearer and brighter in color as he continued to speak. He pressed forward. The words dropped from his lips like stones that struck the surface of the water, shattering the complacency that had become normality.

"For I am convinced that neither death nor life, neither angels nor demons, neither the present nor the future, nor any powers, neither height nor depth, nor anything else in all creation, will be able to separate us from the love of God that is in Christ Jesus our Lord."

The darkness within her departed and she fell to her knees, shaking. Her dark hair waved in the wind, whipping across her tear-streaked face and flourishing about with every breath of air. It reminded him of tall grass in a windstorm.

No darkness remained in her. He saw it on her face, in her eyes. Those eyes were beautiful and bright when not shrouded in lies.

A cold prickle raised on his skin again, and he turned. His wife stood before him with sorrow on her face and unshed tears glimmering in her silver eyes. Somehow, deep within him, he knew this was the last time he would ever see her again in this world.

"Goodbye, my love."

She took a step past him, then before he could turn she embraced him. Instead of ice, warmth greeted him, and then it was gone. He turned around, but she was nowhere in sight. He closed his eyes and drew a deep breath. He had forgiven himself for her death. Even forgiven God. He knew the truth now, and the truth? It set him free from guilt and anguish. From his torment and from his prison.

The wind ripped at his coat, bone-chillingly cold again. He shivered, opened his eyes, and gasped, his heart hammering the blood through his veins. Carson stared down the long drop into the inky-black water below and then stumbled away from the rail, the thought of jumping now going against everything within him.

The whizzing of cars flying past in their uncaring way felt out of place with the experience he had just been through. He was different. Lighter, brighter … at peace. He huddled tighter under his coat. Had it all been a dream? His knees stung with a cold blast of air and he looked down, surprised to see that his jeans were torn and his knees skinned. He had fallen on the rocks, but perhaps that was just what it had been in his dream. He could have easily scraped them on the cement of the bridge. He ran a hand over his beard, trying to rid himself of the impression that it was real. Everything was back to the way it had been, even the mysterious stranger had disappeared.

Then he saw her.

She stared at him with the same startled look he was probably giving her. Everything was the same. Her blue eyes, the dark hair whipping in the wind. Even her black clothes that hung off her as if they were too big. Even the tears wetting her face.

She stood not far from him, her hand on the rail. She looked between him and the water below, and then took a step back.

She was the girl he had saved in his dream ... but, was it really a dream? The darkness he had seen in her eyes when he first caught her gaze as she stood above him on the cliff was gone. She looked at him as if she knew him. A sob racked her shoulders and her eyes were wide. He reached his hand to her out of instinct.

She swallowed and took it. Neither of them said a word as they walked through the cold winter wind to the edge of the bridge. More than one life had been saved today. Whether the circumstances Carson remembered were real or not, it didn't really matter.

All that did matter was that he had been lost.

And now he was found.

THE FOREVER DOOR

By Rachael Ritchey

https://www.rachaelritchey.com/

History has seen its share of violence and the conquest of man. And now that same history has caught up with Owen McFadden when his archaeologic-expert sister's passion for the unimaginable unknown leaves him no choice other than to join her on the quest of the millennium … a dangerous hunt for the forbidden, deep in the cloud forests of Peru.

As a bonus, I've provided a prologue on my website: https://rachaelritchey.com/2018/11/03/the-foreverdoor-prologue/

Owen rehung his and Julianna's matched quartz crystals around his neck and tucked them under his shirt. He replaced the cell phone against his ear and watched his guide Jorge, the stranger his sister sent to fetch him from Seattle and bring him to Peru, hang up the airport pay phone and rummage through his dusty backpack.

"Boss! Boss, I know. I'm sorry," Owen said, his voice elevated over the noise of the Peruvian airport. He'd never been to Peru before …. "Like I said, Stephen is your guy. He's trustworthy, and he knows my plans maybe better than I do. The build will be fine in his hands while I'm gone." He nodded as his boss replied over the phone. "Yeah. You bet. See you in a couple weeks." He hung up the phone and slid it into his cargo shorts, securing the flap over the top. He did have a few misgivings about the construction of the skyscraper, but Julianna took priority.

"This way, Señor McFadden," Jorge said, grabbing Owen's arm and dragging him through the hubbub of activity outside the main door to the airport. A taxi, or whatever it was the locals called it, sat out front. Owen didn't pack much, so he tossed his pack on the seat. Jorge kept his satchel on, and they both climbed in—or rather Owen folded himself into the back of the tin can for the eleven-hour drive to Chachapoyas in the Amazonas province.

Owen searched his bag for his last granola bar, cursing himself for not thinking to bring more or even buy a water bottle before leaving the airport. His concern for Julianna had definitely hindered his decision-making process; he really needed to get his head on straight. Instead of eating the granola bar, he shoved it in the other pocket of his shorts. While he had his head down, the car lurched forward, but the driver slammed on the brakes. Owen's face jammed into the head rest of the front seat. "Ow!" he said, more surprised than hurt.

Jorge mumbled something, but Owen caught one word for sure. *Dios.* If only he knew Spanish. "What's up?" A shadow fell across him and Owen peered out his passenger side window to see a man's loose peach cotton button-down blocking the view. The man tapped on the glass.

Owen frowned but rolled down the window. "Can I help you, amigo?"

He leaned down and smiled. Even though outwardly exuding hospitality, something ominous lingered behind his eyes. "Ah, Mr. McFadden, welcome to Peru," he said with a barely discernable Peruvian accent on his excellent

English. "I am shocked Jorge did not tell you to expect us. Come. We will fly you to Chachapoyas. This is much closer to Kuelap and the other sites. No need for this … less-than-comfortable accommodation," he said, indicating the old car with a flip of his manicured fingers and a repressed sneer.

"Do I know you?" Owen hesitated, his attention now divided between this Casanova and the 'muscle' standing in front of the car, arms crossed, sunglasses on, and looking every bit the stereotypical bodyguard.

"Ah, no." The man reached into the deep pocket of his pristine, white linen pants and pulled out a wad of American bills while he continued to speak. "But we will remedy this on the flight."

The driver, too poor to hide the greed in his eyes, reached across Owen, grabbed the bundle as it was offered, and turned off the car.

"You see, I am an associate of your honorable sister."

Jorge groaned softly but Owen remained clueless. The driver said something in Spanish. Jorge argued, but without knowing what they were saying, Owen could only guess it was about the drive. Jorge grumbled but stepped out of the car, and Owen followed suit, though with a measure of reluctance.

He watched the taxi driver take off and leave them on the curb and couldn't shake the feeling that the eleven hours in that car would go more smoothly than flying in a plane with the South American Casanova grinning next to him.

"Come, come, Señor. Luis will carry your satchel." He signaled the bodyguard.

"No, I got it." There wasn't anything particularly important in his bag, other than the journal Julianna had insisted he bring, but it felt wrong to trust his personal stuff to these guys.

"This way." Casanova spun and sauntered back into the building.

Owen looked askance at Jorge who refused to make eye contact and scuttled after Mr. Smooth. Luis, the bodyguard, stood with arms crossed, staring at Owen. There was no use arguing, so he shrugged and followed the other two. He felt more than heard Luis move behind him, bringing up the rear. A fleeting image of getting himself kidnapped by South American drug lords flitted through Owen's head, but he pushed the ridiculous thought away.

***

After being offered a plush leather seat on the plane, the man finally introduced himself. "Mr. McFadden, my name is Miguel Alvarado. If you have not heard that name, I am a direct descendant of an explorer associated with

Pizzaro."

The name—Alvarado—was one he recognized. The power-hungry man of South American lore whose thirst for the gold of the Incas drove him mad. Just hearing the name sent an unexpected shiver down Owen's spine.

He nodded by way of acknowledgment, and Miguel Alvarado, Pizzaro's buddy's descendant, rambled on about his position within the government and his work in preserving Peru's history through archaeology. The influence this man held should have been impressive, but Owen grew warier with each new revelation. It might have been better to be kidnapped by outlaws ….

His host grew quiet, sipping a glass of ice water, and Owen stared out the window of the private jet. The rapidly changing exotic and beautiful landscape differed immensely from the northwest U.S. Fall crept over the land without much change, but as they drew near Chachapoyas, awe relieved his exhaustion by degrees. He drank in the lush green of the jutting hillsides as they peeked in and out of the cloud cover. They'd flown east from the arid coast, and still within sight were high plains, both stark and barren. He knew that beyond the Andes lay the Amazon, a wild and lush rainforest that regularly swallowed up everything in its path.

But to add to Owen's unease, the entire plane ride Jorge sat hunched in the corner, his arms crossed over his own dirty bag. When the flight attendant tried to take it from him, it looked to Owen like he might have snarled at her. She'd left him alone the rest of the flight.

His introduction to the animated Peruvian had been more cordial. Jorge had claimed friendship with Julianna and brought her crystal necklace as evidence, insisting Owen needed to return to Peru with him. He couldn't reach Julianna on her phone, so here he was on a private plane with strangers whose first language he didn't speak. He wanted to kick himself for that one. Should have chosen Spanish instead of French in high school … and paid better attention.

Owen brought his attention away from the window and reached into his bag where it sat on the seat beside him. He pulled out the old journal Julianna had asked him to bring. Why she wanted him to do it, specifically, he didn't know, but the way she asked for it and him to come by sending her necklace was enough to make him drop everything.

They'd been given those necklaces by their uncle, an archaeologist who they'd spent summers with at dig sites across the world. One particular time had been in Turkey. That summer Julianna saved Owen's life when a pillar fell from its support beam. After that, their uncle had given them the twin the necklaces and said they were talismans of protection … to always keep them close. For Owen and Julianna, they'd become a sort of promise, but Owen suspected maybe more for him than her. Julianna would always look out for him, but her head was so much in the clouds it was a wonder she was so good at her job.

He thumbed through the pages of the journal, all written in an almost unrecognizable script. Jules had said it was written in Spanish and dated back to the early 1500s. On occasion, pictures accompanied the words. One looked just like their crystals. He stared at it for the hundredth time and had to wonder. He smiled to himself and thumbed the spots where she had desecrated the pages by adding her own scribbles. For all her love of archaeology, she sure had no problem with adding her personal mark to history.

Owen stopped to study the loose paper she'd stuck inside—a hand-drawn map. Spanish names popped out at him. The center displayed a halfmoon with a waterfall.

"We are almost arrived." Alvarado's tone betrayed nothing while he stared at the leather-bound book.

Owen folded the map in half and held it under the book, snapping it shut with a soft thump. He found it interesting when Alvarado's eyes flitted up as if he'd been caught doing something he shouldn't.

"Tell me, Mr. McFadden, do you know much about your sister's work?" He crossed his legs and rested his hands on his knee. "What she does?"

Instinct and caution fired warnings in his mind. "I used to work with her … more a personal assistant. She's an antiquities expert, dating things found at archaeological sites." Alvarado laughed and Owen frowned. "Something funny?"

"Oh, nothing, nothing. She has certainly kept her expertise … how do you say? Narrow."

"I thought you said you're her associate. Why does that surprise you?"

"May I?" Alvarado asked. He leaned forward, indicating the book and ignoring Owen's question.

Owen ran his thumb across the cover and slowly passed the old tome. Alvarado almost snatched it from Owen's outstretched hands like a greedy child getting a sweet. With a strange reverence, he opened the cover and ghosted the tips of his fingers over the first page as if it might crumble under his touch.

"Do you know what that book is?" Owen's curiosity led him to ask the question he'd wondered since his sister asked him to hold on to it eight months previous. He also wanted to feel out Miguel Alvarado's motives.

"Do you not?" Alvarado asked, his dark eyes meeting Owen's. "This is a treasure trove of knowledge. How your sister came to own it, I do not know."

The fasten seatbelt light dinged, alerting their upcoming descent. Owen frowned, something Alvarado said having set off its own alarm bell in his head. He held his hand out for the book, and with obvious reluctance Alvarado handed it back.

"My sister's work gives plenty of opportunities to find and collect objects of varying value. This is probably just one of the things she's been given by some grateful boss or village leader she helped along the way. She's good like that."

The look of hunger in Alvarado's eyes added to the pit of growing unease in Owen's gut. He slid the book back in the bag but hesitated midway when he realized he never told Alvarado that the journal belonged to Julianna. He shoved it deep in the bottom. The sooner he could find Jules and put distance between himself and this guy the better.

***

The plane coasted down the one-lane tarmac to the terminal. As soon as it came to a stop, before the fasten seatbelt light turned off, Owen sprang from his seat—at least as far as his six-foot frame would allow.

"Well, thanks for the ride. C'mon, Jorge, let's go find Jules."

Jorge scrambled out of his seat in the far corner and shuffled toward Owen, but Alvarado's voice stopped him mid-stride.

"Nonsense, my friend. We will take you to your lovely sister. How could we not show you true Peruvian hospitality?" He unbuckled and stood, his movements smooth and confident.

Owen shoved his sister's hand-drawn map in his pocket and looked at Jorge who continued to avoid eye contact. The hairs on his neck rose, and Owen tapped his other pocket where his phone was secured. He gave Jorge one last questioning glance before following Alvarado off the plane. The flight attendant's seductive smile was surely meant to distract him and told Owen more than enough as he slid past. Her slim fingers grazed his arm, but Jorge crowded his back and whispered in his ear.

"We must not go with them."

"What?" Owen said, turning halfway to better see his skittish new friend.

Jorge's eyes darted toward Alvarado. He shook his head and gave Owen a small push to keep moving.

Alvarado, four more of the bodyguard guys—clearly sporting some serious firepower—and three dark SUVs shrouded in shadow under the setting sun lined the tarmac. None of it fit this exotic locale where time seemed to have stood still a hundred years before.

"Luis will take your bag, Mr. McFadden."

"I'll hold on to it, thanks."

"I insist." Alvarado nodded to Luis, and the bodyguard stepped forward. He gripped the pack on Owen's shoulder, forcibly taking it from his grasp.

"Can I ask what exactly's going on here?" Owen's fractured attention darted between Luis walking to an SUV with his bag and Miguel Alvarado's self-satisfied expression.

Without a second glance, Alvarado raised his hand and swiveled all in one dancer-like motion. The other bodyguards moved forward and circled Owen and Jorge who stepped close to his side and mumbled some sort of prayer before surreptitiously crossing himself.

Owen shook his head and walked after Alvarado. The escort moved with eerie precision around them and directed Owen toward the second SUV. One of the big, silent dudes opened a door for Owen, motioning him in. Owen pulled Jorge up next to him and gave him a light shove to get in first. The bodyguard reached a hand out to stop him. Owen sized him up out of habit … maybe a little bulkier than himself but not taller.

"Jorge and I have some business to discuss. We'll do it here on the tarmac for however long it takes or in the vehicle. Take your pick."

The burly dude glanced at the front SUV where Alvarado had climbed in. He dropped his hand. Owen raised a brow, and then he stepped in behind Jorge.

The three SUVs snaked down the road, away from the airport and into the heart of the city of Chachapoyas. Owen took note of the majority of red tile roofs on white Spanish-inspired buildings. He'd love to study this style in an authentic city like this, but he was getting distracted.

"Beautiful, is it not?" Jorge asked, leaning toward Owen to peer out the window.

"I had no idea a place like this existed in the middle of nowhere."

"Alvarado's ancestors built the first city here," he replied, a serious tone adding extra weight to his words.

Owen looked Jorge in the eye who nodded slowly as if to say this was important.

"Danger is around the corner."

"Huh?" Owen asked, losing patience by the minute.

"Be ready." Jorge mumbled something else, undoing Owen's seatbelt, and then, without a breath between, he struck the driver's head. The gun-toting driver snarled and slammed on the brake. Both guys in the front turned as if to grab Jorge, but he was ahead of them. He'd already reached across Owen and opened the door, pushing him out while the vehicle remained motionless.

"Wha—"

"*¡Apúrate!*"

Owen stumbled out, Jorge gripping the back of his shirt, choking him in his haste to exit right behind. The last SUV stopped and the men within jumped out, guns drawn. People on the street screamed and scurried for cover.

"*¡Apúrate!* Hurry!" Jorge yelled and shoved Owen toward the alley in front of them.

A gunshot blasted and echoed between the buildings, the bullet splitting the air and shattering the corner of the building next to Owen's head. A spray of shrapnel blistered his bare arm and neck. The surreal moment broke into a cacophony of pandemonium. He ducked, but a frantic Jorge, still shouting at him in Spanish, beckoned him into the alley.

Owen looked back to see one of the goons take aim at Jorge. Without thought, he rammed Jorge to the side, the bullet grazing his left shoulder. Owen cried out, the gash burning like a hot poker on his skin, but he didn't stop moving, yanking Jorge back into a run.

Alvarado's clear tenor could be heard above the ruckus. *"Lo dejó ir!"* Owen glanced back again to see him hold up the journal, a wicked grin on his face as his men slowed their pursuit and lowered their guns. Owen's pace faltered, but Jorge gave him an insistent tug and kept him stumbling down the alley.

"I will see you again, Mr. McFadden," Alvarado yelled. "Either in this life or the next. Tell Julianna 'thank you' for me!"

His laughter melted into the distance as Owen and Jorge dashed across the next street and into another alley. ***

Jorge kept running. All Owen could think about was that some guy just shot at him—*had* shot him—and Alvarado had his sister's journal. Touching the bleeding graze on his shoulder, he hissed through his teeth and looked up again at the stranger dragging him farther into an unfamiliar city in the middle of an unfamiliar country … where people shot at him.

This could not end well.

Panting and a little dizzy, he caught up to Jorge and saw a fountain in the middle of a square, but Jorge stopped before they could exit the cover of buildings and doubled over at the waist, gripping his knees. The public area teemed with passersby and people milling about, enjoying the setting sun and each other's company. He and Jorge had only come four or five blocks. These people must have heard the gunshots, but most of them moved about as if nothing out of the ordinary happened.

Jorge gasped for breath. "My apologies, Señor McFadden." His words came out on a wheeze. "I hope you have not injured."

Owen, in much better shape than Jorge, breathed hard, but he guessed that was only because he needed to adjust to the high altitude. He aimed his shoulder where Jorge could see. The smaller man grimaced.

"What the hell was that?"

Jorge stood tall and stretched his back. He looked around in the gathering darkness and seemed to be thinking while he spoke between puffs of breath. "It is best we not go with Señor Alvarado."

"You know what, I don't care right now. Just get me to my sister."

"*Sí*. Come. We go to my amigo. He will borrow to us his *mulas*."

"*Mulas?*"

"*Sí, mulas*. Eh … mules. And you can clean this injury," Jorge said and started limping at a brisk pace that morphed into a slow jog once they reached the other side of the square. Owen had garnered a few open stares, but for the most part everyone tended to glance and quickly look away.

He'd entered some kind of twilight zone where people shoot at you just for fun and no one speaks the same language. He needed to see Jules … to make sure she was all right. Owen pulled his cell out of his shorts pocket and held it up. "Seriously?" The signal read nil, nada, zilch, zippo.

"Do you coming?" Jorge called to him before he continued his lumbering, lopsided pace.

Owen shoved his phone back in his pocket and caught up to Jorge in half the smaller man's strides.
***

It turned out when Jorge said they were going for mules, he meant they were driving in an old duct tapewrapped, rusty 1960s era Jeep the ten or so miles it took to get to Cocachimba, and then borrowing mules for the trail Jorge swore would take Owen to Julianna.

A couple times during the drive, Owen pulled out his phone and stared at the empty signal bars, but he gave up after the twentieth try and prayed he hadn't been led on a wild goose chase. This unassuming Peruvian guy had brought him his sister's necklace and knew Owen had that journal, so either she was friends with Jorge, or Julianna was in even deeper trouble than he thought.

He rubbed his eyes with the heels of his palms and couldn't remember the last time he'd slept. Maybe for a minute or two in the Jeep between the jostling.

"*El loco mula!*" Jorge swore through gritted teeth, but that was one phrase he'd said often enough Owen had no problem interpreting. Jorge slid off the stubborn animal's back and pulled the reins over its head, dragging him.

Owen urged his own mule to move forward again, following behind Jorge and his grumpy mule who both grumbled and protested respectively. The last thing Owen wanted was to get separated from his guide in the middle of the forest—a high altitude jungle swathed in heavy darkness. It was a wonder they stayed on any kind of trail.

Even at the pinnacle of night the trees and bushes buzzed with unseen life. Owen shoved thoughts about what might lurk beyond his sight away as he pulled down the sleeves of his borrowed ratty jacket, the only one even remotely his size.

Another sound joined that of the wildlife. The distant rhythm of rushing water. A river?

The tree line broke and in the distance loomed a waterfall cloaked in mist and moonlight.

"Gocta Cataracts," Jorge said with a satisfied lilt to his heavy accent as Owen stopped next to him and dismounted.

"Wow. Not what I expected." If not for the waxing moon he'd never be able to see the falls, but somehow the reflected light seemed to make the waters glow with an otherworldly light.

"Come."

Jorge took the reins from Owen's hand and tied both mules to a fallen tree that had obviously been used for just such a purpose many times before. The mules skittered and brayed, but Jorge shushed them. "Don't worry, stinking *mulas*, your master will come for you in the morning."

Owen danced his flashlight over the slick green surface of the log, following it to its end where two eyes reflected what light could be gathered from the darkness. When the flashlight's beam touched near, a screech rent the air and the eyes disappeared with a crash of underbrush.

"Watch your back," Jorge said just to the right and behind Owen. "*Otorongo.*"

"What's that?"

"Big cat. Eh … jaguar." Jorge slung his pack over his shoulder and motioned Owen to follow him down a handdug set of dirt stairs that looked more like a mud slide in the flash of his light. "*Otorongo.* They guard the mermaid of Gocta and her secrets."

"Mermaid?" Owen only half-listened as Jorge spoke in a hushed voice on their trek down through the thick brush.

"*Sí.* Gocta's legend. Our grandparents told us to stay away from here. That we would die. That we would be … eh … enhanced and never leave."

"Entranced, you mean? Or … enchanted?

"*Sí.* Enchanted."

Owen looked up at the towering falls and imagined that the warning was probably accurate. This place exuded danger, and there was definitely something mesmerizing in the atmosphere.

"The legend says a mermaid pulled her lover into the waters to escape his jealous wife, and he was never seen again."

"Brutal."

Jorge made a noncommittal noise and led Owen on in silence. The thin, steep trail twisted back and forth, snaking its way into the basin of the upper falls where the water pooled before escaping over the second fall to the base.

Jorge suddenly stopped and raised his hand for Owen to do the same. He executed an animal call reminiscent of a monkey, and Owen held his breath to listen, but the rush of the falls in the distance disrupted the stillness of the forest. Seconds ticked by at a snail's pace until a reciprocal call greeted them.

Jorge whooped and grabbed the strap of Owen's borrowed 1970s army pack, dragging him forward. "Woah there, dude, slow it down," Owen said and pried Jorge's fingers off.

He looked up and stumbled to a halt when a small camp nestled in the cover of underbrush and tree canopy emerged from the darkness. A tight fire burned at the center of two tents and two hammocks strung up nearby, but it was Julianna's giddy face and bright eyes surrounded by the halo of her white-blond hair that struck him.

"Jules!"

"Owen? What? Owen!" She hurdled the fire and ran at him as if she were a spirit unhindered by the physical world.

Owen dropped his pack to the forest floor just as she launched herself into his outstretched arms.

"You came!" Her words were mixed with a laugh.

Owen grunted at the stab of pain in his shoulder, but he didn't let go and didn't let on that he'd been injured.

She pressed away and grabbed his beard to give it one swift tug. "You should have just sent the book with Jorge, but I'm glad you're here."

Owen frowned and glanced at Jorge who busied himself with the straps on his worn-out pack. "He didn't mention that. But you knew I'd come if you were in trouble."

"Me? Trouble?" She laughed again, a guilty lilt coloring her tone. "Come on over to the fire. You've got to be exhausted. I'll let you sleep a couple hours, but then we've got to get on the move."

"Jules, there's a lot more going on here than anyone has been willing to tell me."

"Oh, you have no idea!"

"Talk. Where exactly do you think you're going?"

"We. We're going. And I'm not exactly sure, but that's why I needed the book."

Owen sank to the log by the fire while Julianna stood over his shoulder and held out her hand expectantly.

"Alvarado has it." He tamped down a twinge of guilt.

Julianna leaned in and gripped Owen's shoulder, digging her fingernails into him. Thankfully the borrowed coat protected him from the worst of it, but the movement still pulled at the gash and made him take a sharp breath.

"What?" She gasped, and then smacked him in the head.

"Oww!" Owen said and rubbed his head before standing to face his sister and the sparks flying from her eyes. "Take it easy."

"Take it easy? How could you let Alvarado have my book?" She stamped her foot, emphasizing her words. "Alvarado! My book!"

"He didn't exactly give me a choice, and once his guys started shooting at me, well—"

"What!" Her eyes widened and the color drained from her face.

"Yeah. That happened." He lifted both crystals, hers and his, from beneath his shirt and took hers off, placing it around her neck as a sort of peace offering, and then he pulled the crinkled hand-drawn map from his pocket.

"But I still have this."

She tucked the crystal under her shirt and looked up. Owen watched her face run the gamut of emotions over the course of the short conversation, but he had to admit her look of relief at that second made him the most curious about the whole ordeal. She gingerly slid the paper from his grasp and pressed it to her chest, and then without batting an eye she stepped past Owen on a path to one of the tents.

"Hey, don't worry, sis, I'm fine. Barely a scratch on me," Owen said to her as if she were actually listening, which she obviously wasn't. Her mind had already moved on to bigger, better things. That was Jules. He tucked his crystal safely away again.

"Brian! Get up. We have the map," she said.

A zipper whirred open and a bedraggled man with graying hair and a week-old beard stepped from the tent.

"If you hadn't already woken me, I'm sure that news would have been enough to do it." He zipped the tent back up and stood tall, stretching before bestowing his full attention on Julianna with the map.

Owen watched them, speechless. Jorge stepped near and grinned. "That is Señor Doctor Brian. He and Señora Julianna are … what is the word … colleagues."

"I gathered." Owen folded his arms over his broad chest and watched the two as they spoke in hushed voices, pointing at various positions on the map. "Where can a guy get a little sleep around here?"

Jorge showed Owen one of the hammocks and how to use it. The lightweight material also had a micro-mesh cover to keep out the bugs, which Owen appreciated.

"Wake me in a couple," Owen said.

Jorge yawned and made some noise that might pass for an affirmative.

***

Owen woke with a start, his hammock shaking violently in the predawn light. He went to sit up only to encounter the mesh cover. A wave of claustrophobia rolled over him for a brief second until he could get the zipper undone.

"Quiet," Julianna said in a hushed whisper. "Jorge thinks you might have been followed. Don't want unwelcome visitors."

Owen had no idea who she was talking about but as soon as he opened his mouth to ask, she shushed him with a loud *shhhhhh* and a glare. He settled for grumbling and shook out his boots before putting them on. Julianna tossed his borrowed backpack at him.

"I'm not your dog, Jules." Owen's whisper had the quality of a growl, and when Julianna smirked, he frowned. "Why are we whispering? Why are people shooting at me? What kind of trouble are you in this time?"

"Sheesh! Too many questions, O." Julianna shoved a machete into a loop on her belt and handed a sheathed knife to Owen. "Here. Just in case."

He took it and slid it into his boot. "Haven't you ever heard you shouldn't bring a knife to a gun fight?"

"Oh, hardy-harr-harr," she replied, rolling her eyes but fighting a smile. On her way past him she smacked his cheek. "I missed you."

Owen half-smiled and followed her into the brush. Twenty yards in they met up with Jorge and that Brian guy. The tense atmosphere relaxed and Julianna poured over her map, leading them into the denser jungle in a round-about way—it seemed—toward Gocta Falls. Owen pulled the mangled granola bar from his pocket and ate it while they trekked.

"Jules, what is that map?"

"It's the way to *La Puerta de Siempre*. 'The Forever Door.'" She pulled his hand close and bit off a chunk of his granola bar.

Owen shifted to walk behind her as what might pass for a trail narrowed. She handed him the map and pulled out her machete to chop at the overhanging vines and brush that blocked the way.

"Here, let me do that," he said. "You can read this. It's in your atrocious handwriting." Owen took the machete from her hand and shoved the crinkled map in its place.

She shrugged and smoothed the paper. "Have it your way ... Muscle."

Owen ignored the jibe. She'd been calling him 'Muscle' ever since he took up weight lifting and rock climbing their sophomore year of high school as a way to deal with bullies. She said if he couldn't out-fight them at least he'd be able to climb out of reach, but since then he'd filled out quite a bit and the name actually fit. He never told her he did it for her. To protect her ....

As he hacked away, he said, "So give me the rundown."

"Okay—"

"Julianna, is that such a good idea?" Brian Shaeffer piped up from just behind her.

Owen glanced back and saw Jorge raise a brow.

"He's my brother. I trust him with my life. And yours, so yeah."

Brian's lips pressed together in a thin line and his eyes narrowed as he looked back at Owen who smiled and resumed bushwhacking. They moved forward at a slow pace, but other than the noises of nature, they were alone.

"It all started when I got that journal last year when I was in Spain," she said. "The conquistador who wrote it claimed it to be a firsthand account of their time here in the cloud forest. It covered ancient sites like Kuelap, but what they discovered farther north at the base of a waterfall caught my attention." She paused for effect.

"*La Puerta de Siempre.* A local told them a story of one of their elders who went in and never returned."

"Hey, Jorge, that's kind of like that story you were telling me last night."

"*Sí.*"

"As I was saying …" Julianna shoved Owen. "The man showed them the place buried deep underground. The journal guy wrote about the experience but not how to get there. At least, he didn't put it in order. He actually made a cipher of directions throughout the journal, Owen! Can you believe it? How clever is that?" "Not very if you figured it out."

"Shut up and swing that machete. Let me finish. Where was I?" Juliana said. "Anyway, I found the clues, lined them up, and drew this map and the instructions for opening the door.." The trail widened again, and Julianna pushed her way to the front. "I happened to meet Dr. Brian Schaeffer here at an archaeological convention in California, and when we were talking we discovered that the place this map led was somewhere near Gocta Cataracts …." She stopped and waited for Owen to stand next to her. "And here we are!"

The falls spilled over the towering cliff and mist floated off the surface from top to bottom like fog on the lakes back home. The fine droplets of water condensed on his bare skin and raised goosebumps along his arms.

"What are we looking for?"

"Can't you just enjoy the view for like two seconds?"

"I spent fifteen hours on planes yesterday, got maybe four hours of sleep in the last thirty-ish hours, and have a gunshot wound on my shoul—"

"What!" Julianna cried and yanked Owen around to see where he was gesturing. She pulled his jacket down over his shoulder and saw the crude patch with blood soaked through. "Owen! You didn't say they shot you!"

The anguished look on her face brought a sense of satisfaction to Owen for a brief second before he took pity on her.

"Yeah, well, you can blame it on Jorge—" "Oye!" Jorge said from behind them.

"It was your idea to punch a guy in the face and shove me out of the car," Owen said, his dry humor lost on Jorge who glowered. Owen couldn't help adding, "And I did push you out of the way of that bullet."

"*Si*, you did." Jorge paused and his ire softened. "*Gracias.*"

Julianna smiled at Jorge and squeezed his hand before turning her attention back to the falls. "Now that that's settled and no one is dead, can you see a mermaid anywhere in the rocks?"

Owen stared through the thick mist but couldn't make anything out. He dropped the machete over the edge of the cliff where they stood and sat, dangling his legs. He flipped to his belly, lowing himself over the edge. There was a drop beyond his reach of another three feet, but he landed with ease on the soft earth.

"Coming?"

Within seconds a rope flew over the edge, landing with a soft thud against the steep slope of the twelve-foot cliff. Soon, Julianna came down, followed by a clumsy Dr. Brian Shaeffer, and lastly Jorge who made it look like he'd been climbing ropes his entire life.

Julianna pulled flimsy rain ponchos from her pack and handed them out before they moved closer to the falls. Finally, once enveloped in the mist, Owen could make out the back walls. There, on the left was the faint appearance of what might pass for a mermaid in the formation of the rock. "The tail is pointing there," Owen said and motioned toward a spot where the misty water was thickest.

Julianna jumped across to a rock and nearly fell in, but she caught herself at the last second. Owen followed behind her and didn't bother to see if anyone else was coming.

"Jules, why are we even looking for this forever door?" he yelled to be heard.

"If you had the book I could show you." Her words were almost lost in the thick cacophony of the falls.

"Jules."

"All right, all right. It's real, Owen. I know it is," she yelled, her poncho whipping in the falls-generated wind. "And I believe it's a portal ... to ... to I don't know where, but the explorer who wrote that journal swears he passed through and came back. Can you imagine?"

"No. It's crazy, but if such a thing exists ..." His mind traveled over all the possibilities.

Owen crossed the slippery rocks to wait for Julianna and the others on the sloping edge of the deep pool. Everything around him appeared like a dream, lost in the foggy mist.

Owen helped Julianna along the edge until they reached the place just behind the falls he'd pointed out earlier. The water's roar overpowered speech and the wind blew harsh around them, a prickling of freezing water stabbing them like a million tiny needles.

Julianna's lips moved as if she were repeating some memorized detail, and she searched out the wall with her hands, pressing and feeling every inch. Brian joined in the task. Owen and Jorge stood close and watched, the former skeptical but alert and the latter alight with anticipation.

Owen scanned the distance as far as he could see through the fog, but the muffled scream of Julianna stole his attention. Her arm disappeared into the rockface and the ground beneath her feet seemed to raise and crumble away, pulling her down with a torrent of water gushing from where she'd stood only seconds before. It carried her underwater and beneath the crush of the falls.

"Julianna!" Owen's cry was lost to all but his own ears as he dived after her. Under the surface, everything in the world disappeared except the thunder of his heartbeat and the dull pelting of water hitting water. Too murky to see anything, he pushed himself deeper in the direction he thought Julianna had been swept. The machete hindered his movement, and he yanked it off, discarding it to the torrent.

Owen battled against the current of the swirling force, but to no avail. In seconds he'd gone from sure of his path to out of control. The pool moved like a drain, circling and pulling him downward. He swam upward and gasped for air, and he saw Julianna at the eye of the whirlpool just before she disappeared. Owen dove after her.

He lost himself in the tumult. Time disappeared. Distance didn't exist. And then blackness.

***

The hushed whisper of his name called to him from a million miles away. He floated on the night sky, stars glittering all around, no ground beneath his feet.

"Owen," the familiar voice whispered again. "Owen," she said, firm and a little harsh.

Stinging pain shot through his cheek and he groaned, the stars fading into the blurry face of Julianna, her wet white-blond hair matted and hanging limp around her face. He blinked several times and rubbed his cheek. "That wasn't necessary."

"Sure. And Vesuvius never blew." Julianna flopped back and leaned on a rock at her back, shivering.

Owen groaned as he rolled to his elbow and pressed up into a sitting position. Cold and battered, he didn't care. He grabbed Julianna and pulled her into a bear hug. "Don't ever do that again."

She laughed and squeezed him back. "Yeah, getting sucked down a giant toilet drain was totally my intention." He held her by the shoulders and looked her in the face, "Seriously, Jules, you take too many risks."

"But you're always there to catch me when I fall."

He knew she was half-joking, but the thought of really losing her took all the fun out of it. "I'm serious. You could have died."

She pried his fingers off and sobered. "I know, O. I'm sorry. Thank you for being stupid and coming after me."

They stared at each other for another second before Owen relaxed and pinched her nose. "I guess we can call it even."

It dawned on Owen as he looked at her that they were in a cave, but there was plenty of light illuminating their facial features. He took in the immensity of the space. Light filtered in from somewhere above, and he could still hear the falls but in a distant way. His rain poncho hung on him in shreds, so he pulled it off, and instead of dwelling too much on his sudden fear of being trapped, he stood and helped Julianna to her feet.

"Where are w—"

Words escaped him when he looked up over the piled, moss-enveloped rocks to see a structure so far out of place his mind could not grasp it as reality. A Taj Mahal-like arch reached toward the roof of the cavern, light spilling in to illuminate it.

"*La Puerta de Siempre*," Julianna said, her voice soft with reverence. "It must be."

Before Owen could stop her, she charged up over the rocks, along the mossy path, up ancient dilapidated steps. He could hear her laugh, her joy and amazement bright enough to rub off on even him. He followed her at a slower pace, rubbing just below the wound on his shoulder. With a wary eye, he scanned the dark corners of the unbelievable cave.

Most of the light concentrated on the arch atop the timeworn, mossy hill of rock.

A shot rang out in the cave, reverberating off the walls and only matched by the scream of his sister. She ducked, covering her head with her hands.

Owen stumbled but immediately broke into a run up the slick steps toward the top where Julianna slowly stood, her hands raised in the air. He slowed to a stop near the top as Miguel Alvarado, his five bodyguards, and Jorge came into view. The goons had all guns pointed at

Julianna.

Jorge's hands rested at his waist and were tied with rope, and he sported a dark, puffy bruise over the left side of his face where his eye had disappeared in the swelling.

Alvarado leafed through the ancient journal. "You know, Mr. McFadden, I underestimated you. I do not know how you hid that map without my seeing. If not for Dr. Shaeffer, we would not have arrived with such haste, and who knows what damage you and your sister might have done here."

Dr. Brian Shaeffer stepped out from around the edge of the arch, oblivious to their conversation. "This is amazing!" He held up a strange instrument that made soft beeping noises that sped up the closer he came to the center arch.

"Brian, why?" Julianna asked, her imploring tone unable to conceal her hurt.

Shaeffer distractedly glanced at Julianna while also drawing the attention of the group. Owen used the opportunity to inch up a stair. One of the men with guns noticed and swiveled his pistol to aim at Owen.

"We'd never have made it this far, let alone been able to gain clearance in Peru, without Mr. Alvarado's help," Brian said. Dismissing the tense scene before him, he pressed buttons on his device.

"You b—"

"Señora, temper-temper."

"Put down your guns and we'll leave. Julianna, Jorge, and I will let you do whatever it is you think you need to do, no questions asked."

"Owen!" Julianna scowled at him. "This is the great discovery of our time. We can't leave these grave-robbing thugs to claim it."

"If it's your life versus claiming discovery rights, I'd take your life."

"Sibling banter. Precious. Mr. McFadden, join the señora."

Miguel Alvarado shoved Jorge forward and motioned one of his henchmen toward the group as Owen stepped cautiously up to the main level, just fifteen feet from the opening of the arch. A heavy vibration hit him in the chest, and then hummed with energy; Owen wasn't sure if it was this electrical charge or fear that caused his heart to skip a beat.

"It'll be okay, Owen," Julianna whispered.

"Are you kidding me?" Owen glowered, flexing his fists as the man with ropes approached.

"Don't try to fight, Mr. McFadden, unless you want to see your sister hurt." Alvarado watched with a satisfied expression.

The muscle in Owen's jaw twitched, and he lifted his foot to take a step forward, but Julianna rested a firm grip on his arm. She was right to try to stop him. They were no match for the firepower they faced.

Two of the gun-wielding men stepped up, pointing the unfriendly ends of the barrels at them while the guy Owen recognized as Luis tied his hands behind his back. Once done, Luis grabbed Julianna by the arm.

"Why are you doing this?" Owen asked, the angry words ground out between clenched teeth.

Alvarado meandered near. "Dr. Shaeffer searches for *aliens*. But what my great-great-great-great-and-so-forth grandfather discovered here was much more. He discovered El Dorado. A city of gold and unimaginable power. I cannot trust you to keep my secret. Through that gate is a world beyond your imagining. This journal," he said and held up the old book, "is only the map to this place. I have more of the same with detailed descriptions of what he saw through the portal."

Alvarado held up a smooth, crystalline ball the size of a jawbreaker that definitely looked foreign—otherworldly—like nothing Owen had ever seen before. The sleezy coward reached out to touch Julianna who spit and called him a name, but Alvarado just laughed and rubbed the sphere across her cheek. Owen struggled against his restraints, leaning toward Alvarado. One of the goons punched him in the mouth and sent his head whipping to the side.

Julianna gasped. "Owen!"

He groaned and tasted blood. Owen blinked to clear the black spots from his eyes and glared at the perpetrator.

"Now, señora," Alvarado said, ignoring Owen, "I need you to tell me the rest of what you discovered from deciphering the coordinates so that we can activate this door to my El Dorado."

"Go to hell."

He raised a brow and motioned to the man who'd punched Owen. The stoic brute hit him again, this time in the gut, sending a rush of air from his lungs.

"Stop!" Julianna shouted.

Jorge scrambled forward, but the man holding a gun to him slammed the butt of his pistol into Jorge's head, knocking him out cold.

"I'm all right," Owen said between coughs while he stared at Jorge to make sure he was breathing.

"This will continue unless you agree to help."

"Leave Owen and Jorge out of this." Julianna's voice warbled with unshed tears and rage. A steely glint shone in her eye.

"I can't," Alvarado said, his annoyance evident. "You brought them here. Now you are responsible for what happens to them."

Owen's anger boiled in his blood, but before he could encourage Julianna to keep quiet, she said, "You let them go. Now."

"You know I cannot do that."

Owen sensed her danger. "Jules—"

"Mr. McFadden. You are useless to me beyond insurance that your sister help me. I suggest you keep quiet or risk Sacha's wrath."

"Owen, please."

Luis dragged her after Alvarado as he walked away, and she whimpered, obviously in pain. Owen's instincts screamed at him to do something. Tugging at his restraints, he stepped toward Julianna, but again Sacha slammed his meaty fist into Owen's stomach. He grunted against the pain, bent at the waist, and nearly fell to his knees.

Anger outstripped the pain. Still bent forward, Owen watched Sacha pull out his gun. He growled and rammed into the brute like a raging bull, knocking him to the ground. His gun clattered against hard stone.

Owen's hands were still tied, but he used his body weight to hold Sacha down and fought against the ropes all while the big man's fists flew like battering rams against Owen's head and upper body. Then, suddenly, two men physically lifted him. Sacha, swearing worse than a sailor but in Russian, scrambled to his feet and landed another hard fist to Owen's gut. And another.

Owen collapsed to his knees. The last time he remembered being outnumbered and beaten was by a gang of high-class jerks his sophomore year after he defended Julianna from their harassment.

He coughed and sputtered, his eyes looking past Sacha to see her shake her head at him. She turned away and started pointing out places on the wall on either side of the main arch that Dr. Shaeffer and Alvarado immediately went to.

Sacha turned to search out his gun, but Owen noticed him dividing his attention, giving away his interest in the arch and what they were doing there. The other goons pulled Owen back to his feet and dragged him forward. He watched as Alvarado and Shaeffer turned stone dials in the walls, ones barely perceptible from a distance. Each held those same clear quartz-like orbs in their hand, and counting down, they pressed them into the center of the dials simultaneously.

Awed by what he saw, Owen thought he must have stepped onto the scene of a *Stargate* episode as he watched a wall of undulating blue electricity or … or plasma? … or something unbelievable spread from either side of the archway to its center.

"Now let my brother and Jorge go."

"Oh, señora, you are naive if not foolish."

"Mr. Alvarado," Dr. Shaeffer said, hesitant, "she has given us what we needed to open the arch. Shouldn't we …" He flittered his fingers. "… you know."

Alvarado's lethal stare was his only reply, and the good doctor clamped his lips closed. Instead, Shaeffer squatted down in front of a body-sized black case and opened it to reveal all manner of advanced tech and a suit that looked like a cross between a wetsuit and space suit.

"Now," Alvarado said, turning to Julianna, "my dear, please test the door."

"T-test? The door?"

"Now."

Julianna hesitated and approached the gateway with cautious steps. Her hand visibly shook as she reached out toward the surface.

Owen pulled against the restraining hands of his guards but to no avail. They forced him to his knees, one of them aiming his gun at Owen's head. "Jules, don't do this."

Her fingers reached, tentative and so small, toward the wall of unstable energy; Owen could feel it pulsing against his body and briefly wondered if anyone else could.

Their collective breath held as she placed her hand on the surface. She jerked back, but a half laugh escaped her lips. "It shocked me." She waved her whole palm over the surface before pressing it into the liquid.

The image of her arm disappearing into the rock wall from earlier flashed through Owen's mind and he frowned, no longer awed by what he saw. "Careful, Jules."

"This is amazing," she said, her voice full of wonder as she pulled her hand back out of the portal and examined each digit.

"Doctor," Alvarado said and stepped close to the rippling wall with a hungry look in his eye, "once you have established the safety of the atmosphere, et cetera, the rest of us will join you."

The man on Owen's right stepped forward to gear up alongside Shaeffer, and Sacha took his place next to Owen. It seemed the excitement stirred by the mindbending gate was too much for them, and other than a limply aimed gun, they ignored him. Owen kept working at the ropes on his wrists, the angry burning sensation they caused reminding him he was still alive.

Julianna inched her way toward him and his guards, away from the rhythmic hum of the archway. No one seemed to notice or care. Luis hadn't even bothered to keep an eye on her. She kneeled behind Owen and yanked at the ropes.

"They won't budge," she whispered, lament filling her voice.

"Boot. Knife," he whispered back.

She gasped softly and retrieved it. She went to work on the ropes at his wrist, but before she could get all the way through sawing the rope, Alvarado's attention swung around to take in the scene behind him. She quickly slid the knife into the back of her belt and reached to hold onto Owen's arm.

Alvarado stared at them a few seconds longer than Owen would have liked, but the maniac's mind was obviously so preoccupied he didn't seem to register what they'd been up to.

"It is time," Alvarado announced.

Dr. Shaeffer and the two men, all in their high-tech suits, stepped up to the archway gate and faced it together. The two guards on either side of the doctor started a second ahead of Shaeffer and made it halfway before their screams rent the air. Dr. Shaeffer had stepped one leg through the surface and tried to pull back, but it was too late. He too dropped to the ground, agony contorting his face.

The doctor toppled over, his leg completely gone from the hip down, the flesh where it had been removed totally seared. The two men who'd made it further in also crashed to the ground, or what was left of them did. Owen looked away in revulsion, his stomach rebelling.

At the gruesome sight, Julianna dug her face into the space between his ribs and triceps and screamed.

Alvarado's cry of rage raised above every other sound except Dr. Shaeffer's shrieks of agony. Without mercy— *or maybe it was mercy* was Owen's fleeting thought— Alvarado aimed his gun at the doctor and put him out of his misery. Julianna buried her face further into the back of Owen's bound arm at the sound and cried. There was nothing he could do, but there was no way he was going to let this maniac hurt his sister.

He yanked harder at the ropes on his wrists and looked around frantically for any way to escape. "Jules, run," he whispered.

She gripped his arm tighter in response.

"Send him through," Alvarado said, barely masked rage twisting his tone as he pointed his pistol at Owen.

"No!" Julianna cried as Luis, who'd just realized she wasn't standing next to him anymore, strode over and pulled her off Owen's arm.

"You're hiding something from me, señora,"

Alvarado said, "but by Dios, I will find out what it is. Send him through!"

"Please!" she cried, hitting Luis with her free hand.

The other men grabbed for Owen again, but before they could get ahold of his arms, he gave the rope one last hard pull and snapped it. But he was too late. They dragged him up and toward the pulse of the gate. Struggling, he ripped his arm free of Sacha and kicked him in the gut, sending him sprawling through the gate with a terrible scream cut off by his momentum through the opening.

"She dies right now, Mr. McFadden, if you do not comply!"

Owen whipped his head around to see Luis holding Julianna's own knife to her throat. The fight drained out of him, and he allowed the other guard to grab his free arm, trapping both in a firm grip.

"Owen, don't!"

He thrashed around, forcing his captor closer to the gateway. "Let her go. I swear, if you don't, you'll regret it." He caught a glimpse of Jorge's head peek out from behind a rock and forced himself not to do a doubletake. He was hidden from Alvarado's view.

The battered Peruvian nodded once.

"She'll be safe so long as you comply," Alvarado said, his voice nearly back to normal.

Owen could feel the energy from the door's surface like a thrumming heartbeat. The crystal under his shirt burned into his skin. He stared at Jorge and nodded slowly, and then he looked at Alvarado whose grim smile revealed the devil inside.

"Owen—"

Julianna shook her head. Twins. He could swear he felt everything she felt. She knew him better than anyone, and by the look on her face, he could tell she knew what he was about to do.

In a split second, Owen whipped around, grabbed the arm of Alvarado's other grunt, and yanked him through the gate with all his force and then let go.

At first, Owen was sure he was dead. He'd heard the scream of the man he pulled and thought it might have been his own, but there was no pain. He only felt a surge of hair-raising power like when he was a kid and would rub balloons on his head to create static electricity. The feeling had been fleeting, and now a cool breeze drifted over his skin.

Prone, he opened his eyes and couldn't believe what he saw. He scrambled up. The blue sky, bluer that any he'd ever seen, and the grass—if it was even grass it was so green and moss-like—looked like it had been painted by a child. A deep valley separated him from crystalline spires in the distance, but he tore his gaze away to look behind. The arch rose like a mirror image, and the portal continued its lazy undulations.

The foreignness of the place struck him like a dream, but Jules was in trouble and he didn't believe he was dead. He took a deep breath and walked back through the gate, but this time he was aware of the passage. It took only a second or two. The surge of power rippled through him, and the crystal at his chest burned again until he was through. All that remained was the pulse of energy from the gate at his back.

In the cave, Alvarado's empty hands were in the air. His gun lay on the ground several feet from him, and Jorge had a gun—probably the one Sacha lost earlier—pointed at his head.

"Let her go," Alvarado said in a growl to Luis who relaxed his arm but didn't lower it or step away.

"Owen!" Julianna yelled, a smile breaking across her dirty, tear-streaked face.

In a matter of seconds chaos ensued.

She turned on Luis, grabbed his knife wrist and twisted at the same time as crushing his foot with all her might. He dropped the knife but grabbed her by the hair.

She screamed.

Jorge aimed his weapon at Luis. Shot. His aim surprising and fatal.

Alvarado dove at the ground and grabbed his discarded gun. Momentum sent him rolling toward Julianna. He crouched with pistol aimed at Jorge, then Owen and back again.

"Stay back!" He moved in on Julianna, pulling her back to her feet, and used her as a human shield. He walked her toward Owen.

"How did you not die?" Alvarado asked, suspicion and awe strong in his tone.

"Let her go, Alvarado." Owen raised his hands. "You can't win here." He was unable to take his eyes off the pistol against his sister's neck.

"No. Not until you tell me the secret of the gate. Who *are* you?" He asked, circling closer but keeping Julianna between himself and Owen. "My men say you are nothing but a builder. You have no knowledge—no skill that could possibly help you here."

An image flitted through Owen's mind of the drawing of the crystal like the one around his neck from the old journal. Slowly he said, "Let her go. I'll take you through the gate, but you have to let her go. I swear to you, I'll help you, but only if you do it. Look. I'm unarmed."

Alvarado considered him and pointed the gun at Owen's chest, "Tell your dog to drop the gun." Owen's frown deepened into a glare.

"Now!" Alvarado's veins bulged on his forehead, his eyes crazed and sweat soaking his shirt.

"Don't help him, Owen," Julianna said.

"Trust me," he said to her. "We'll be okay."

She opened her mouth to protest but closed it again almost as quickly.

Owen looked at Jorge who lowered the gun but didn't drop it.

He held out his hand to Alvarado. "Take my hand. It's the only way."

Alvarado shifted Julianna forward, the gun pointed at her back, and stepped closer. He grasped Owen's hand.

"Don't move," Alvarado said in warning to Julianna.

Owen pulled Alvarado's hand to the surface of the gateway and thrust their combined grip into it. Alvarado gasped and lowered his gun. After a second, he smiled. "What is this? Why doesn't it burn us?"

Owen inwardly sighed, relieved it had worked. He pulled their hands back out.

Alvarado stared at the surface of the gate, greed glinting in his eyes.

Owen used his distraction to make eye contact with Julianna. He looked from her to the far wall of the archway and tilted his head a fraction. At first she looked confused, so he did it again. The second time understanding dawned and she nodded.

"Let's go. It's safe on the other side." Owen took a deep breath pulled Alvarado through the gate.

Alvarado yelped but grabbed Julianna around the neck with his gun arm. He swore once they were through, but as realization dawned his only response was to shout in triumph. He released Julianna, and then

Owen's hand, and spun around, his arms raised and still gripping the gun. "I have found El Dorado!"

Owen backed a step away, letting Alvarado have his victory. He nudged Julianna toward the opposite side of the arch and moved as close to his side of the gate as he could get.

Alvarado turned to them with a sinister grin twisting his face. He raised the gun to point at Owen. "What do you—"

"Now!"

Owen swiveled and jumped through the gate, a bullet whizzing past the back of his head before the energy enveloped him again and he stepped through on the other side. "Now, Jules!" His cry came before he'd fully come through; he prayed she'd understood his unsaid plan. He immediately went for the strange crystal orb in the opposite side of the arch from where Julianna should have gone through. He looked over, immediate relief flooding his body to see her scrambling to her feet. She lunged for the orb on the other pillar, and he did the same on his side, yanking the spheres from the wall.

Owen stumbled back and watched the gate ripple closed, disappearing, but not before a bullet whizzed through and shattered the corner of the arch wall near his head, sending bits of shrapnel spattering the area around him. He raised his arm to shield his eyes.

"Owen!" Julianna cried and raced toward him. She jumped at him, crying through her smile as he caught her and sank to the ground. "You're alive. You're okay. Oh, thank God you're okay! I'm so sorry. I'm so sorry. I should never …! Oh, I'm so glad you're okay." The words kept spilling from her mouth almost like the tears pouring out of her eyes. She hit him and hit him again. "Why did you do that? You can't always be trying to protect me, you big dummy. We're even!" She hit him again, and then hugged him so tight around the neck she nearly cut off his air supply.

"It's okay, Jules. It's over." Numbness filled his chest at the carnage around them.

She let go and sat on the ground facing him. They looked around, and Jorge came into view where he rested against another boulder, the gun in his limp grip. He smiled and waved his free hand. Owen smiled, still more relieved.

He looked at the orb in his hand and ran a finger over the surface, but words couldn't express the confusion he felt over what he'd seen on the other side. It must have all been a dream. But looking around proved it wasn't. And Alvarado's absence was further evidence.

A soft groan broke the stillness and they both looked to Jorge. He'd set the gun down and was holding a wound on his leg that Owen hadn't noticed before. Blood seeped between his fingers. Owen pulled Julianna to her feet, and they staggered to their friend, pocketing the orbs.

"You saved my life," Julianna said and kissed Jorge's unbruised cheek. He winced but smiled through the pain.

"It is nothing." Jorge grinned at them, even with the distortion of his swollen eye, and let Julianna take his hand.

Owen pulled his shirt off, what was left of it, and wrapped strips of it around the bullet hole in Jorge's leg. He pulled the makeshift bandage tight, and Jorge screamed, arching his back for the seconds it took to endure the new sensation on his injury.

"Sorry," Owen said, cringing.

Jorge waved his apology away and worked to slow his breath. Owen stood and looked around the cave, the light beginning to wane.

"Now, how do we get out of here?"

***

Julianna and Owen stood together on the upper most cliff of the Gocta Cataracts with a small group of locals from the village and Jorge's people. An old man dressed in an ancient Incan custom stood nearest the edge and yelled words Owen couldn't understand, but many in attendance nodded their heads or said things as if in response. The old man held a jar with a lid carved like a jaguar. He removed the lid and turned the jar upside down, spilling its contents—gold dust ... an offering, Jorge told them— into the wind that swirled down and amongst the tumbling waters of Gocta.

"Thank you, Jorge," he said as his friend limped up next to him with an unfamiliar yet fitting confidence. Owen placed both orbs into his outstretched hands.

"We are even," Jorge said and smiled bright, his eyes on the ceremonial leader.

Owen had come to find that Jorge had saved his life more than once in the short time he'd known him. The people of his village explained that after Julianna had sent Jorge to get Owen they'd been told of a plot to have

Owen murdered in order to get the book and leave no witnesses to its existence. They assured Owen that Jorge's insisting he come with the book had saved his life. He tended to agree … they were definitely not even.

It was also Jorge who, from his capture, showed them how to escape the cave through a tunnel and up a stairway leading to the very spot Julianna's arm had disappeared in the wall at the base of the falls.

When they'd emerged from the cave and made a precarious crossing of the rocky pool, they were met by friends of Jorge. After getting him home to his family and much needed medical care, Julianna and Owen went to the authorities about what had happened in the cave. The local police had gone to investigate and found nothing. They discovered no evidence to the cave or the entrance. The authorities told them Alvarado had probably gone out on his yacht and to stop wasting their time.

The only believers were the locals and Jorge's own village. And they swore the McFaddens to secrecy.

A distant cry, like the roar of a jaguar, haunted the breeze. Owen absently reached for the crystal at his neck and wrapped his free arm around his sister's shoulder as he looked out over the misty cloud forest. No one would believe their story anyway.

"O?"

"Hmm?"

"What did you see? On the other side."

AFTERWORD

Now that you've found yourself at the end of this compilation of adventurous science fiction and fantasy stories, you might wonder where to go next. You probably noticed that many of these tales end in such a way that there is potential for something more. And in this, I'd encourage you to reach out to the authors of the stories you enjoyed (or contact me and I'll pass on the word) and let them know you'd love to read more. Trust me, authors love hearing from readers, especially those who express an interest in continuing their tales.

And, of course, we would be honored to have you declare your enjoyment of the anthology by leaving a simple, brief review at your preferred retailer or even on Goodreads! It is a huge kindness, and there's nothing better than knowing the stories we write have touched the minds and tickled the fancies of readers across the globe.

We cherish the time you've put into these stories and thank you for being our reader!

- Rachael Ritchey

BONUS AUTHOR BIOS & LINKS!

R. J. Rodda is an Aussie Christian mum living on a mandarin farm in an ex-Soviet country. Her inspiring nonfiction has been published most notably in *The Age and Stories of Life 2018* anthology. *Chosen for the Fox-dance* is a teaser for her upcoming novel *The Vixen-Trials* about the Hattavah being ordered to kill his childhood sweetheart.

https://www.wattpad.com/user/rjrodda
https://twitter.com/RebRod40

Joy E. Rancatore writes fiction, nonfiction and everything in between. When she's not doing horrible things to her characters or dreaming up faery creatures and fantastic weapons, she beats her husband at card games, homeschools her two children, snuggles her two stinky dogs and lets her cat, Tolkien, do whatever he wants. They'd prefer to live in Middle-earth or Narnia or Hogwarts or in a galaxy far, far away; but, for now, they live across Lake Pontchartrain from New Orleans.

www.joyerancatore.com
www.facebook.com/joyerancatore
www.instagram.com/joyerancatore

After a career as a librarian, **Audrey Driscoll** communes with plants in her Victoria, British Columbia garden, and with fictitious characters in her head. Since the turn of the millennium, she has written and published the Herbert West Series, and is preparing to launch her latest novel, She Who Comes Forth, a paranormal adventure set in Luxor, Egypt. Information about these books, as well as Audrey's opinions on a variety of loosely connected topics, may be found on her blog at https://www.audreydriscoll.com.

Materials Scientist by day, writer by night, **David Jesson** is a Research Fellow at a British university and the cohost of Fiction Can Be Fun which is a collaborative writing blog. In reality, he's not quite as dapper as his photo would suggest.

https://fictioncanbefun.wordpress.com/
https://www.twitter.com/breakerofthings/

E.E. Rawls is the product of a traveling family, who even lived in Italy for 6 years. She loves exploring the unknown, whether it be in a forest, castle, or in the pages of a book, and finding a mushroom is like finding a hidden treasure. Ever since childhood, she's been fascinated by fairy tales and folklore, which later on inspired her to begin creating stories.

She now runs on coffee and delicious things to keep the story wheels of her mind turning, as she works hard to create books that will both capture and inspire readers, giving them worlds they can explore and become lost in.

www.rawlse.wordpress.com
https://mailchi.mp/22a2f2dce8c0/eerawls
https://www.instagram.com/eerawls_author/

Barb Taub: a humor & urban fantasy author. Caffeinated Aussie Dog wrangler. Daring daytime escapee to UK to live in medieval castle, Hobbit House, & magic Scottish Isle.

https://barbtaub.com/
https://www.facebook.com/barbtaub

**K. R. Ludlow** is an Australian supply teacher, composer, and writer for Christian magazine, "Girls4God." She holds degrees in both Music and Education and currently shares a townhouse with her guinea pig, Bonnie.

https://www.facebook.com/krludlow/
https://soundcloud.com/kr-ludlow

Although a 'tech' by trade, **Sha'Tara** has always liked writing. Her common expression is through essays but she prefer short stories and micro short stories, most of which involve very few characters, sometimes only one, but usually two or three with some just being hinted at. When she retired in 2011 she was sure to have plenty of leisure time to indulge writing. Unfortunately techs are in high demand these days and she find myself as busy, if not more, than when a corporate employee. Not complaining, she enjoys the challenge of work. She's managed to write one fantasy novel in the last couple of years but done nothing with it yet and is considering publishing, time permitting, this Winter— "Wouldn't want to rush it, hey?" Meanwhile, she's grinding out short stories and opinion pieces on her blog at https://shatara46.wordpress.com.

Avid reader & incurable story-spinner, **Angie Thompson** also enjoys volunteering in her church's children's program and starting (but not always finishing) various kinds of craft projects. She currently lives in central Virginia near most of her incredible family, including two parents, six brothers, one sister, and five siblings-in-law—plus four nieces, nine nephews, and several assorted pets!

https://www.quietwaterspress.com/

https://www.goodreads.com/author/show/17342653.Angi e_Tho mpson

Briar Shea is a high school student who uses her writing as a way to escape from the stress and anxiety that comes with the life of a teenager. The worlds she comes up with are inspired by her love of reading, where she discovers new writing techniques from the realities written by other authors. This being her first published piece, this story gave her a wonderful experience and she cannot wait to introduce more pieces soon.

https://www.fictionfanaddict.wordpress.com/

https://www.instagram.com/fiction.fanaddict/

V. P. Grey is the author of short fiction and poetry with her first novel well on its way to completion. She is a reader, writer, dreamer, and survivor.

Deb Whittam is a graduated from Macquarie University Bachelor of Arts and is traversing the great continent of Australia in a caravan. She seeks to explore the many forms of reality in her writing and examine how perspectives can alter when life is viewed through an alternate lens. Her ebooks are available at Smashwords.

https://twitter.com/DebbieWhittam
https://www.smashwords.com/profile/view/DebWhittam

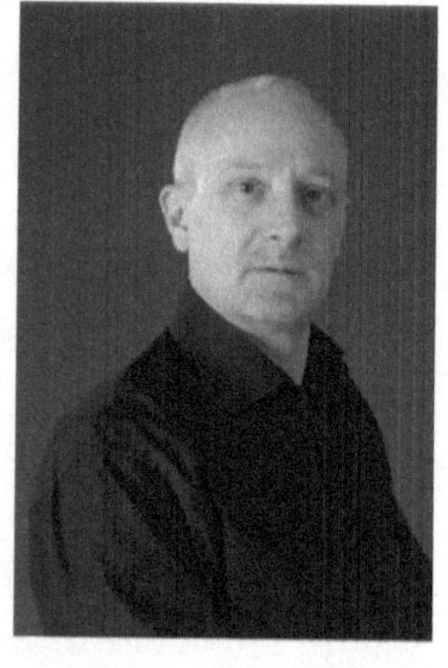

Gary Jefferies is a former research scientist turned primary stay-at-home dad of two fantastic children. Writing was always factual in the previous life. Yet a fascination with fiction lingered nearby, even though he thought himself not brave enough to develop it further. A comfort zone thing. Science writing was familiar, fiction was not. Blogging has opened up doors and instilled confidence to pursue his passion for writing by combining his knowledge, expertise, and creativity to build a career in writing from home around children!

https://www.fictionisfood.com
https://twitter.com/GaryJefferies10
https://www.facebook.com/Fictionisfood/

Victoria Lynn has a passion for creativity. Writing keeps her busy as well as her repertoire of careers at Victoria Lynn Designs with graphic design, sewing & creating music. Her passion for writing started at a young age. She weaves stories of real life, historical happenings, and extraordinary circumstances with hope to strengthen readers in their faith and draw them closer to the Lord all while entertaining with a good book.

https://www.rufflesandgrace.com
https://www.facebook.com/victorialynnauthor/
https://www.instagram.com/victorialynnauthor/

Rachael Ritchey is a writer of YA fiction and a book designer. With a passion for beautiful books, cover and interior design are high on her list of hobbies. When not writing or designing, she loves spending time with her four kids and husband. The beautiful lakes and forests of Washington and N. Idaho inspire her writing almost as much as the hope that drives her gratitude and passion.

https://www.rachaelritchey.com
Facebook: @RachaelRitcheyAuthor
Instagram: @RachaelRitchey

Dear Reader,

If you enjoyed any of the stories in this anthology, please leave a review at your preferred retailer and/or Goodreads!

When you do, it helps keep the book in the sights of other potential readers and helps them know if they want to give it a go!

9 780099 720336 3